Miss Seeton Paints
the Town

Also by Hamilton Crane
in Large Print:

Miss Seeton Goes to Bat
Miss Seeton Cracks the Case

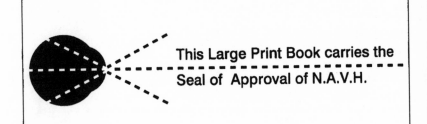

Miss Seeton Paints the Town

HAMILTON CRANE

Thorndike Press • Thorndike, Maine

Published in 2000 by arrangement with Curtis Brown Ltd.

Thorndike Large Print® Mystery Series.

The tree indicium is a trademark of Thorndike Press.

The text of this Large Print edition is unabridged.
Other aspects of the book may vary from the original edition.

Set in 16 pt. Plantin by Al Chase.

Printed in the United States on permanent paper.

Library of Congress Cataloging-in-Publication Data
Crane, Hamilton.
    Miss Seeton paints the town / Hamilton Crane.
        p.   cm. — (Heron Carvic's Miss Seeton)
    ISBN 0-7862-2339-1 (lg. print : hc : alk. paper)
    1. Seeton, Miss (Fictitious character) — Fiction.
    2. Women detectives — England — Fiction.   3. England —
    Fiction.   I. Title.   II. Series.
    PR6063.A7648 M567 2000
    823´.914—dc21   99-057825

Miss Seeton Paints the Town

chapter
1

"Good grief!" Superintendent Chris Brinton of the Ashford constabulary blinked, and stared, rubbing his eyes. "What in heaven's name did you have for breakfast today, Foxon?"

Detective Constable Foxon looked puzzled. His superior did not normally display so much interest in his dietary habits. "Just the usual, sir. Porridge to start with —"

"Porridge? In the middle of summer? I always suspected you might be mad, Foxon, but being a good copper, I've been waiting for proof. Proof which you've now given me."

"But, sir, I like porridge. Soaked overnight and cooked properly, of course, and none of this serving it with sugar, or honey, or treacle. A good sprinkling of salt, that's what decent porridge needs, sir," said Foxon, warming to his theme. "Sea salt, if you can get it —" He broke off as the superintendent groaned. "Something wrong, sir?"

"Everything's wrong, if the investigation

of crime in this part of Kent is being carried out by lunatics like you — and don't remind me that I gave you the job, laddie. It's too early in the morning. Go on telling me what you had for breakfast — for the sake of my own sanity, I need a solution to the mystery."

"It's no mystery, sir. I have the same every day: first the porridge, then a good fry-up — bacon, sausage, a couple of eggs, and some fried bread, then a few slices of toast and marmalade to finish up with, sir."

Brinton shuddered, then sighed. "Well," he said, "it had to happen in the end, I suppose. I fought a good fight, Foxon, but now it seems I'm just as crazy as you. I must be — it's taken longer to lose my marbles, but they've definitely rolled away to join yours. Because I could have sworn, laddie" — he leaned forward across his desk to jab a menacing forefinger at his baffled subordinate — "that you must have eaten a good sack or two of fertiliser for breakfast and washed it down with a few gallons of weed killer. What other explanation could there possibly be for that horrible flowery excrescence sprouting on your chest? Or is it merely the delusion of a lunatic?"

Foxon, who had been growing increasingly bemused by his superintendent's words, now relaxed and grinned. "You've hurt my feelings, sir. Don't you like my tie? Someone I'm very fond of gave it to me — it's the latest fashion."

"It's hideous. It looks as if you've been molested by a manic exhibit from the Chelsea Flower Show. The very least you could do is hand out sunglasses to poor beggars like me who've got to look at it first thing in the morning. And, talking of glasses, if you don't want some short-sighted old dame to do you a spot of unwitting bodily harm with a pair of shears, better keep well away from herbaceous borders in case you get picked by mistake." All of a sudden, Brinton became serious. "You're sure this is what the youngsters — heaven help us all — are wearing nowadays?"

Foxon knew his chief's thought processes almost as well as he knew his own. "I'd fit in fine, sir. No question."

"You may have to." Brinton shuffled the papers on his desk. "Petty vandalism may be what they're calling it now, but if these yobs're allowed to get away with it, they won't be stopping there. Things will start to hot up, Foxon, and we want to be ready with the extinguisher before they burst into flames. I hoped we'd seen the last of the Choppers. We popped 'em all inside for a fair old stretch after that business in Plummergen and anybody normal would've learned their lesson and come out of the nick like a flock of little lambs — but this lot stirring up trouble now is the younger generation, if you ask me, been taught a few tricks by its older brothers, who're too wise to get involved again themselves, but don't mind passing along the odd tip on how to make our lives a misery. And then, while we're busy sorting out what baby brother's been doing, we haven't the time to keep an eye on anybody else — or so they hope."

"You want me to try infiltrating the gang, sir? Find out what they're really up to?"

Brinton eyed him thoughtfully. The flared trousers of deep, rich burgundy, artfully concealing the platform-soled shoes of sparkling white; the wide-collared shirt, almost emerald in its greenness; the flapping floral neckwear that had prompted the superintendent's outburst; the shoulder-length hair which Brinton could never quite bring himself to comment on. He suspected Foxon of putting his wavy locks in curlers every time he washed them, and dreaded finding out that the young man used conditioner as well.

"But you certainly look the part," he acknowledged with a scowl. "Maybe a bit long in the tooth for the Choppers, revised version, and you're rather too clean-looking to mix unnoticed with gentry of the sort we're worrying about — if they take a bath more than once in a blue moon, I'd be very much surprised. Still, perhaps they'd take you for some kind of harmless eccentric."

"Doing my own thing, sir," suggested Foxon. "Peace and love, tolerance, letting everyone do what they feel like."

"And a better recipe for anarchy I never hope to hear," snorted the superintendent, thumping his fist on the desk. "Where should we be if everybody did exactly what they felt like whenever they felt like it? These damned Choppers, now — what *they* seem to feel like is smashing windows and bashing chunks out of people's garden fences, breaking into telephone boxes and helping themselves to the cash, joyriding in stolen cars all over the place hooting their horns in the middle of the night — need I go on?"

Foxon, despite everything, tried to be fair. "No, sir. But I think the peace-and-love lot always add 'provided it doesn't upset anybody else' to the basic theory —"

"Upset? I'm more than upset, laddie, I'm furious. With the Choppers and their friends who're starting to make life such a

11

misery for the people in this town — and with us, for not being able to catch 'em. They've grown cunning, Foxon, and I don't like it. Their big brothers have been coaching the blighters rather too well." He glared once more at the sheaf of papers on his desk. "And if we're being realistic — don't let's try kidding ourselves, Foxon. You're far too normal, despite your ghastly taste in clothes — you'd stick out like a sore thumb among that shower, no matter how good a detective you might be. You'd never carry it off."

"I could try, sir." The detective constable's expression was grim. "They had a go at my grandmother's cottage a few nights ago — uprooted her new bedding plants and made a bonfire of 'em in the front garden, with her gate, as well. She's not on the phone, and she was scared half to death — said they were dancing and yelling like mad things, enough to curdle your blood to hear 'em at it, she said."

Brinton nodded. "I've read the report, of course, but with the surnames being different I didn't realise . . . and I'm sorry about it, Foxon." He sat up suddenly. "So that's why you asked for a couple of days off!"

"Compassionate leave, sir, and I've got

the backache to prove it. Every one of those blessed plants was replaced, and the burnt patch of the front lawn seeded over, and when she's chosen a new gate, I'm going to fit that for her, too." Foxon rubbed his lumbar region thoughtfully. "The tie's by way of a thank-you present from her, sir, though of course I chose it really. Gran just came along for the fun — and she was even more, er, forthright about my choice than you were, sir. She's not afraid to speak her mind — not usually, that is." His face hardened again. "But she was sure as hell scared the other night . . ."

"You're itching to nobble them, aren't you? For which I can't say I blame you in the least, Foxon, but if it's got personal with you, it could turn nasty — distort your judgment, maybe make you take risks you wouldn't otherwise have done — and I don't like the thought of any of my men running unnecessary risks."

"I'd take care, sir —"

"No. And that's an order, laddie — no heroics, understand?" Brinton glared. "Foxon?"

"If you say so, sir. I suppose you were right in the first place, about me not fitting in very well, anyway . . ."

"And there's always the risk — the biggest

problem of all — that they'd recognise you, remember. That they'd recognise anybody from Ashford, if it comes to that." And the superintendent began to brood.

While he did so, Foxon slumped lower on his chair as he tried to polish the toe of one shoe on the back of a convenient trouser leg. When he dropped his eyes under Brinton's challenge, he'd spotted a few specks of dust, which offended his fashionable sensibilities. Not for Foxon the dirty sneakers, unsavoury-looking jeans, and ripped old leather jacket of —

"Sleaze Arbuthnott, sir!" Inspired, Foxon sat upright. "He'd be perfect for the job, if we could get him."

"Who? No, wait — the name sounds familiar — Arbuthnott . . . something's saying 'tennis' to me. But I don't think he could possibly be our white hope for Wimbledon. Why are you pulling those horrible faces at me, Foxon?"

"Trying to give you a clue, sir. I'm twitching my nose, like a rabbit does, and" — he stamped his foot hard on the floor — "I'm thumping a warning signal, sir —"

"Of course, the Thumper case! How could I forget? For a moment there, Foxon, I thought you really had gone out of your tiny mind. But it's all coming back to me

14

now. Trish Thumper, one of England's genuine Wimbledon white hopes, and that poor devil who tried to kidnap her, and asking Sussex if they wouldn't mind keeping an eye on the suspect once we had him in the frame. Harry Furneux at Hastings sent the Arbuthnott lad to play the slot machines in that Cranhurst pub with a microphone stuck in the back pocket of his jeans — and wasn't he in at the kill with Bob Ranger when chummie tried to snatch young Trish at Glyndebourne?"

"That's him, sir. He's a scruffy-looking chap" — Foxon regarded his own natty attire with satisfaction and tried not to smirk — "but he's a damned good detective. I bet he could infiltrate the Choppers easily, no question."

Brinton brooded a while longer, then made up his mind. "It's always worth a try," he said, reaching for the telephone. Then he withdrew his hand as if it had been burned. "Hang on a minute, Foxon. You called him Sleaze, and no doubt it suits him, but that's surely not his real name. I can hardly ask the Fiery Furnace to lend us a plainclothes man if I don't know what he's called, can I?"

"I think he was christened Julian, sir."

Brinton gazed heavily at his subordinate, but Foxon's face showed no hint of mischief. "I'll take your word for it, laddie," said the superintendent, dialling briskly. "And as this was your bright idea, you might as well hang around to find out what happens . . . Hastings police? Could I speak to Inspector Furneux, please? . . . Superintendent Brinton from Ashford . . . Yes, in Kent." He rolled his eyes. "Over the borders, in the wild country . . ."

The telephone receiver informed him that he was being put straight through, and there followed a series of clicks and a dull buzzing sound. Brinton sighed; then brightened.

"Hello, Harry? Chris Brinton from Ashford here."

"And let me congratulate you, sir, on the arrival of the telephone in the sticks," came the greeting from Inspector Harry Furneux of the Sussex constabulary. "I'd have expected communication by tom-tom, or smoke signal — or carrier pigeon, if things were desperate. Which I suppose," he added "they are, or you wouldn't be ringing me. Always glad to be of service to our less fortunate colleagues. So, what can I do for you?"

"You can lend me Sleaze Arbuthnott," Brinton informed his flippant friend. "If you can spare him, that is."

"Now, he's a good man. One of our best youngsters —"

"Which is why I'd like to borrow him Harry. Our own youngsters are too well-known around here, never mind being not young enough really — they wouldn't fit in so well. But your sleazy character'd be just the ticket . . ." And Brinton gave Inspector Furneux a potted version of what the Choppers had been up to, and what he feared they might do next. The Fiery Furnace listened in an understanding silence to the gloomy narration of his colleague.

"Well," he said as Brinton concluded his summary, "yes, I see what you mean, because we've been having similar problems down here. One theory is that it's the summer sunshine boiling their stupid brains and sending them cuckoo — that, and possibly drugs, just to spice things up a little."

"That's what we're wondering about, too. But it's hard to infiltrate a local crowd like the Choppers with everybody tending to know everybody, the way they do in a town like Ashford — or Hastings." Brinton sat forward, his eyes bright. "You'd like to nobble your lot, and I'd like to nobble mine and we face the same difficulties. Shortage of manpower being not the least among them. But, Harry, suppose we did a deal? You lend me Arbuthnott, and I'll send you one of my men, who wants to see a bit of action on this." Foxon's yelp of delight echoed round the superintendent's office and evidently made itself heard in Hastings. Brinton grinned at the receiver in his hand.

"Yes, Harry, that was him. Foxon by name, and a regular contrast to young Sleaze, from what I recall. None of this merging into the background for Foxon — he dresses like an artist's palette, so I'll send over a pair of sunglasses with him when he comes . . ."

"Which reminds me," remarked Furneux, "talking of artists — when they said it was you on the phone, I began to wonder — how's that Miss Seeton of yours nowadays?"

A groan burst from the superintendent's lips, which had suddenly turned pale. "For heaven's sake, Harry, don't go tempting fate! This Chopper business is nothing to do with Miss Seeton — thank goodness." He scowled at Foxon "And you can stop grinning like that, laddie, or the deal's off, garden gate or no garden gate, understand?"

"Sorry, sir," said Foxon, not sounding it, while the telephone remarked in the stricken superintendent's ear:

"You're forgetting what you told me once, sir. About how if she can get herself

tangled up in a case somehow, she will —
your Miss Seeton, that is. There was that
affair of the Lalique jewellery, and the Dick
Turpin crowd I gather she pretty well
caught single-handed — so what you really
mean, surely, is that it's nothing to do with
her . . . *yet.*"

chapter
2

Miss Seeton was not thinking about the Ashford Choppers and their vandalism; she was not even thinking about Mr. Jessyp's recent proposal — or, she hastily corrected herself, perhaps one should say *proposition* — though that also might lead to a degree of . . . misunderstanding. Miss Seeton, even in the privacy of her bedroom, blushed. *Suggestion,* she decided in a fluster, would be the best word . . . although even that . . .

"Oh, dear," said Miss Seeton with a guilty sigh as her eyes fell upon her well-worn copy of *Yoga and Younger Every Day,* and she forced her wayward thoughts back to the candle flame upon which she had been attempting to focus. But her guilt had been so great, her sigh so gusty, that the flame of the candle had flickered out.

"Oh, dear," said Miss Seeton. She was beginning to suspect that she would not achieve even *pratyahara,* the withdrawal or preliminary stage of yogic concentration, never mind the deeper techniques of *dharana, dhyana,* and — rarest and highest of all — *samadhi*. It was doubtless easy for the author to say that the ability to concentrate at will came as a result of strict self-discipline: years of practice and learning, Miss Seeton knew, went into the makings of a yogi. Her own half-dozen years of practice had certainly resulted in a suppleness of body — especially her hitherto troublesome knees — that she would never have believed possible: the advertisement had promised so very much, and for once an advertisement had not misled.

Perhaps — she blushed again — it had been an unsuspected hint of unladylike pride in her physical achievements that had prompted her, after all this time, to think about extending her daily routine to include some of the more esoteric pages at the end of the book. Perhaps she should have left well alone . . .

And yet . . . although she had bought neither candles nor matches for the especial purpose — living in the country, one should be prepared for stormy weather and power cuts even in summer — Miss Seeton felt that it might be regarded as wasteful, as well as weak-willed, to give up the attempt at *trataka* without one final effort. Apart from other considerations, she was curious to learn whether the facility of inner visualisation would (if she ever managed it) in any way assist her artist's outward eye. Not that one regarded oneself as a particularly gifted artist, but maybe for that very reason one should explore every avenue . . .

Miss Seeton leaned forward from her suggested straight-spined pose and picked up the box of matches. She slid it open, shook out a match, and struck it briskly along the side: the familiar acrid smell spiraled through the air as she applied the flame to the smoking wick of the candle, and she held her breath as the flame flickered a little, then in a quick burst caught the wick and began to burn.

Miss Seeton smiled, turned her head carefully to one side to blow out the match, and turned it back again to fix her steady gaze, as instructed, upon the fiery gleam. With her legs — how thankful she was that her knees no longer bothered her as they had done — neatly crossed in the Lotus posture, she began her rhythmic breathing.

She must concentrate on the flame — must empty her mind of all distraction — focus her gaze and regulate her breathing in time with her slowing pulse — must allow nothing from inside or outside herself to interrupt her . . .

And then, through the open bedroom

window, wafted on the delicate summer breeze, floated a burst of loud, resonant barking. It sounded as if two large and determined dogs had sighted a quarry they disliked and were making their dislike all too plainly known.

"Bother," said Miss Seeton, realising that *trataka* and *pratyahara* were not to be hers; realising, too, with a hidden sense of relief, that she was rather glad of the fact. She blew out the candle and unfolded herself from the Lotus posture without a click or a creak from her knees, and to celebrate what she saw as her liberation immediately coiled herself into the Dancing Serpent, such a picturesque name — such a pleasant, stretching sensation along one's spine . . .

It had sounded as if two large and determined dogs, sighting a quarry they disliked, had been making their dislike all too plainly known.

"Those animals," sniffed Mrs. Norah Blaine, "are simply too dangerous, I've said so more than once. If people can't control them, they shouldn't be allowed to keep them." With her angular friend Miss Erica Nuttel, whose knees were still shaking from shock, she warily crossed The Street and made once more for the Plummergen post-office-cum-general-store. On the same side of the road, but heading well away from The Nuts (as these ladies are popularly known) strode a tall, distinguished-looking man holding the leads of two elegant and muscular dogs with thick, silky coats. The man did not once look back; the dogs, their long, lean heads alert, kept staring over their shoulders, watching The Nuts every bit as closely as Miss Nuttel and Mrs. Blaine watched them.

Mr. Stillman's well-stocked establishment is patronised by the entire village and is normally the first port of call on any shopping expedition: it is also considered the hub of village life, for it is here that most of the gossip upon which Plummergen thrives is exchanged, exaggerated, and enjoyed by almost everyone. Foremost of the fermenters on Plummergen's grapevine are Miss Nuttel and Mrs. Blaine, who can be safely relied upon to worry away at even the smallest item of vague interest until it has become a full-blown saga destined to linger in local folklore long after the truth — often mundane and lacklustre — is forgotten.

No village comings or goings are safe from the keen eyes of The Nuts. Their house, with its acres of plate glass, stands directly opposite Crabbe's Garage in the centre of The Street — and Crabbe runs a twice-weekly bus service to Brettenden, the nearest town. Lilikot's windows are the best-cleaned in Kent, and the house has perhaps the best-weeded front garden in the county: The Nuts cannot bear to have anything escape their notice. And very little does, for the location of Lilikot is doubly convenient, being diagonally opposite the post office . . .

The bell pinged merrily as Mrs. Blaine pushed open the post office door. Her blackcurrant eyes glittered as she spied her audience within, although she was far too wise in the ways of the world to commit herself to any direct statement. Norah Blaine, in another life, would have made a good — that is to say, skillful — politician.

"Good morning, Mr. Stillman. Carefully now, Eric, and do ask Mr. Stillman to find you a chair. After the shock you've just had, I think you should sit down."

"Could be worse, Bunny," murmured Miss Nuttel bravely a faint echo of her normal gruff self. "Don't like to fuss."

"Too like you, Eric, but there's a time and a place for being stoic, and this isn't it. Or them," added Mrs. Blaine, in an anxiously grammatical moment. She hurried on: "Such a very hot day, too — we don't want you fainting, do we?" And she turned to glare at Mr. Stillman, who had not yet responded as planned.

"Oh," remarked Mr. Stillman, who disliked hearing remarks directed at him in the third person, and decided to reply in kind. "Miss Nuttel feeling faint, is she?"

Which gave Mrs. Blaine the opening she wanted. "Surely you must have heard the commotion a few minutes ago? Those huge dogs growling at us and showing their teeth, too grim and scary for words, and poor Eric terrified to cross the road with them tied up outside on the pavement."

"Ah," said Mr. Stillman, and nodded. "So the dogs didn't, as you might say, bite either of you, then?"

"They would have done, if we'd gone near them," replied Mrs. Blaine smartly. Mr. Stillman smiled a faint smile.

"So you didn't get near them, either? Ah, well, no harm done, is there, and no need to fuss," Mr. Stillman said in a mischievous echo of Miss Nuttel's own words earlier. He pointedly turned his back on the aluminium steps which he kept behind the counter and which, with their folding top, sometimes did service as a stool. "Was there anything in particular you wanted, or shall I serve Mrs. Spice while you have a look around?"

"Well," bristled Mrs. Blaine, "I must say, I wouldn't wish to be thought to jump the queue, but if Mrs. Spice isn't in a hurry . . ."

Mrs. Spice had been edging nearer during the exchange, as had her fellow shoppers. "Not too much of a hurry," said Mrs. Spice. "So Miss Nuttel feels poorly, does she? Those dogs, I'm not surprised, great savage-looking brutes, and tying 'em up outside like he does, it's enough to put anyone off shopping till he's gone."

The postmaster was content to ignore the remark, but his wife, whose feet were aching even at this early hour, sprang at once to the defence of the departed dog walker. "To my mind, Mr. Alexander is a very thoughtful gentleman. There are some people will bring their dogs in the shop no matter how many notices we put on the door that it's not allowed, but he's never once done so since that first time, and very apologetic he was about it, too, when we explained the health regulations to him."

"He shouldn't have needed it explained," Mrs. Spice said firmly. Since none of the notice-flouting dog owners was to be seen in the post office, she could say this without fear of hurting anyone's feelings — Plummergen generally reckons not to care tuppence for what it says behind anyone's back, but face to face is another matter altogether. "There's the notice, plain as you please, *No Dogs Allowed*."

"Plain enough, to the likes of you and me," pointed out Mrs. Henderson, "but then he isn't, is he? Like us?"

"Foreign," breathed Mrs. Flax, in doom-laden tones, and a murmur of agreement rippled round the post office interior as everyone settled down to the discussion that promised so very much in the way of speculation.

"Not a thing do we know about him," Mrs. Henderson said, "*or* his employer, *if* that's really what she is."

"Bold as brass I heard him come out with it!" exclaimed Mrs. Spice, "and so did Mr. Stillman, didn't you, that first time when he came in to buy stamps — '*My* mistress and I have just come to live in your charming village,' that's what he said, and could anything be more brazen than that?"

"Proper scandalous," opined Mrs. Bulman.

Emmy Putts, who brooded daily on the dullness of her life behind the grocery counter, added that he certainly was a good-looking man, if you liked the more mature type, and that funny foreign way he spoke made him sound, well, interesting.

"Shame on you, Emmeline Putts, for saying such things," chided Mrs. Stillman, who had frequent cause to worry about her young employee's flights of fancy. "And as for — that word he used, well — he's foreign, anyone can tell, and he just got the translation a bit wrong, I'm sure that's all there is to it. And even if it isn't," she added firmly, "it's nothing to do with you, Emmy." *Or with anybody else* hovered on her lips, but she restrained herself. With luck, they would take the hint.

Plummergen can be oblivious to the heaviest of hints, if by oblivion the torrent of gossip is permitted to thunder on unchecked. Mrs. Blaine leaped swiftly into the brief pause left by Mrs. Stillman's admonition.

"Surely it must be of concern to everyone in Plummergen, too mysterious, nobody ever seeing *her* at all, and guarded by those Bolshoi dogs of hers as the house is —"

"Borzoi, Bunny," corrected Miss Nuttel, who had regained strength and animation as the discussion progressed. Norah blinked at her friend, surprised at the interruption.

"What was that, Eric?"

"Borzoi, those dogs. Russian wolfhounds —"

"Guard dogs," insisted Mrs. Blaine, and

everyone nodded.

"And what's there to be guarded against in Plummergen?" demanded someone whose village pride had been hurt.

"Outsiders," suggested Mrs. Bulman. "If you ask me, that woman's in hiding, and that's why we never see her, with those dogs running free about the place behind that great high wall to chase 'em off — whoever," she appended darkly, "they might be. Or her, come to that."

"Could be anybody, right enough. Look who used to own the place, after all." Mrs. Spice led collective memory back several years. "Mrs. Venning . . ."

"She went to Switzerland so they said at the time."

"Nothing to stop her coming back once her poorly heart'd been cured, is there? Maybe that's why we never see her out and about — because she knows we'd recognise her."

"They said Mrs. Venning wasn't like to recover."

"Doctors," pronounced Mrs. Blaine with authority, "make mistakes more often than they'd care to have it known — and especially when it's in their best interests." She looked about her at the throng of eager faces. "After all, wasn't it drugs that was the cause of all the trouble? Too convenient for any doctor, a supplier right on his doorstep . . ."

There was a moment of speculative silence as everyone considered the relative positions of Dr. Knight's private nursing home on the outskirts of Plummergen, and, almost directly opposite, up a narrow lane, behind that all-too-mysterious high brick wall — The Meadows, former home of the notorious Mrs. Venning.

"Don't even know that she sold the place, do we?" Miss Nuttel contributed a further spoonful of surmise to the merrily simmering brew. "Never saw an estate agent's board go up, after all."

"It might be rented," came the hesitant suggestion from someone who lived in the council houses at the northern end of The Street. All the home-owners, with mortgages and tax relief ever in their minds, turned to gaze at the proposer of such a — to them — novel concept.

The speaker was young Mrs. Newport, who had three children under four and another on the way, sister to that Mrs. Scillicough who had taken sibling rivalry to its limits by producing triplets already notorious in village legend for their utter frightfulness, though they were barely past the toddling stage. With such an awesome inheritance, Mrs. Newport was used to standing her ground on the rare occasions when she felt strongly about something.

"It might be rented," she insisted, gaining courage from the way nobody contradicted her. "To someone Mrs. Venning maybe met out in Switzerland — foreigners, see? Like this Mr. Alexander, if that's his real name."

Which left the field open to the development of several rival theories. One school felt that the mystery woman was Mrs. Venning, disguised, in hiding, having escaped the police-watch set on her in Switzerland for some enterprise which was bound to be illegal; another opinion held her to be (her particular identity being still unknown) certainly a foreigner, probably Swiss, and definitely up to no good at Mrs. Venning's instigation, whatever "no good" might be.

A vociferous minority obstinately clung to the theory, supposedly debunked by P.C. Potter, that the man living in The Meadows had done away with the woman almost as soon as they arrived in Plummergen, burying her body somewhere in the grounds. Even though he continued to buy provisions enough for two, the theorisers maintained that he bought it solely in the cause of verisimilitude; the testimony of P.C. Potter, who (on learning from his wife, Mabel, what was being said) had insisted on speaking directly with the mystery woman, was not considered sufficient proof that the woman still lived. Potter had reported her safely alive, but eccentric in that she had received him in a veil: which only, as the theorisers said, went to show.

The distinguished dog-walker himself was thought to be of slightly less interest (unless, of course, he was indeed a murderer), as the very fact that he permitted himself to be seen in person suggested that he had (possibly) less to conceal. He was variously thought to be the mystery woman's lover ("Perhaps the vicar ought to have a word with them," a suggestion vetoed on the grounds that the Reverend Arthur Treeves wouldn't know what to say, in the first place; and, in the second, they'd never find out what happened anyway, as his sister would certainly not tell them) or manservant, although Emmy Putts was horrified at this. Mrs. Stillman quenched her again even more promptly than before.

"But it's definitely all too mysterious," concluded Mrs. Blaine, to the satisfaction of everyone. "I mean — nobody would just *turn up* in a village out of the blue like that unless there was something strange about them, would they?"

And Erica Nuttel cleared her throat. Every eye focussed upon her. She stared back, nodding wisely. "Not the first, by a long chalk," she said in portentous accents. "Maybe old Mrs. Bannet's goddaughter, inheriting her cottage, but — exactly what Miss Seeton did, isn't it?"

chapter
3

On such a very hot day Lady Colveden had wondered whether her menfolk might prefer a salad, such as she had prepared for herself, to their usual roast beef and vegetables. But working farmers, she knew, required calories with which to work, even if her own appetite had virtually vanished. She watched in amusement as Nigel polished off his second helping of richly gravied potatoes, and when Sir George gave the satisfied little cough which signalled repletion, she shook her head at the empty serving dishes and sighed.

"I don't know how you manage it," she said enviously. "You never seem to put on an inch, Nigel, even with all that starch, but in this weather even a lettuce leaf seems to be fattening, as far as I'm concerned."

"You could come out with us this afternoon," suggested Nigel, "and help bale the hay: think of the exercise."

"Think of my aching back," retorted his mother as she began to collect the dishes together. "You know I haven't the faintest idea how to use a pitchfork —"

The newspaper behind which her husband lurked twitched in his hands. Nigel coughed. Lady Colveden hurried on:

"Besides, it's the Best Kept Committee this afternoon, so I couldn't spare the time even if I wanted the exercise. Which I don't believe I do — do I?" And she glanced down at her still-trim waistline, frowning.

"Best Kept Committee?" echoed Nigel as he reached round *The Times* to retrieve his father's plate. "Do you mean you all have to dress up in your garden party hats and white gloves and posh frocks? I suppose that'll be the first time since you went with Miss Seeton to Buck House — better make sure the outfit's had a proper airing. We wouldn't want the Committee choking on mothball fumes. You know how they can linger, if you're not careful."

"Nigel, don't be irritating. You know perfectly well what I mean. The Best Kept Village Competition Committee, if you want me to say it in full, though it's rather a lot to keep chanting every time. And anyway, we all know what we mean, which is what counts."

Lady Colveden vanished into the kitchen while her son began to load plates and dishes ready to hand through the serving hatch. The percolator had been busy during the meal, and soon the tray laden with cups and coffee pot was being carried into the dining room while Sir George turned over a page in his newspaper and his wife settled herself to pour. "As a matter of fact . . ." she began as Nigel took his father's cup and manoeuvred it into place. Sir George uttered a grunt of thanks and turned another page.

"As a matter of fact," repeated Lady Colveden, "you may be interested in our committee, George." An agonised denial erupted from behind the newspaper before she could say more. "I meant," she corrected herself hastily, "in the work of the committee — I'm not suggesting you should join."

"Over my dead body," muttered Sir George Colveden, KCB, DSO, JP. "All those women nattering nineteen to the dozen — enough to make a man's blood run cold."

"I," his wife reminded him, "am on the committee, and if my presence makes your blood run cold, then all I can say is, what a waste of twenty-five years. Nigel, stop sniggering. It's hard enough to talk to your father at mealtimes when it isn't anything important."

Sir George lowered his newspaper.

"What's important?" He glanced at Nigel. "Don't let her co-opt you," he advised his son, who was grinning. "Fate worse than death."

"It isn't the fete," Lady Colveden rushed in to reassure her spouse. "It's the Best Kept Village Competition, and we haven't won it for years —"

"High time we won again, then. Good luck to you. Plant a few shrubs at the front of the house, if you think it'll help." And Sir George resumed his reading, thankful to have escaped so lightly.

"George, come back, please. Of course it would be nice to have some new flowering shrubs, if you could spare the time to put them in for me, but I wasn't thinking about this house so much as The Street. The judges are far more likely to wander around the main part of the village, rather than turning off up Marsh Road just to look at the Hall."

"They might try to catch us out," Nigel said, helping himself to more coffee, his voice grave. "You can't afford to be too relaxed in your guard at times like these."

Behind his newspaper the major-general uttered a cough which sounded, to his wife's suspicious ears, very similar to a laugh. "George, please! And Nigel, stop it.

This is important — we all think so."

"And who," enquired Nigel, "is *all,* exactly?"

"The Competition Committee, of course. Matilda Howett and Molly Treeves, and me — and Phyllis Armitage," added Meg Colveden. Nigel grinned.

"Poor Miss Armitage! Fated always to be an afterthought. I wonder if she's glad or sorry she doesn't spend too much time in the public eye?" Miss Armitage was a quiet soul who seldom offended anyone; she had once taken second prize at the Women's Institute Regional Show for her flower arrangement, yet not a soul had grudged her this brief glory.

"She's very artistic," said Lady Colveden quickly, "and she has a good sense of colour, and balance, and, well, that sort of thing. In fact, this business with your father and Miss Seeton" — she raised her voice to penetrate the barrier of newsprint — "was originally her idea, though the rest of us agreed to it at once . . ."

As her startled spouse lowered *The Times,* wide, innocent eyes met his. Meg Colveden smiled. "Why, George, how very kind of you to join us. Was it something I said?"

"Why you said it," Sir George said. "Wasn't it?"

"And it worked," said Nigel. "Mother is obviously privy to your guilty secret, Dad — you and Miss Seeton! What the Plummergen tabbies will make of *that* little item, I daren't think — and how I'm going to show my face in the village in future, I can't imagine."

His mother picked up the coffeepot. "Nigel . . ."

With a shrug, a grin, and a wink at his father, Nigel subsided. Sir George stroked his moustache reflectively. Lady Colveden smiled again.

"I never realised, all these years, that you were paying attention, George, but I'm so glad to find out at last. Now I shan't have to explain too much."

"Have to explain from scratch," he told her. "Something about the Howitzer, and the Competition, that's all I know."

"No, George, not Major Howett — it was Miss Armitage's idea. About you taking photographs of The Street, and Miss Seeton doing sketches of how everywhere could look if people followed the Committee's suggestions. Not that you were the person Miss Armitage thought of — she just said, someone who knows what they're doing with a camera. And of course, you were the obvious choice."

Sir George quietly began to preen himself as his wife explained. *The Times*, for once, was forgotten. Nigel gaped at the miracle his mother had wrought.

"Like tickling trout," he murmured in admiration. "Like catching monkeys — softly, softly . . ."

"Your father's not in the least like a trout," protested Lady Colveden, "and certainly not at all like a monkey."

"Not if he's going to use a camera, he's not," agreed Nigel. "Rather a bright scheme, really — before and after, with Dad's box Brownie doing the Befores and Miss Seeton and her paintbox producing the Afters. Which reminds me" — and he shook the coffeepot hopefully — "Does anyone else . . . ?"

His parents ignored him, and he was able to fill his cup for the third time. Sir George was preoccupied with more serious matters. "Sent my box Brownie to the church fete years ago," he reminded his family, with a sigh. "Sorry to do it, too: fond of the old memory-trap. Don't make 'em like that anymore."

"And they don't make film like that anymore, either," said his wife. "They stopped humouring sentimental people like you ages back, which is why I decided it was a waste having the place cluttered up with a camera you couldn't use. But if," she said, in the coaxing voice of Eden's serpent, "you were thinking of taking up the hobby again — which you said you were, remember, when Cedric Benbow first came to the house . . ."

"So I did," remarked Sir George, brightening. The grand old man of fashion photography, Cedric Benbow of worldwide renown, had first made the acquaintance of the Colvedens at the time of his much-publicised search for the Lalique Lady. This young woman, chosen by Cedric himself to model designer clothes and to wear the priceless jewellery borrowed from museums in Lisbon and Paris, had needed (according to Cedric Benbow) the decorations of William Morris to display her and her adornments to best advantage; and Rytham Hall boasted two of the finest Morris rooms in the country.

Nigel Colveden had lost his heart, albeit briefly, to Marigold Naseby, Cedric's prize model; Cedric and his crew had nearly lost some of the jewellery, in a daring daylight robbery thwarted, at the very last minute, by Miss Seeton, in a manner which forged firm bonds of friendship between Sir George Colveden, the great Cedric Benbow, and two other visitors to Rytham Hall who could duly relish the recherche character of the whole adventure.

"Benbow," nodded Sir George. "Haven't seen him for a while — time we all got together again." For, every few months, Sir Wormelow Tump (custodian of the Royal Collection of Objets de Vertu) and Ferencz Szabo (dealer in fine art, whose gallery was in Bond Street) would join their new friends Benbow and Colveden at Sir George's club, for an evening of cheerful and reminiscent sodality. "Could pick his brains about the best camera to buy," reflected Sir George. "Maybe learn a few tricks of the trade at the same time — nothing like asking an expert for advice if you want a job done properly."

Lady Colveden sighed with gentle relief that her husband had taken it so well. When Miss Armitage had first made her tentative suggestion, clearing her throat and politely waiting for a suitable pause in the conversation before daring to speak, nobody had for one minute supposed that she had been volunteering her own services as Plummergen's wizard of the single-lens reflex. Phyllis Armitage belonged to the age of tripods, black cloths over the head, and glass plates — which, even supposing such items to be more obtainable than the film for a box Brownie, nobody could imagine her using with particular success.

The thought of a box Brownie had at once brought to the mind of Lady Colveden her husband, and his long-neglected hobby, and his friendship with Cedric Benbow . . .

"No point in hanging around," said Sir George, briskly folding up *The Times* and pushing back his chair almost in the same movement. "Might as well give him a ring now, if he's at the studio — if not, daresay someone can take a message." He glanced at Nigel and returned his son's faint grin. "Important matter, after all — practically life and death, this competition. Utter nonsense about Miss Seeton, though — pleasant little soul, but not my type." He nodded to his wife as he made to disappear out of the door. "Tell 'em I prefer blondes," he advised, and vanished.

"That's one in the eye for you, Mother." Nigel drained his cup and set it in its saucer. As Lady Colveden smiled, he began to collect together the other cups and crockery and tidied everything on the tray. "Blondes, indeed!"

"Oh, he's talking about Daphne Carstairs — ages before we were married," she said, frowning. "Miss Seeton — now, I wonder —"

"For heaven's sake, Mother, I was only teasing," broke in her son, in some alarm.

"Surely you don't think —"

"Of course I don't, and neither would anyone else with any common sense. But do take care not to say anything of the sort down in the village, won't you — you know how they delight in getting hold of the wrong end of the stick, and the poor little soul comes in for quite enough gossip as it is. No," said Lady Colveden, "what I was wondering was, is she going to be able to fit in the After pictures, with all the other projects she has on hand? Not just the Scotland Yard business, though I notice she hasn't seemed to be doing so much recently, although I'm sure there was more in that Dick Turpin affair than anyone ever knew, but then, I am a school governor, and when Mr. Jessyp rang me yesterday, of course I had to say it was a good idea, only I'd forgotten about the Before and Afters when I agreed."

"Mother darling, has the shock of Dad's secret obsession turned your brain? What has your being a school governor in any way got to do with — oh." Nigel grinned. "At least you aren't suffering from Seeton Disease, after all — disjointed ramblings that only make sense if people sit down with wet towels wrapped round their heads and flash back in slow motion. I hadn't," he said, "realised that Miss Maynard's mother was ill again . . ."

It was not one of Martha Bloomer's days for "doing" in Miss Seeton's cottage, and now that her yoga session was over, Miss Seeton had Sweetbriars to herself. She had made herself a fresh pot of tea and was sitting now in thoughtful solitude to reread the letter which she had received by the first post that morning — a tribute to the professional dedication of red-haired Bert and his fellow post office workers, for the writer had only committed his missive to the mail the previous evening.

> The School House
> Plummergen
> Kent
> Thursday, 10th July

Dear Miss Seeton,

Although it is rather short notice, I wonder if you would possibly be able to help out as a supply teacher next week as you have done on previous occasions. Miss Maynard's mother, who as you know has been ailing for some time has become suddenly so much worse that an operation has been proposed, and naturally her daughter wishes to be with her. As it is fairly near the end of term, your duties would certainly be less onerous than on previous occasions: general supervision of previously set lessons, with the occasional excursion, also already planned, to Ashford Forest for nature study rambles, and to Greatstone, to visit the Shire Horse Stud. They have a splendid collection of harness and farm machinery, as well as a flock of Suffolk sheep and other animals which the children might like to draw. Perhaps you would be able to organise some form of competition for the best picture? It is planned to hold a small exhibition of the children's handiwork in the school during the final week of term, so that the parents of our pupils may see and admire their efforts from the whole school year.

Pay and conditions would be as before, and I very much hope you will see your way to helping us out in this slight emergency. Perhaps you would be kind enough to telephone me on Friday, at some time convenient to yourself, to let me know your decision.

Yours sincerely,
Martin C. Jessyp

It was a simple enough request, and of a kind which she had fulfilled more than once in the past, as Mr. Jessyp, the village school's headmaster, acknowledged.

Then why did Miss Seeton feel a slight twinge of unease as she read the letter for a third time?

chapter
4

Chief Superintendent Delphick, The Oracle of Scotland Yard, who first was instrumental in annexing Miss Seeton's unique artistic skill for use by the forces of law and order, once described his remarkable protégée as everybody's conscience — the universal maiden aunt, humanity's backbone, going to the stake again and again throughout history as a matter of principle. Detective Constable Bob Ranger, who was the astonished recipient of this profound assessment of Miss Seeton's character, came over the years to see how very true it was. Indeed, he and his wife Anne, daughter of Plummergen's Dr. Knight (whose private nursing home, following Anne's matrimony-induced defection, was in the capable charge of retired Army Major Matilda Howett), very early in their acquaintance chose to adopt Miss Seeton as their own Aunt Em, conscience and all . . .

Certainly, Miss Seeton's conscience was ever vigilant — some, less scrupulous than Miss Seeton, might say troublesome — and especially now. So very thoughtful of Mr.

Jessyp, trying to spare poor Miss Maynard any anxiety about deserting her post, although of course one could not really see it as such when a daughter's duty was surely to be with her mother at a time like this — yet was it not equally true that one had one's own duty, to Scotland Yard? And to be committed to two or more weeks (Miss Seeton, so happily retired, was now vague about when the school term ended) of teaching, when perhaps the police — who were, one had to admit, so very generous with their fees — might call upon one's services — and naturally must have first claim upon one's time . . . The awkward phrase *conflict of interests* had been dancing in letters of fire around Miss Seeton's mind all morning: fire which might subconsciously have been the reason she decided to essay the exercise with the candle flame, failure though it turned out to be.

Miss Seeton has no proper understanding of her true value to Chief Superintendent Delphick and his constabulary colleagues. She believes that the annual retainer she is paid for what she calls her IdentiKit sketches is a measure of her artistic competence; she tries her conscientious best to provide likenesses of such persons as the police request her to draw, and genuinely does not realise that a proper IdentiKit would probably do the same job much better. Miss Seeton's importance lies in the quick-fire, almost instinctive — some would say psychic — drawings of which she is always slightly embarrassed. She regards them as cartoons, almost doodles, and tries not to let anyone know when she has, at some urging she never fully comprehends, produced one. Rather, she is more proud of her ability to turn out *proper likenesses of what one sees,* not realising that a photograph would have the same result.

The police send for Miss Seeton, known to their stubborn computer paymaster as MissEss, when matters seem out of the ordinary — for Miss Seeton herself is the most ordinary and conventional person in Kent: the contrast is piquant, and to Scotland Yard very useful. It is also not strictly true, for Miss Seeton is a conventional only in her own eyes — Scotland Yard, and the newspapers, know better. Adventure follows Miss Seeton — no, is stirred up by herself when, behaving in a purely conventional manner, she produces a far from conventional result; and does not even appear to notice herself doing it. In Miss Seeton's eyes she has done nothing remarkable or noteworthy: she would greatly prefer neither to

51

be remarked upon or noted; when she is, she regrets it, but sees it as the price one has to pay for doing one's duty. Miss Seeton has taken, not the King's Shilling, but the Queen's, in the form of the Scotland Yard retaining fee, and her duty to the police is plain.

But, mused Miss Seeton now, had one not also a duty to the community in which one lived? Poor Miss Maynard — and Mrs. Maynard, so unpleasant, being in hospital — the anxiety over the schoolchildren which might be lessened were one to speak the word — and Mr. Jessyp, always so courteous and considerate of one's feelings, arranging the lessons as far as possible to fit in with one's abilities — and such amiable children, always polite and interested . . . a pleasure to teach again, just for a change, although one would never wish to return to such employment full-time — not that one needed the money, although it was always welcome, but there had been the surprisingly generous settlement from the insurance company after those pictures belonging to the Duke of Belton were found in the gallery in Switzerland, and the interest from the deposit account was gratifyingly high . . . but then the police might wish for some IdentiKit drawings, and if one had accepted a prior commitment . . .

Miss Seeton sighed and shook her head. No wonder she had been unable to achieve mental calm this morning: there was far too much for her to worry about. Perhaps it would be best if she were to ask someone for advice . . .

When the telephone bell rang on his desk, Superintendent Brinton was frowning over a report that had just come in. Almost without thinking, he groped for the receiver; why, he found himself wondering, did the rhythmic ringing sound so, well, hesitant? As if whoever was on the other end of the line were clearing his or her throat and preparing to apologise for disturbing him . . .

"*Who* did you say wants to talk to me?" he demanded when the switchboard relayed the message. The message was carefully repeated.

"Miss Seeton." Brinton sighed, clutching at his hair. "Well, you'd better put her through — but you can stop that sniggering before you do." The switchboard apologised, but still with a choking quality to its voice that told Brinton his paranoia concerning Miss Seeton — and who, he silently asked the empty office, could really blame him? — was known to the whole of

53

Ashford police station, if not the entire Kent constabulary. He groaned, and cursed.

"I do beg your pardon, Miss Seeton — a frog in my throat — hay fever," he gabbled when a polite voice enquired if he was indeed Superintendent Brinton, and if he was quite well. "Oh, yes — a nuisance, but I've learned to live with it. Never mind me, though — I'm sure you didn't ring up to hear me sneezing, did you? What exactly can I do for you?" And he crossed mental fingers that her request, whatever it was, might not be too exotic.

He'd been right: the first thing she did *was* to apologise for disturbing him. And the second, and the third . . . but that, he could cope with: and he made the right noises at her, soothing, friendly, trying to stop her saying the same thing fifty different ways. Trying also, he realised, to put off the evil hour when she managed to get down to brass tacks and tell him why she'd really rung . . .

"I felt, you see," she explained, "that it would be best to speak to you — as you are nearer than London, and I first thought of asking P.C. Potter, except that his wife told me he is out on patrol, and you are his superior officer, are you not? And, having first approached Mr. Potter, even though he was not there, I thought it might be unethical to telephone Scotland Yard."

She paused. Brinton, who had been shaking his head in an attempt to clear some of his confusion, realised that Miss Seeton was hoping he would reassure her, although for what, exactly, he wasn't absolutely certain.

"That's quite all right, Miss Seeton." It wasn't easy to sound convincing when you were as baffled as Brinton was, but he did his best. "Don't worry about it — forget it, and just tell me why you rang. There's nothing," he repeated, "to worry about at all."

"And I told her," he lamented, ten minutes later, "there was nothing to worry about at all — I must have been out of my tiny mind even to dream of saying something like that to your Miss Seeton, Oracle. Stark, staring mad."

"*Our* Miss Seeton," the amused voice of Chief Superintendent Delphick corrected him all the way from Scotland Yard. "She's as good as on the strength, remember — attached to the force by being paid an annual retainer for her sketches. She's a professional colleague, Chris, and — what's that strange noise? Interference on the line, no doubt."

"That was me," Brinton corrected him unnecessarily. "Me uttering a hollow groan. You know as well as I do — but what's the use? I should have guessed this was coming, what with Harry Furneux this morning going on about her and young Foxon, blast his eyes, saying she was bound to get involved somehow — fated, that's what she is. And what can anyone do except resign themselves to fate? Or," he added, brightening, "resign, full stop. It'd be a pity about such a shortfall in my pension, but believe me, Oracle, there are times when I'd say the sacrifice was worth it."

"How about telling me what the problem seems to be? You know what they say about a trouble shared —"

"The trouble," broke in Brinton, "is arson."

Which drove the laugh from Delphick's voice at once. He said, "Arson? Miss Seeton?" and then, not for the first time in his association with MissEss, could think of nothing further to say.

"Oh, she isn't going round setting fire to things — but somebody is, and she seems to have known about it almost as soon as I did. It makes me nervous, Oracle. I can't help wondering what she's going to come up with next."

"She knew about it as soon as you did . . . because it was in Plummergen, you mean?"

"No, I don't. That," pointed out Brinton, "wouldn't be so well, spooky — at least if someone had burned down Plummergen village hall, or the church, you'd *expect* Miss Seeton to know about it."

"Then has she drawn you one of her pictures?"

Brinton shuddered. "Not yet, no, thank heavens. When she gets going along *those* lines, it makes me really jumpy — how you manage to interpret 'em, I'll never know, but between the pair of you it strikes me as downright creepy . . . Which, I suppose," he reflected, "is what this yoga business is, in any case, so . . ."

Delphick gave him ten seconds to explain, then prompted his old friend with: "What's so creepy about Miss Seeton standing on her head? She's done it for years."

"She wasn't standing on her head," Brinton said. "From what I gather, anyway. She was sitting staring at a candle flame — that's what made her decide to call me, she said, I think, though you can never be sure, with Miss Seeton." He clutched at his hair again. "Listen to me, will you? She's got me as confused and woolly as she is! I might as well write out my resignation letter this minute."

Delphick ignored all but the basic facts. "Why should Miss Seeton's staring at a candle flame worry you?" Never mind why it made her think of telephoning the Ashford police — minor matters could wait. "Did she, er, see a vision?"

Brinton took a deep breath. Then he released it and took another. "Well, I feel such a fool now. But it was too much of a coincidence. I was reading a report from the fire brigade just as Miss Seeton rang — we've been having a spot of trouble with the Ashford Choppers, or rather their younger brothers — vandalism, stealing cars, you know the sort of thing. But last night two haystacks went up in flames, and, now there's been time to check, the brigade doesn't believe it was spontaneous combustion."

"Krook," interjected Delphick with delight.

"Or crooks," said Brinton who hadn't read *Bleak House*. "Your average arsonist usually does it for kicks, or for the insurance — but a bunch of yobboes, egging each other on for the sheer hell of it, that's vandalism in a big way, and in hot weather like we've been having . . . Haystacks *can* catch fire spontaneously, you see, which is why they weren't too worried at first. The hay has to be perfectly dry, for a start, and then the middle of the stack has to be built properly — the right proportions of hay and air, or it overheats — you sometimes see farmers who're a bit bothered shoving wooden poles into the heart of the stack to see if they come out charred. If they do, then it means dismantling the whole thing before it bursts into flames . . . But these two last night apparently began burning from the outside in, they found out once it was daylight."

"Not spontaneous combustion," Delphick agreed. "And you feel that somehow or other Miss Seeton's got hold of this, almost before it happened?"

"You," bristled Brinton, the countryman, "may not think a couple of haystacks worth worrying about —"

"I didn't say so, Chris. In fact, I —"

"— but how do we know where it's all going to end?" the superintendent went on, ignoring his friend's attempts to soothe him. "The Choppers'll get a taste for it, the same way the kinky ones do, and they'll be burning places down left, right, and centre — which'll bring the *regular* kinky ones out of the woodwork, and Lord knows what sort of bother we'll have with sex crimes as a result — you know it always seems to get worse in summer anyway, girls in short skirts and panties hanging on the line overnight to dry . . ."

Brinton's predictions of gloom might, to one unused to Miss Seeton, have appeared more than farfetched. Delphick did not think so, however; and this time, as the superintendent drew breath, managed to say so. He expressed his concern and only wished there might be something more he could do. Short of gagging Miss Seeton, or taking away her pencil and sketchpad, however, he could think off-hand of nothing.

"You can be ready," growled Brinton, "to drop everything else and come down here when I shout for help, you and that young giant of yours who calls her, heaven help him, his own dear Aunt Em. The pair of you seem to be able to understand her — I don't. The only thing I understand right now is, to go by her previous form, she knows we're in for a long, hot summer — and I'm in the firing line . . ."

"Firing line," repeated Delphick thoughtfully. "Fire — oh, yes, I do see."

chapter
5

The sun shone bright in a cloudless sky as Miss Seeton rose on Monday morning, prepared to do her duty by the youth of Plummergen. Reassured by Superintendent Brinton during the brief conversation they'd had last week, she had telephoned Mr. Jessyp and said that, unless the police required her to sketch for them, she would be at the disposal of the Education Authority from now until the end of term, and Miss Maynard need now worry about nothing more than her poor dear mother's health. Mr. Jessyp had expressed his delight and gratitude, and Miss Maynard, before she left the village on her errand of mercy, had brought round to Sweetbriars, with tears in her eyes, the biggest box of chocolates Miss Seeton had ever seen.

"Come, come, I love you only, tum, tum ti tum," hummed Miss Seeton as she performed her toilet. She was sorry for the Maynards, of course, yet it was pleasant to be in harness once more, to know that one was still needed and that one's former skills were not forgotten. "Come, come, tum ti tum, tum ti tum . . ." The song from *The Chocolate Soldier* — Oscar Straus, not Johann, but the music was just as delightful as those charming waltzes — somehow seemed expressive of her mood today — and such lovely chocolates, although quite unnecessary, when one was only too pleased to be able to help in such an emergency.

Having performed her yoga exercises — without even an attempt at *trataka:* so far as that was concerned, the flame of the candle would remain forever unlit — and break-fasted, Miss Seeton said a cheerful goodbye to Martha Bloomer, who had popped across from her cottage to ensure that her Miss Emily went off to work in good time.

"Now, don't forget your umbrella," Martha reminded Miss Seeton, mischievously. But Miss Seeton had already stopped at the stand in the hall and was unclipping her second-best brolly even as Mrs. Bloomer teased her. No matter that the sun was blazing down, and the songbirds, their beaks aboil, were thinking about staying silent for the rest of the day: Miss Seeton had never, since she'd been of an age to think ahead, gone anywhere without her umbrella; and she didn't plan to begin now.

"After all," said Miss Seeton as Martha

gazed up at the cloudless sky, "it is a very hot day. And parasols, more's the pity, are no longer fashionable — waxed paper, with such splendid floral patterns, as I recall, and so cooling, to be in the shade — I once made my class draw a still life, with an open parasol behind, and summer fruit, and a Chinese jar in willow-pattern, for contrast, although during recreation some of the naughtier children crept back in, so greedy, and ate it before the drawings were complete. The display of fruit, I mean. And it taught me," said Miss Seeton with a smile, "only to use flowers in future. I might try to ask the children to draw summer flowers in one lesson, although there is the timetable to consider, of course. Mr. Jessyp has said that so near the end of term a certain amount of flexibility is in order, and especially when the weather is so hot — their concentration you see, and only natural, for a child, to wish to be outside playing instead of indoors at one's lessons. There are to be," said Miss Seeton pleased, "a number of school excursions, which will be interesting as well as educational, I feel sure. A nature study ramble in Ashford Forest, I understand, and there will be plenty of wild flowers there. Perhaps we could have a little contest to see which child could find the greatest variety . . ."

Still happily planning her lessons, Miss Seeton found herself being gently pushed out of the cottage and down the short paved path towards the wooden gate in her neat picket fence. "You may have left plenty of time to start with," warned Martha Bloomer, "but if you don't get a move on, you won't reach the school until every kiddie in Plummergen's at their desks and waiting. Off you go, and don't worry about a thing — I'll dust around and have everything sorted out by the time you come home again."

Dear Martha, such a treasure, and so concerned for one's well-being. Miss Seeton's eyes glistened as she turned on the corner by the bakery opposite to wave to Mrs. Bloomer, who still stood in the doorway, before starting to make her way down The Street towards the school.

The main street in Plummergen — indeed, virtually its only street — runs almost due north and south. It is wide, more or less straight, and a quarter of a mile long; shops and houses of various architectural styles and periods line it on either side. Miss Seeton chose this morning to walk northwards along the westerly side of The Street, to catch the morning sun; the sun whose rays glittered merrily on the panes in the tiny, bow-fronted windows of the bakery: which, now that it has become an outpost of Winesart's empire, is also a sweetshop and tobacconist, though Miss Seeton seldom uses either of these facilities. But she began to wonder now about a Battenberg cake for afternoon tea, once she saw what a tempting display Mrs. Wyght had set out in the bakery window: peeling off the marzipan, so sickly but in small amounts so tasty, to release the little pink and yellow squares of sponge sandwiched together with apricot jam . . .

The yellow doors of the blacksmith's forge next caught her eye as she continued on her way: they were propped open, and Miss Seeton, fascinated by the sight of a craftsman busy with his craft, stopped to watch. During the course of the weekend Daniel Eggleden had received more orders than he normally took in a month: all of them rush jobs, and all with the deadline of Judgement Day, as village wags were starting to call the time when the Competition should reach its climax.

The whole of Plummergen had caught Competition Fever. Sir George had bullied Cedric Benbow into meeting him for dinner and a concentrated discourse on the art of photography the very day after his telephone call, Lady Colveden and her committee had held a meeting in the village hall to which everyone had been invited, where a preliminary plan of campaign had been set forth.

"We've already won once, but that was some years ago," said Lady Colveden at the end of an inspiring speech. "Now it's up to us all to see what we can achieve towards winning again. Major Howett, Miss Treeves, and I — not forgetting Miss Armitage's invaluable assistance, of course — have been busy drawing up a list of suggestions for improvements that might be worthwhile, but of course we'd appreciate it if any further ideas were to come from you. Then we'll put everything together, and see if we can't come up with a joint effort. We really will have to try our best," concluded Meg Colveden cunningly, "if we're going to win the trophy when Murreystone are so keen," and she sat down, delighted with the stir her final words now made.

The village of Murreystone is to be found five miles due east of Plummergen, as the crow flies, in the middle of Romney Marsh; but as, in the windswept marshlands, no crow will fly in a straight line, so is Murreystone more like seven or eight miles from its neighbour and rival by road, depending on which route is taken. Some people feel that the distance between the two could do with being even greater, for something in the nature of all-out hostility had been enjoyed by the villagers for generations.

Murreystone boasts a more skilful darts team; Plummergen which claims cricket to be the superior sport, never fails to wipe the floor with the smaller village when the needle match is played at the end of each summer. Murreystone's population has never crept above the three hundred and fifty mark, whereas Plummergen hovers at just on the half-century. The church at Murreystone is larger and far more interesting, historically; Plummergen's congregation always raises more money at the annual village fete. Both churches have as their vicar the Reverend Arthur Treeves — but his residence is in Plummergen, which Murreystone sees as a calculated affront. The Reverend Arthur regrets the rivalry between his two parochial charges, and in earlier days, before he lost his faith, would try to bring about a reconciliation: an older and wiser man now, he has not attempted such a thing for years. And woe betide any young man from Plummergen who goes courting a

Murreystone maiden: it is not her father, but her brothers who will be after him with a shotgun, and that to drive him out of the parish, not force him to the altar.

Lady Colveden's final words, therefore, had been chosen with deliberate cunning, and they did not fail of their purpose. The meeting applauded vigorously, and then everybody began talking at the tops of their voices. People leaped from their chairs to besiege the committee's table, clamouring to submit their pet suggestions for the beautification of Plummergen, and as Lady Colveden scribbled frantically on her notepad, Matilda Howell was forced to remember her old Army training, barking brisk commands at the villagers until they formed a more or less orderly queue and gave everyone time to think.

Wrought-iron gates, house numbers, and decorations such as flower baskets or lamp brackets were thought likely, if applied to Plummergen homes in prime locations, to catch the favourable eye of the competition judges; blacksmith Daniel Eggleden was known to be a skilled worker with a good aesthetic sense and could be relied upon not to turn out every gate looking exactly like the rest. The items he made would harmonise, but retain their individuality: Dan's

abilities are renowned. Samples of his handiwork are on display in two glass cases outside the forge for customers to ponder when
he is not there and the yellow doors are
closed.

This morning, however, the yellow doors
were wide open and the smith was already
hard at work. From the depths of the forge
came the roar of the bellows, the clang of
hammering, and sudden clouds of dancing
scarlet sparks which made Miss Seeton, in a
gesture that was instinctive, put up her umbrella for protection.

"Things getting too hot for you, Miss S.?"
enquired an unexpected female voice in her
ear. Mel Forby, old friend to Miss Seeton
and demon reporter of the *Daily Negative*,
had crossed the road from the George and
Dragon, where she'd just come to stay, to
stand beside the little figure in the neat
tweed suit. Miss Seeton, having jumped at
being startled out of her concentration,
smiled.

"Miss, er, Mel, how delightful to see you.
You've come back, then, as you said you
might?"

"As I said I *would*," Mel corrected her.
"After all that Turpin business a few weeks
back, and me missing out on it, you think
I'd run the same risk again? My spies are ev-

erywhere, you know. Just as soon as Anne Ranger warned me how her mother'd told her things were starting to hot up for the Best Kept Village Competition, I told that editor of mine I was going to write a series on the Rural Revival — so here I am." She nodded towards the labouring figure of Daniel Eggleden. "There's a whole generation growing up that doesn't know one end of a horseshoe from another, let alone wrought-iron twiddly bits for lamp posts, so I see it as my journalistic duty to enlighten them, before it's too late."

Miss Seeton nodded but was too busy studying Dan at his work to reply for a moment. An artist herself, she could appreciate another artist, even in so very different a discipline. "You see," she remarked, after a moment, "how even when he has no need to hammer the iron he keeps hammering on the anvil? He keeps up the rhythm all the time — saving his muscles, I suppose, for comfort, so like the *Anvil Chorus* — the strong beat, I mean, keeping time."

Mel shot her a quick look. "You're perfectly right, and I'll make a note of it for my article. You don't miss much, do you? The artist's all-seeing eye, I guess it must be." Miss Seeton blushed. "Say, Miss S., how about a couple of illustrations for my article? You know the sort of thing — *The Village Smith at Work* — and I promise not to mention the muscles of his brawny arms in the text even if you draw 'em. A nice little fee for you, plus my editor getting the chance to see some genuine Seeton drawings, which he's said for ages he'd dearly love."

Miss Seeton went even pinker, but regretfully shook her head. "I fear I would hardly have the time, Mel, dear, even if my contract with the police allowed me to sell my drawings elsewhere, which I'm not sure that it does, and though Mr. Brinton or Chief Superintendent Delphick would doubtless know, I hardly feel I could ask them, when they're so very busy. Sir George and Lady Colveden have asked me to do some sketches of Plummergen — suggestions, you know, for the Best Kept Village Competition — Before and After, as Nigel calls them, and of course I am delighted to assist, but when Lady Colveden offered to pay me out of parish funds, I would in any case have refused, living here so happily as I have done these past few years — which is why I was so glad to be able to help when poor Miss Maynard's mother was due to have an operation — and it hardly seems entirely proper, does it," Miss Seeton concluded, "to be paid twice? Though very flattering, of course, to be asked."

Mel could see from her friend's anxious expression that Miss Seeton, tying herself into ethical knots, desperately wanted the young reporter to understand. And Mel was quick, and bright: brighter than she seemed. Originally noted for the tough manner, acid tongue, and mid-Atlantic accent which she had assumed during her early years in Fleet Street, Mel had been influenced by Miss Seeton's admiration for the interesting bone structure of her face, and the beautiful eyes she had disguised with heavy black shadow. Both her makeup and her manner had mellowed; she felt confident enough now to face the world as she really appeared and let the world be fooled, if it so chose. Looking soft and acting tough rendered Mel a highly effective service: by the time the people she dealt with had worked out what was happening, it was too late. She might look too gentle to take advantage: but the advantage was always on Mel Forby's side now.

Not that Mel would ever have dreamed of taking advantage of Miss Seeton. "Don't worry, honey," she said, patting the older woman gently on the shoulder. "Relax — I won't badger you again, though it was a pretty good idea, while it lasted — but if you've got other commitments, why, I understand."

Miss Seeton sighed with relief. She did not care to let her friends down, but really, she was so busy — although it might be possible for her to let dear Mel use one or two of the sketches she had promised the Colvedens, for the Competition — entirely without payment, of course, that must be quite understood. and provided also that nothing of Plummergen's plans would be made known, in case Murreystone learned of them — but it might be rather interesting, to find out if and how the printing process altered one's work, which would have to remain anonymous, as well, for fear of upsetting the police, when they'd already been so good about allowing one to — what was the word . . .

"Moonlight, of course," decided Miss Seeton at the end of a long, thoughtful silence — silence, that is, from Mel and herself, though not from the blacksmith. Dan Eggleden had been hammering and working the iron all this time, and a small crowd had gathered to watch.

Mel jumped. "Moonlight? You mean sunstroke, don't you, Miss S.? It's going to be another scorcher of a day. Unless you've got something planned for later this evening?"

"Oh, dear." Miss Seeton had suddenly remembered where she was supposed to be. "This morning — and I'm late — the children will be waiting, such a bad example — but so interesting to watch, the sparks falling in such graceful curves, and no fear of burning, it seems unless one goes too close, which it would be most unwise to do." Briskly she furled her umbrella. "Do excuse me, my dear. I hope to see you again before too long . . ."

And she hurried off up The Street.

chapter
6

With a smile Mel watched the little figure trot anxiously away until an overhanging hedge partly hid her from view. That, thought Mel, had better be pruned before the Best Kept judges get here: she wondered who it belonged to, though it hardly mattered. Plummergen, she knew well enough, would bring every citizen to order at a time like this: the offending greenery was as good as firewood already.

Not so strange that she should be thinking of fires just now, as there was a rumour that a pyromaniac, or a group of them, might be going into action in the Ashford-Plummergen area. As Mel had said, she had spies everywhere — or rather, the editor of the *Daily Negative* had them, and when anything to do with Kent came up, he allowed Mel, the acknowledged Seeton expert, to make use of their intelligence. He'd hardly made any complaint at all when she'd dropped hints about another holiday when she'd barely come back from the cruise she'd taken with Thrudd Banner, fellow (though freelance) reporter and extremely close personal friend. Thrudd had been called away on a foreign assignment by World Wide Press, leaving Mel free to scoop whatever story there might be burgeoning. And if it was anywhere near Miss Seeton, then burgeon, Mel felt sure, that story certainly would . . .

But her cover of a series on the Rural Revival was something more than that. She'd enjoy writing up the blacksmith and his beautification of the village; she'd try to talk to the farmers who were having their haystacks burned down, and learn about combine harvesters and thatching and whether the rabbits enjoyed all the excitement. And she might just slip in a few artless questions about spontaneous combustion . . . give the cunning yokels a chance to score over the ignorant townies, and let slip more than perhaps they ought. Mel had every intention of fooling the rustics as much as she fooled her fellow reporters — and especially if there was likely to be a Battling Brolly angle to the story when it eventually broke. Which was more than likely, seeing how Ashford was no more than fifteen miles away from where Miss Seeton lived — and that umbrella of hers seemed born to trouble as, well, as the sparks fly upwards, thought Mel.

Her eye was drawn back to Daniel Eggleden and his brawny — yes, there was no other word for it, hackneyed though it might be — arms wielding the hammer and periodically thrusting the cooling iron back into the fire to be heated again. The sweat dripped from his brow, and the red gleam of the fire brought out gold highlights in his hair. Mel watched his muscles ripple and thought wistfully of Thrudd.

There was a movement at her side as someone materialised just out of her line of vision and, clambering against her, planted a warm, moist kiss on the back of her neck. With a yelp of surprise, Mel turned.

To find herself gazing at two huge brown eyes set in an aristocratic face: a face long-boned and finely featured, a narrow face framed by two drooping ears.

"Your dog," Mel complained to the man on the other end of the lead, who was clearly struggling to frame an apology, "has just accosted me. The least you can do is introduce us properly." Firmly she removed the huge silky paws from her shoulders. "And to his friend," she added, noticing that he held another, better-behaved dog on a second lead. "His, or hers? With all that fur it's not easy to tell."

"I most humbly request your pardon,

madame." The man, a tall, distinguished figure almost as elegant as the two dogs he now kept firmly at his side, bowed low. "Such a disturbance has never before occurred — I regret that I allowed my attention to wander." He gestured briefly towards the forge and the busy figure of Dan Eggleden. "Happenings of this nature I have not witnessed previously, and it was of great fascination to me — too much so, if it permitted such a lapse. I apologise again, for the sorry behaviour of my companions. Their only excuse must be that they are still in high spirits after the walk they have taken in the fields by the imperial waterway."

He hadn't spoken more than a half-dozen words before Mel was wondering about his accent. Something exotic, foreign — eastern European, but cultured, nevertheless. Almost like a stage Russian aristocrat, with the dogs as props. Weren't they — Mel had vague memories of once covering an Exemption Show where the judge went berserk with a stainless steel water bowl and laid out the presenter of the Sit, Stay, and Come Cup — those Russian Wolfhounds, indeed? And to call the Royal Military Canal the Imperial Waterway was, okay, a logical translation perhaps, but rather overdoing it . . .

So what was a phony Russian doing in Plummergen? And why was he so busy staring at the blacksmith's forge? Could he be admiring Dan Eggleden's muscles just as she'd done, in a purely aesthetic way, of course — or were there more sinister overtones? Maybe he wanted the smith to forge him a picklock or something, and was wondering how best to phrase the suggestion . . .

All the while she was furiously thinking, Mel was making a fuss over the two Borzois, stroking their gracefully arched spines and admiring the plumes of their gently waving tails. And the man was ignoring her, still intent upon what Dan was doing at the anvil, though the dogs began to whine and lick and reciprocate Mel's advances. They pulled on their leads and panted with pleasure, their long tongues slurping along her hands as she caressed them.

They really were splendid creatures, it almost didn't matter that their master had an aura of mystery — and phony mystery, Mel was willing to bet — about him. "What are their names?" she enquired and forced the man to drag his attention back from what the blacksmith was doing and to direct it towards her. After all, she'd been slobbered on by one of his dogs, which was as good an introduction as any, and one Mel would turn to her own use.

"Boris and Sasha." Yes, that figured. Keeping up the pretence right along the line. "It is Boris who took such a startling interest in you, for which I must again apologise. He is normally a most well-conducted animal."

"Boris and Sasha," said Mel, duly patting both dogs as she spoke. "Forby — Amelita Forby," she introduced herself with a smile, and an inquisitorial glint in her eye.

There was only the briefest of pauses before the man, with another bow, said: "And I am Mr. Alexander. An unexpected pleasure to have made your acquaintance, Miss Forby, but a pleasure indeed. However" — he glanced at his watch, and twitched one eyebrow in a gesture of polite dismay — "it is too long this morning that we have been away from the house, and you must, if you will be so good, excuse us. You are staying in the village? Then we may perhaps meet again. It is my duty to accompany Boris and Sasha on their walk every morning, both there" — he glanced back down The Street past the point where it narrowed between Sweetbriars and the row of cottages where Martha Bloomer lived, then headed southwards over the canal — "and, as you see, back."

He bowed again, a stately inclination of his silver head which reminded Mel of the courtiers in *Anastasia*. What was with this guy, hamming it up like that? And what a name to choose — *Mr. Alexander,* indeed. Why not call himself Alexei and have done with it? Talk about obvious.

And Mel glared after Mr. Alexander as he and his two dogs departed north up The Street, following in the footsteps of Miss Seeton. "I'd like to see what Miss S. makes of him and his oh-so-Russian act," she murmured, thinking of various occasions when Miss Seeton had, with her sketches and their insight into human nature, shed light on behaviour which had other people puzzled. "Yes, I'd like to see it, very much indeed . . ."

What Mel in fact now saw was a car — one of the taxis from Crabbe's Garage — driving slowly down The Street, passing the little group that had just left her and drawing up outside the George and Dragon on the other side of the road. Jack Crabbe, who recognised Mel from her previous Plummergen visits, nodded a brief greeting to her as he climbed out of the driver's seat and hastened to open the passenger door.

A woman emerged, dusting herself down with an irritated air. Jack Crabbe looked hurt: evidently he'd picked her up from Brettenden railway station, but she could hardly have become covered in grime during the six miles to Plummergen. His cab, as Mel well knew, was always spotless.

Above the continuous clanging of Dan's hammer in the forge behind her, Mel was unable to hear the conversation between Jack Crabbe and the newcomer; but from the toss of the latter's head, and the wink Jack tipped in Mel's direction when he climbed back into the taxi, it required fewer investigative skills than those possessed by Amelita Forby to guess that the townie had come off worse in whatever little exchange there had been. Normally Jack carried his passengers' bags into the hotel and stopped for a chat: not this time, however.

Leaving Daniel Eggleden to his work, Mel strolled back across The Street and smiled at the woman who stood outside the George and Dragon's ivy-covered frontage scowling down at the two tweed-covered suitcases dumped by Jack Crabbe at the edge of the road. "Need a hand?" enquired Mel, gesturing towards the luggage. "I'm staying here, too," she added with a further smile as the woman's eyes narrowed. "Name of Forby, Amelita Forby. Miss," she found herself appending in a way she'd never done before.

Mel found the woman unnerving. She was tall and thin, her bony features made more prominent by the steel-grey bun into which her hair was scraped. Balanced on her hooked nose were spectacles with what looked like steel rims, and the thickest lenses Mel had ever seen outside mad professors on children's television. And through that thick wall of glass glittered eyes full, Mel could tell, of strong convictions; an uncomfortable personage, indeed.

"Hawke," returned she of the spectacles, after something of a pause. For goodness' sake, surely she didn't suspect Mel of designs upon her luggage — a craving for that bulky shoulder bag, of all unlikely things? She could at least have said thanks for the offer, Forby, but I'd prefer to manage on my own.

"Ursula Hawke," she said gruffly after having favoured Mel with one of her piercing glances. "Thank you."

Without another word, Miss (Mel had spotted her ringless left hand) Ursula Hawke bent her bony knees with a series of creaks and picked up the smaller of her two cases. Mel was not sure whether to be amused by the effrontery or annoyed; while she was making up her mind, she began to grapple with the larger case and followed

Miss Hawke towards the white-pillared doorway of the hotel. By the time she had climbed the two low steps, breathing hard, Ursula Hawke had reached Reception and settled her case on the floor beside her.

There was nobody there: but there was a small brass bell standing on a handwritten label instructing visitors to ring if attention was required. From the brisk tintinnabulation Miss Hawke produced, it seemed that attention was very much required. Mel dropped the case and clapped her hands to her ears.

"Careful with that," barked Miss Hawke, then took no further notice as she shook the bell once more.

In response to the urgent summons, Doris appeared from a back room somewhere, breathless and red of face. Head waitress at the George and Dragon, she served also as part-time receptionist; but not, she was quick to inform Miss Hawke as the latter checked in, as a porter.

"Not with my back, I couldn't, not if you was to pay me a thousand pounds. You'll have to wait till Mr. Mountfitchet gets back" — Charley Mountfitchet was the landlord — "unless Miss Forby might like to, er . . ."

Mel pushed her features into a smile of resigned cooperation and waited for Miss Hawke to express her gratitude. "Pretty poor state of affairs," opined Miss Hawke, without a word to Mel, then picked up her case again and trudged off towards the stairs. Evidently Mel was supposed to follow with the larger case without being asked again.

Oh, well, it took all sorts, and the reporter in Mel had been intrigued, as well as a little unnerved, by Miss Ursula Hawke. What was she doing in Plummergen? Was she always so brusque and ungrateful, or had something happened today to make her worse than usual? And what — Mel wheezed as she mounted the stairs, reduced to bumping the case from step to step while Miss Hawke trod briskly upwards — had she packed in her suitcase to make it so heavy? Journalists, jetting around the world at short notice after stories, of necessity travel light. If they don't, they must be on holiday. Mel, not for the first time, wished Thrudd Banner were with her.

Miss Hawke paused outside her bedroom door and checked the number on the key Doris had given her. "Fine," she said as she slipped the key into the lock and began to twist it. Mel puffed to a standstill beside her, thankfully dropping the case and contriving to bump against the smaller one Miss Hawke had elected to carry. She wanted to know just how hard-done-by she ought to feel when she brooded over this cavalier treatment in the privacy of her own room, or when — if he managed to get through on the international telephone system — she was telling Thrudd of her adventures.

The smaller case never even wobbled as Mel collided with it. Maybe Miss Hawke wasn't quite as ungrateful as Mel had thought: the thing must be at least as heavy as the larger case, if not — Mel nudged it questingly once more — heavier. Much heavier . . . almost, Mel thought, what might be called a dead weight.

"Come far with this little lot?" asked Mel, when, having got the door open, Miss Hawke seemed likely to vanish inside without another word. But the reporter was going to end up with some sort of information if it killed her. After all, they were guests in the same hotel. There was an etiquette about these things. "I'm down from London," she offered, making to pick up the case she'd struggled with. Maybe if Miss Hawke believed the privacy of her room might be invaded by this inquisitive Samaritan, she'd let out something — anything —

to get rid of her. There was a pause.

"Maidstone," said Miss Hawke at last, then seized the handle of her case and hefted it over the threshold. Mel's efforts, it seemed, deserved some explanation. "But it was too far. Plummergen is more convenient. Much."

And, dragging her other suitcase with her, Miss Hawke disappeared inside her bedroom, and closed the door; and, to Mel's surprise, carefully locked it behind her.

chapter
7

"Eric, don't open the door!" squeaked Mrs. Blaine as Miss Nuttel, shopping bag in hand, was about to summon her friend forth. "There's that man with his dogs, right outside our house — and on our side of the road, too!"

Norah Blaine was peering through the white net curtains which allowed The Nuts to see out of Lilikot's plate-glass windows, but nobody to see in. "He's smiling," she hissed. "Too sinister — what's he got to be so cheerful about?"

Miss Nuttel sat down heavily on the stripped-pine bench in the hall. She pressed a bony hand to her side and gave a gasping little cough. When nothing happened, she uttered a groan and dropped her shopping bag on the floor.

"Eric!" cried Bunny, startled, as her friend had intended. "Are you all right?" She came scuttling out of the lounge and rushed down the hall. "Eric — what is it?"

"Those dogs," muttered Eric, shuddering at the memory. "Barking — ready to attack —"

"Oh, I know, we could be eaten alive in our beds. We're hardly safe with them wandering loose through the village at any time of the night or day." Mrs. Blaine was being unfair to Mr. Alexander and the Borzois in saying this, for the dogs were always kept on the lead when walked along The Street, which only happened twice a day, morning and evening. And only in the meadows beside the "imperial waterway" were they allowed to run loose. "Too dangerous," said Mrs. Blaine. "It makes one wonder why anybody would need such ferocious guard dogs without something to hide, doesn't it?"

She was voicing the same opinion as they finally entered the post office opposite, Miss Nuttel having been reassured that the mysterious Mr. Alexander and his dogs were well out of range. Miss Nuttel was ready to back up Bunny's opinion with a few choice words of her own; but for once The Nuts were not the centre of attention.

The post office was humming, and Emmy Putts was preening herself as the cause of all the excitement. Her mother, who worked in Brettenden's biscuit factory, had been on night shift during recent weeks and consequently found out what had been going on in the area long before anyone else.

"Burned down the school, so they've done, fire brigade there half the night and poor Wully Boorman with his leg broke falling off the turntable ladder trying to save the caretaker's cat, that climbed down by itself anyway and not a whisker singed, and the police snooping about in the ashes looking," said Mrs. Skinner, who'd button-holed Eric and Bunny before they'd reached the grocery counter behind which Emmy Putts held court, "for clues. Deliberate, that's what they say it was — and them haystacks on Ted Mulcker's cousin's farm over Brettenden way, they was deliberate, too."

"Arson? But that's too terrible!" cried Mrs. Blaine, all fears of canine savagery driven from her mind on learning of this new threat. "Why, we could be burned alive in our beds every night for a week, with a maniac at large! What about the police?" She glared round accusingly, looking for Mabel Potter, wife to the village constable. But Mrs. Potter, her husband having warned her of the likely mood abroad today, had decided that her shopping could wait for a while. "What are the police," demanded Mrs. Blaine, "doing about it?"

"Looking for clues, so me mum said," Emmy Putts informed her, a little peeved that Mrs. Skinner had stolen her thunder and left her, really, with little to add to what had already been said. Nothing to stop her putting forward her own idea about what had happened, though. "They say," she announced with a delicious shudder, "that it's sort of kinky, like, to want to go around setting fire to places — sex, and that."

"Emmy," warned Mrs. Stillman, "get back to your work, and don't talk nonsense. Mrs. Henderson wanted some tomatoes, if I remember rightly."

But the postmaster's wife was too late: the seed, once sown, flourished on the fertile soil of Plummergen's hyperactive mind. "A sex maniac?" squeaked Mrs. Blaine in alarm. She turned to look for Miss Nuttel, who was gazing thoughtfully at the selection of garden gnomes Mr. Stillman, in deference to the Best Kept Village Competition, had brought in to add to his usual more subdued stock. "Eric, did you hear what everyone's saying? We must go into Brettenden at once and buy a burglar alarm!"

This suggestion was thought by the majority of shoppers to be well worth following, and the post office would have been vacated en masse by the panic-stricken hordes if someone had not remembered that, since the powers-that-be had reduced the bus service to one day a week, the only other way of travelling into Brettenden was on the twice-weekly bus run by Crabbe's garage.

"Bus don't run today," lamented Mrs. Skinner. "We'll have to lock all our doors and windows tonight, you mark my words no matter how hot the weather. But to-morrow . . ."

Mrs. Henderson had once quarrelled with Mrs. Skinner over whose turn it was to arrange the church flowers, and never missed a chance to score over her. "And what use would such a thing as a burglar alarm be," she asked, "when we all know what trouble that one of Miss Seeton's has always caused her — and us, too, going off at all hours through not being set proper and a good job, if you ask me, that she's not fixed it after the lightning struck t'other week. More bother than they're worth, such contraptions are, and there'd be a sight more sense in getting a dog about the place."

"Like the ones at Mrs. Venning's house," breathed Norah Blaine. "That man was prowling up and down The Street with his dogs this morning — we both saw him, didn't we, Eric? And he was *smiling*, too sinister for words. Why would he do that if he hadn't been up to something? Something," moaned Mrs. Blaine, "in Brettenden last night — they say that sort of person gets a, . . . a *perverse pleasure* from setting fire to — well, even the most ordinary places — like a school."

"Thinking of all them poor innocents frying alive, make no mistake," suggested Mrs. Skinner. "Gloating, that's what he'd be about, depend on it." Everyone shuddered: everyone except Mrs. Henderson, that is.

"Then he'd have done far better to set fire to the place during the daytime, when there'd be some kiddies inside, and a spot of sense to his carrying-on," she remarked.

"But that's surely the point!" Bunny Blaine turned upon her at once. "When a maniac's involved, there's absolutely no sense to his behaviour whatsoever — they're completely irrational, everyone knows that, which is what makes them so dangerous. Unpredictable," said Mrs. Blaine, and everybody shuddered once more.

"Like I said," sulked Emmy Potts, "kinky."

"Pyromania," announced Miss Nuttel in an authoritative tone. It was her first contribution to the discussion, and everyone's eyes focussed upon her. "Well-known form of sexual deviation." She flushed slightly as Bunny's mouth dropped open in shock.

93

"Best keep a lookout for anyone behaving oddly," she suggested. "Fit locks on windows and doors as well, of course."

"First thing tomorrow," decided Mrs. Blaine, "we'll be on the bus for Brettenden, and we'll go straight to the ironmonger's and buy locks for every window in the house! And I know," she added in a plaintive tone, "I'll never sleep a wink tonight, with worrying about what will happen next . . ."

A sentiment which was echoed by almost everyone in the post office.

The mingled delights of shock, scandal, and shopping must not be indulged in for too long, lest they lose their force. Plummergen knows this well, and instinctively. Thus, after a pleasurable half-hour or so threshing out the finer points of pyromania, the merits of guard dogs, and various systems of burglar alarm, people began to drift homewards in moods of enjoyable anxiety, casting worried glances over their shoulders and vowing to make Jack Crabbe drive tomorrow's bus to Brettenden earlier, and faster, than ever before.

The Nuts crossed the road in a thoughtful silence. Poor Bunny was still upset by Eric's blatant use of the shocking words her friend had hardly realised she'd known, let alone be able to come out with in public like that. Erica Nuttel was brooding on the garden gnome Mr. Stillman had procured; its face wore a lopsided grin which quite unnerved her. And Mr Stillman had chosen it deliberately! Outside the gate of Lilikot, she paused.

"Didn't like to say anything in the post office, Bunny, but Mr. Stillman's in a bit of an odd mood recently. Touchy — snapped at us the other day, didn't he? Wouldn't let me sit down after those dogs . . . Might just be worry over the Competition, of course — unlikely, though. No front garden, is there?"

"Oh, Eric, surely you don't mean . . ."

Miss Nuttel put a long finger to her lips. "Walls have ears, Bunny. Best not say too much. Just felt you ought to be warned."

"Oh, Eric! And the post office so near the house — we'd never know until it was too late! What shall we do?"

Before she could collapse in the hysterics which seemed likely to develop, Miss Nuttel opened the gate and shoved her sharply inside. Bunny squeaked with startled indignation, but her squeak was drowned out by a sudden horrified yelp from Miss Nuttel.

"The lawn!" she cried and dropped the shopping bag to point with a shaking finger.

"My lawn — look at it!"

"Oh, Eric," gasped Bunny, following her friend's gaze. "How — how peculiar, those brown patches. Surely they're not supposed to be there, are they?"

Normally Miss Nuttel humoured her friend's ignorance about the more practical aspects of home ownership. Bunny cooked the meals, Eric grew the fruit and vegetables essential to their back-to-nature lifestyle. Bunny turned sheets sides-to-middle and hemmed towelling bought by the yard in bargain basements, while Eric slapped paint on peeling woodwork and waged war on black beetles. Bunny pushed the broom and the vacuum cleaner; Eric mowed the lawn.

"Of course they're not supposed to be there!" snapped Miss Nuttel as her friend repeated the artless question. "Never seen anything like it in my life — ruined, ruined!" She might have been a mother bewailing the lost virginity of a cherished only daughter. "My lawn . . ."

Mrs. Blaine had been staring about her during the lament of Miss Nuttel for the loss of the billiard-table verdure which was the result of so much toil. In times of drought, not a drop of washing-up water was allowed to run down the kitchen drains; Miss Nuttel collected it all and stored it outside in the waterbutt, into which she would siphon bath and shower water, as well. The flowers might be allowed to wither, but the lawn was treated as lovingly as those parts of the garden which produced good, wholesome food . . . Small wonder, then, that Eric was upset. But there was a limit to the length of time Bunny was prepared to stand staring at the mottled greensward: her gaze wandered . . .

"Eric!" she clutched Miss Nuttel's arm. "Eric, do look at the Cape Daisy!"

"*Dimorphotheca aurantiaca,*" Miss Nuttel corrected her automatically, turning to look at the cherished marigold-like flowers edging the path, expecting to see their usual black-eyed centres nodding up at her. "Bunny! It — it's got them, too — whatever it is!"

Once they started to look about them, they could see signs of the mysterious brown wilt on several of their prize specimens as well as the lawn. The morning sunlight showed up every stricken stem, every withered leaf. "In too much of a state about those dogs to notice earlier," Miss Nuttel said, when Bunny, bleating with shock, ventured to ask if it could have happened while they were out. "Must have been during the night — some sort of fungus, maybe, activated by the sun — highly infectious, by the look of it. Better buy a large tin of Cheshunt Compound in Brettenden tomorrow, as well as the window locks."

"I think," quavered Mrs. Blaine, who'd been looking over the hedge at their neighbour's garden, "you'd better make it a really big tin, Eric. Or two, or three — because . . ."

In her turn she pointed, and Miss Nuttel followed her gaze. On the lawn in front of the house next door was a rash of brown patches, more or less regular in shape, as were those on Lilikot's lawn; and Miss Nuttel's knowledgeable eye could see that the same tawny blight had disfigured other prize flowers and shrubs.

She glanced up and down The Street: in other front gardens, returning shoppers seemed to be discovering similar problems. Little cries of horror and dismay filled the air.

"And, oh, Eric," lamented Bunny, wringing plump hands as her friend stood frowning, "*what* will happen now about the Best Kept Village Competition?"

chapter
8

Mrs. Putts had been correct to suggest police suspicions of arson at Brettenden School: Superintendent Brinton had stood and shouted at Detective Constable "Sleaze" Arbuthnott for nearly five minutes before, recollecting himself, he choked out what might have been an apology and motioned the young man to sit down.

"It's so damned frustrating," he grumbled as Sleaze set one of the upright chairs neatly in front of Brinton's desk. "We get you to infiltrate — and now you say it isn't them, or if it is, you don't know anything about it."

"It's early days yet, sir. They hardly know me, and I'm sure they don't trust me." Detective Constable Arbuthnott, having settled himself comfortably on his chair, crossed one leg over the other and began to jog his topmost foot to an unheard rhythm. From a hole in the toe protruded a sock-shrouded lump which marked time; the superintendent shut his eyes briefly, as if in prayer.

"You must fit in with them so well," he

complained, "it seems hard to believe they didn't let *something* slip. Half the Choppers went to Brettenden School — not that it did much good, you can't get most of 'em to sign their names on statements without telling 'em how to spell them — but even the ones who attended Ashford would burn the other place down just for the sheer hell of it."

"They're pleased, of course, sir — you can imagine the sort of comments I've been hearing — but I honestly couldn't swear to it that anyone I've met was involved."

"So far as you can tell, on your brief acquaintance," the superintendent reminded him.

"So far as I can tell on my brief acquaintance," agreed Sleaze, unruffled. "Do I take it, then, sir, that you wish me to continue to further my acquaintance with the Choppers for a few more days, at least?"

"What's a week or two, between friends?" Brinton said, with a despairing shrug. "Just see if you can produce a small miracle at the end of it all." He gestured towards the door. "On your way, laddie, and get infiltrating — and get results, and fast!"

But by the end of that week they were no further forward with the arson enquiry: if anything, they had fallen back. The sports pavilion on Brettenden playing fields had been reduced to ashes, and two empty shops off Ashford High Street had suffered severe fire damage. There were reports of other outbreaks in areas a few miles removed from the Choppers' usual sphere of influence: another fireman was injured, this time by falling masonry. The Choppers, notorious, had evidently spawned a rash of imitators, and there were no clues to the identity of anyone involved.

Brinton began to suspect that Sleaze Arbuthnott would learn nothing from the original gang because in some way he'd broken his cover; and he began to fear that, if the perpetrators of the arson were not caught soon, someone would be seriously hurt. His one consolation in the middle of all this was that nobody, at any time, had mentioned Miss Seeton's name in connection with the series of fires; even P.C. Potter's weekly telephone call from Plummergen seemed to suggest that everyone there was more bothered by a recent outbreak of some peculiar plant disease, and the antics of a few mysterious strangers, than by anything Miss Emily Seeton looked likely to get up to.

"After all," Brinton told Chief Superintendent Delphick, "she's teaching at the local primary school, for heaven's sake, which ought to keep her busy until the end of term, at least. So it looks as if my premonition was wrong — touch wood," he added with a hasty thump of his desk that set the telephone dancing. "I mean," said Superintendent Brinton in a wistful tone, "what harm can she do, keeping an eye on a load of children?"

And the Oracle did not feel it appropriate to remind his friend that Miss Seeton, on top form, never needed to *do* anything at all: adventures just seemed to happen to her, no matter that she would think it improper to encourage them. She had been, after all (he told himself) a teacher before her retirement — surely Brinton was right, that it would keep her out of trouble . . . he devoutly hoped.

If the two anxious policemen who counted themselves as her friends could have observed Miss Seeton at that moment, they would have been uncertain whether to be relieved that she was taking her teaching duties so seriously, or alarmed at the train of thought which appeared to be running through her mind.

During the first occasion of her acting as a stand-in for Miss Maynard, Miss Seeton had taken her entire class to the coast for an afternoon, encouraging them to picture the view in the way they preferred, the resulting works of art to be judged in an end-of-term competition. It says much for her teaching skills that she encouraged one child to write a poem, and others to make collages, and that all were automatically entered: the point of art being, as far as Miss Seeton is concerned, to make people see. *How* people, individually, choose to see does not matter, provided that they don't wander around noticing nothing at all . . .

On subsequent occasions Miss Seeton had demonstrated a variety of techniques such as wax scraping, splattering (Mr. Stillman reported a severe shortage of toothbrushes after that particular lesson), and potato printing (the greengrocer sold his entire week's supply in one afternoon). Every child in Plummergen looked forward to art with Miss Seeton; and, being convinced, as they'd become after that unforgettable excursion to the seaside, of her supernatural powers, they were always almost unnervingly (to their parents) well behaved.

They sat now, arms folded, eyes watchful, waiting, while Miss Seeton delivered her stern warning.

"You must remember, children, that matches are not playthings and that naked flames can be extremely dangerous. I do not wish to hear that any of you have attempted what I am about to show you without your parents' knowledge, and when there is no grown-up with you. Do you understand?"

Fifty small heads nodded gravely, and there was a murmur of thrilled assent. If she caught any of 'em out, there'd be no saying what she might do — not that they'd dare, the way she had of looking at them and seeing right inside. They squirmed on their seats and shivered.

Miss Seeton smiled with pleasure at observing the force of her words. The dear children, so enthusiastic, barely able to sit still with excitement, but unlikely, she felt confident, to disobey. People spoke of the difficulties of teaching in a modern world: certainly, Miss Seeton had found it rather less enjoyable a profession before she retired, but that was due, no doubt, to the strain of living in London. where one barely knew one's neighbours and saw one's pupils once or twice weekly and their parents not at all. Whereas village life, especially in a place such as Plummergen which was so very friendly, meant that one knew not only one's pupils, but their parents, too — so fortunate: the personal touch, mused Miss Seeton, smiling again.

The class hardly dared to breathe. They stopped their squirming and shivering and sat like statues, silently begging Miss Seeton to put them out of their misery and get on with the lesson. But nobody was foolhardy enough to voice the wish aloud: everyone knew, after all, that Miss Seeton was, well, strange. Her lessons were always good fun, and so long's you didn't go upsetting her, she'd be fine — but everybody knew . . .

"I want you all to leave your seats and come up to the edge of the platform," instructed Miss Seeton, "but you are not to climb on the platform itself. The smallest children must stand at the front, with the tallest at the back looking over their heads. Quietly, now."

And while they were arranging themselves, with a lack of pushing and mischief that the strictest of teachers would have envied, Miss Seeton withdrew from the top drawer of her desk a box of matches and a candle — that same candle from whose flame she had tried to win the yogic benefits of *pratyahara*. Waste not, want not: Miss Seeton was of a generation to remember the War, and remember it clearly. She was delighted to have found some practical use for her purchase.

Miss Seeton set the candle carefully in its

holder and struck a match briskly along the side of the box. She set the match to the wick and observed one hundred little flames gleaming in the bright and fascinated eyes watching her every move.

Miss Seeton picked up a sheet of strong white paper from the desk and held it taut and flat above the candle. With a slow and steady hand, she lowered the paper until it was in the smoky part of the flame, left it there just long enough to become smudged, then raised it again. Again she lowered it, again raised it — and again — and again . . .

"Remember, children, that on no account are you to try this by yourselves," Miss Seeton warned as she gradually formed a random pattern of soft smoky ovals on the underside of the paper. "For your lesson," she explained, "I have already prepared some starting sheets for you, but before I hand them out, I will show you how we stop the charcoal from smudging away — watch me carefully, now."

She blew out the candle, moved it to one side, and rose from her seat. "There is no need to follow me, children, if you turn carefully to watch what I do next," she said, and, picking up the sheet of delicate grey-on-white patterns, moved to the rear of the platform, where she had already set a small easel. She pinned the sheet to the easel, picked up the small aerosol can which stood on a nearby shelf, and sprayed the sheet with a fine, colourless varnish.

"Fixative," explained Miss Seeton. "So that the pattern will not become rubbed off the paper. Now we must wait for it to dry — that is, normally we must wait. But, as I told you there is no need for you to wait at all before you all may begin to draw what you see in the patterns."

"Miss," enquired one hardy youngster, who'd been dared to do it by his friends and stood to corner the playground market in gobstoppers if he accepted the dare, "what are we going to see in the patterns?"

"I really couldn't say," said Miss Seeton, beginning to hand out the prepared sheets to her charges. "It's not for me to tell you what you see, but for you to learn to see for yourselves. See if the shapes remind you of anything, I mean — and then you might like to draw round the outlines in pencil, or add other shapes with coloured crayon, to bring out what you see clearly enough for everyone else to see, and to share. Which is the purpose of art, after all. Not to be selfish with our imaginations, that is to say."

She turned to the nearest small girl. "Would you mind letting me borrow your paper for a moment, Genefer?"

"Go on, Jen, give it to Miss . . . Share it like she said, Jen," came the giggling encouragement of her friends as Genefer looked slightly uncertain about having been singled out in this way. Miss Seeton smiled at such evidence of artistic enthusiasm.

"Don't you think," she suggested after a moment's study of young Genefer's paper, "that these patterns might look rather like the tops of trees in a forest?"

"Waving in the wind," agreed Genefer after a moment, "only it's more a storm, with the leaves all blurred because they're moving so fast. Yes, I see, Miss. I see!"

"Those aren't trees," objected the gobstopper boy. "Trees have got trunks. Those smudges haven't any trunks. So they can't be trees, not really."

"Shut up, Marcus." Genefer rounded on the budding art critic at once. "You've got to *see* them, like Miss said, so if you can't, I've got to put them in so's you can. That's right, isn't it, Miss?"

"Absolutely right," Miss Seeton told her with a smile. "And the rest of you must see your own pictures in the smoke — everyone will see something different — and we'll all try to guess afterwards what the pictures are."

There was a general scuffling as the children, clutching their papers eagerly, hurried back to their desks and began to concentrate. "Mine," announced Marcus "is a dinosaur, a triceratops, and I'm going to draw a tyrannosaurus coming to have a fight with it."

"Ssh," hissed his friends. "We're meant to guess . . ."

Miss Seeton beamed as she watched the class settle down to work with every evidence of enjoyment. She would herself be working with them, on the sample pattern she had just produced; she wondered what the Surrealists would have felt about their technique being taught to a class of primary school children, and thought they would be pleased to know that their methods of generating new ideas and images had lasted so long.

Having retrieved her most recent Accidental Drawing from the easel, she sat at her desk to study it. What could she see in the random arrangement of smoke? Not trees, not even one large tree; nor flowers; nor storm clouds, although such hot weather meant, mused Miss Seeton, that there was always the chance of thunder, especially in the afternoon, and rain would certainly be welcome before too long. So many of the lawns in Plummergen were looking most dreadfully brown and scorched with heat, although her own, though it was at the back of the house and faced almost due south, luckily did not. Which must either be due to the excellent care Stan Bloomer lavished on the garden at Sweetbriars, or else the high brick wall, such a mellow, comfortable red, provided a welcome shadow . . .

A face, thought Miss Seeton, coming back to her pattern of smoke with a start. At least — no, now she came to focus clearly, it wasn't a face any longer. Which was probably as well, as it might have been somewhat impolite to draw the face of a stranger with whom one had done no more than pass the time of day earlier that morning . . . a bird, that's what the pattern reminded her of, as she looked at it. A large, wide-eyed bird with soft feathers . . .

But even as Miss Seeton found herself sketching in the sharp claws and hooked beak of a barn owl, she couldn't help seeing in the back of her mind's eye, the hook-nosed face of the tall thin woman who had been talking to her in The Street when she'd been on her way to school.

chapter
9

Sir George Colveden's clubland evening with his good friend, the photographer Cedric Benbow, had definitely been worth the next morning's headache and the smiles of his family. On hearing of the major-general's intention to resume his hobby — and taking a mischievous delight in the thought of fostering a village feud — Cedric had not only brought with him a selection of his cameras, from which he hinted that Sir George would be offered whichever seemed most suited to his purpose, but produced, at the cigars-and-brandy stage, a massive scrap book, bound in watered silk and filled with newspaper cuttings.

"Not about me, though," he explained, displaying it with some pride. "This is how I've been keeping an eye on the opposition over the years — mine are all" — and he stressed the word, smiling — "covered in velvet. Scarlet first, so scandalously sinful, and the next was a heavenly, vibrant orange — California sunlight, you know — my third is like English woodland simply crammed with primroses —"

"No need to put on a performance for my benefit, m'dear fellow," Sir George reminded him cheerfully, puffing a cloud of rich smoke in his friend's direction. Cedric had the grace to flush and chuckle.

"Sorry, I forgot — after so many years, one slips into the spiel automatically, I'm afraid. Marvellous publicity, you understand."

Sir George nodded, grinning, then said: "Going to be a bit awkward when you reach the end of the rainbow, so to speak. Stripes, perhaps?"

"Certainly, the time isn't so far off, now. I've been wondering about going through the whole spectrum again in satin, or maybe suede — but never mind my nonsense. Let's see what we can do to put Plummergen really on the map this summer, shall we?"

There followed what was a virtual monologue on Cedric's part, with Sir George interpolating the occasional remark when his friend permitted. "Of course, it takes years for anyone to reach this sort of standard all the time, but you aren't that bothered about pretty pictures, are you? From what you told me, that is. Get this Competition of yours out of the way first and then you can begin on the fancier stuff when you've time to take it slowly, and learn as you go along. But if you're in a hurry . . .''

Cedric clattered his selection of cameras ("My second-best, dear boy, like Anne Hathaway's bed,") on the table in front of them, and launched into a long discussion of their various merits. Sir George listened and began to think his old box Brownie hadn't been such a bad thing after all. Or was it the third glass of brandy they'd each had which made old Benbow so chatty, and himself so confused?

"But this," concluded Cedric, who'd been carried away by the chance of demonstrating his specialist knowledge, "this is the one for you, in my opinion — and I want you to look on it as a permanent loan until you've, as it were, grown out of it. If you do. Single-lens reflex, and really an easy camera to use — just point and click, dear boy."

"All there is to it, you say?" said Sir George, studying the camera doubtfully. "Idiot-proof, you mean? Sounds just the job, but of course I couldn't borrow it. Expensive piece of equipment like that — write the name down, and I'll pop off to Harrods tomorrow and buy —"

"Nothing of the sort!" intoned Cedric swiftly. "Look on it as my contribution to Plummergen's entry in the Competition —

we all had such fun, didn't we? You, and me, and Wonky Tump, and Ferencz Szabo — haven't seen so much excitement in years. Plummergen's such an *interesting* place, and of course there's that adorable Miss Seeton of yours, too — I'd like your snaps to be as good as you can make them for her sake as well as yours, you know. If she's to draw these After sketches properly . . ."

Sir George was weakening, Cedric could tell, though he still looked anxious. "My insurance policies," pointed out the photographer, in a tempter's voice, "are absolutely up-to-date, you know, so you needn't worry for an instant about that side of things. So that's settled, is it? Let's have another brandy to clinch the deal."

Following her husband's instructions, Lady Colveden had borrowed from Brenenden public library a selection of books on the art of photography, and once he'd recovered from what Nigel insisted on calling his evening's debauch, Sir George could be seen studying them with close attention. Time spent on reconnaissance, as the major-general knew well, was never wasted. Accordingly, over the next few days he bought various speeds of film from Mr. Stillman and wandered about his estate armed with the camera, a tape measure, and a notebook. Not until he felt confident of producing a decent set of pictures would he venture forth to the wider spaces of Plummergen: the village, he knew, was depending on him — on him, and on Miss Seeton.

"Good morning, Sir George." Miss Seeton was on her way to school when she encountered him just outside the bakery. "Is that the camera Clive, I mean Mr. Benbow, so kindly lent you? Will you be starting on" — Miss Seeton blushed delicately — "our, um, project today?"

"D-Day today, certainly. Been casting my eye over this telephone box before I begin — could do with a touch of spit and polish, don't you think? Paintwork is acceptable enough, I suppose, but best have a word with the GPO about putting a new pane of glass in — post office property, after all. Not the thing to go interfering without permission. And none of this nonsense about carpets, and vases of flowers, either, don't want to exaggerate — just make the most of what we've got, that's the way."

Miss Seeton approved this sentiment, then with her umbrella poked at the fringe of drying grass and weeds which sprouted in a halfhearted way around the foundations of the telephone box. "It would be in order, surely," she said, "to tidy up this without asking — I can't believe the post office wants plants to grow inside telephone boxes, which of course in such hot weather they don't — grow, I mean, either in or out. Have you noticed, Sir George, how very brown so many of the lawns in Plummergen have become? It is so fortunate that Stan takes care of my garden for me."

"Odd, that. Turning brown, I mean — some sort of virus, I suppose. Have to take care not to show it in the snaps." Sir George patted his borrowed camera and looked modest. "Thought I'd start with Sweetbriars, if you don't mind — need a focal point to begin with, like your cottage right at the end of The Street. Working my way north this morning, out of the sun, and the other way this afternoon."

He was pardonably pleased with the efficient air of technical knowhow he had managed to display, and Miss Seeton was duly impressed. She knew as well as his wife and son that Sir George was no shirker. If he thought himself able to carry out a task, then carried out, and properly, that task would be. He had sense enough to know when anything might be beyond him, and when expert help was required.

"This camera," said Sir George, waving it proudly under Miss Seeton's nose, "foolproof, so Cedric Benbow tells me — no reason to doubt him, after the results in my album — come to dinner one night and take a look. Meg will ring you."

Miss Seeton thanked him. It was always a pleasure to dine with the Colvedens, and Rytham Hall, such a splendid old building. Sir George must have enjoyed photographing his own property, whether or not it had been for practice. "And I so look forward," she added, "to seeing your picture of the George and Dragon, though I cannot really think of many ways in which Mr. Mountfitchet could improve the front of his property, can you? The delightful creeper, so green over the front wall, and the overall balance of chimneys and windows, most pleasing."

Thus having modestly drawn attention away from her own little cottage, Miss Seeton studied the old inn on the other side of the road. The front door, a dark rectangle between two white square pillars, was open; and on the threshold, just emerging, was the figure of a woman.

Miss Ursula Hawke had quickly gained in Plummergen the reputation of "a queer customer," both metaphorically and literally.

Though she was staying at the George and Dragon, she rarely ate her meals there, included in the price though they were: she asked for sandwiches to be prepared at odd hours of the day and night, and vanished for lengthy periods without telling anyone where she was going or what she was doing. Apart from barked requests to the hotel staff, she seldom spoke to anyone else; and even Mel Forby's best journalistic efforts had been slow to penetrate the mystery.

As usual, Plummergen could not agree on its attitude towards the newcomer. Some believed her to be either a friend or a foe of the unseen woman in Mrs. Venning's house, and up to no good in either case, others (very much the minority) thought her simply a holiday-maker; many more suspected that she was someone important (importance as yet unspecified) in the later stages of recuperation from a nervous breakdown.

"You see if I'm not right, Eric," said Mrs. Blaine. "She has the look of suffering in her eyes — the way she stares, too haunted by her past, I can tell. I'm so sensitive to these things. Some family tragedy, the last of a noble line — her inheritance lost, and coming here to regain her mental and physical health before facing the world again."

"Glares," Miss Nuttel corrected her. Mrs. Blaine blinked at her friend. "Not stares," explained Eric. "Very scornful — almost snooty, I'd call it."

"That's just what I was trying to say, only you do tend to catch one up too quickly sometimes, Eric. But that's her aristocratic blood, too blue, so much interbreeding — you know how these old families are. Maybe," gloated Mrs. Blaine in a thrilled whisper, "she's one of those White Russians we used to hear so much about, in hiding, and that's why nobody ever sees her."

But Miss Hawke was certainly not in hiding this morning. She hesitated on the threshold of the George and Dragon, as if delayed by her leather shoulder bag; then saw the interested gaze of Miss Seeton upon her, observed how Sir George fiddled with his camera, and crossed the road towards them.

"Morning," she remarked. Miss Seeton smiled politely and murmured something; Sir George, who was not wearing a hat, bowed courteously to this stranger who was eyeing his, well, Cedric Benbow's camera with such interest. Even the Colvedens had not been able to avoid the various rumours as to the woman's identity and purpose for being in Plummergen. Quickly he reassured her of the innocence of his actions.

"Best Kept Village Competition," he explained, holding the camera out for her inspection. "Before and After, snaps and sketches, with the help of Miss Seeton here." He bowed again; Miss Seeton's smile reappeared. "Miss Emily Seeton — and my name's Colveden."

"Sir George," interpolated Miss Seeton as the stranger seemed to hesitate once more, "takes a great interest in the affairs of our village, and of course we all try to — do our best that is, and my small efforts in sketching according to the ideas of the Committee will play their part also, I hope. In the Competition, I mean."

"Not a bad camera," said Miss Hawke, after a quick, and would-be knowing, glance. "For amateurs, that is."

Sir George was not one to indulge in name-dropping, but when the reputation of his friends was at stake would not hold back. "Cedric Benbow," he said, with some pride, "lent me this. One of his favourites, he told me. Very kind of him to make the loan. Greatly appreciated."

"His favourite, possibly," countered Miss Hawke sounding as if she doubted it. "But hardly his best, I wouldn't have thought, even for a — society photographer." There was scorn, now, in her tone, as if photographing in society took one utterly beyond the pale.

Sir George grew annoyed on his friend's behalf. "Cedric Benbow's a good man, knows his stuff. Very much in demand."

"Popular," said Miss Hawke, who clearly felt popularity the ultimate condemnation. "If you like that sort of thing, all very well, I suppose . . ."

Miss Seeton observed Sir George growing red in the face and had to confess that she, too, felt a little miffed on dear Cedric Benbow's account. Not that she could count him, as could Sir George, as a close friend: it had been many years since little Emmy Seeton had attended the same college of art as the rising young star Clive Bennet; but after the excitement of the Lalique Lady photographs, and the stolen jewellery, she might, she felt, with some justification view him as an *old* friend. And Miss Seeton's loyalty to her friends must never be in doubt.

On the other hand, one should always extend courtesy to the stranger in one's midst: which meant it had now become rather awkward, knowing what to say, and indeed, it might be better to change the subject completely.

"Cedric Benbow's photographs," Miss Seeton found herself saying, "surely deserve to be popular, since they are so very clever in showing us aspects of life we might otherwise not have noticed. Which must be the aim, I feel, of true art — to make people see things more clearly." And, flushed at her own abruptness in thus defending dear Clive, or rather Cedric, Miss Seeton excused herself and hurried away to the waiting school, whose children, for a guilty moment, she had entirely forgotten.

In the pleasure of finding her class so receptive, she had forgotten her brief encounter with the guest from the George and Dragon. Dear Mel Forby had laughed, over tea, about how even her journalist's skill had not been able to ascertain much more than the woman's name, and certainly not what she was doing in Plummergen: as if, Miss Seeton had thought, it mattered. But reporters, one knew only too well (Miss Seeton sighed at the thought), had a different view of life to one's own. Far less private and much more personal — the questions they sometimes asked, for instance. Not that Mel would ever, Miss Seeton supposed, be too personal in her questions — and one had to admit, now that one had spoken to the mystery woman, that

122

it might be interesting to know just a little about her . . .

Miss Seeton gazed down at her Accidental Drawing in the smoke, and behind the image of the hunting owl saw the face of Miss Ursula Hawke.

chapter
10

This time Superintendent Brinton was not shouting. Things were far too serious for such self-indulgence. He looked at Detective Constable Julian Arbuthnott and sighed.

"I hoped you'd get results, laddie. What's gone wrong?"

"I honestly don't know, sir. I'm sorry — I thought they were coming to accept me as one of them, but, well, if any of the Choppers *were* involved, they're not letting on about it where I can hear them."

"And your gut feeling is that this firebug business is nothing to do with them anyway, isn't it?"

Sleaze nodded. "I'd almost swear to it, sir. These are your typical yobs — talking big about what they've been getting up to, trying to impress the newcomer. I've heard all about Foxon's grandmother's gate, the smashed windows in the church hall, breaking into phone boxes and spending the cash on booze when half of 'em are underage — nicking cars, too — everything we suspected, in fact. We could pull them in on sus for the petty stuff several times over, sir. But, as nobody's let a word out about the fire-raising . . ."

"It means we could well have a kinky one on our hands — and the thought makes me very nervous, Arbuthnott. Could be that any night now he'll go for the big time. I've made a check in my diary for the date of the next full moon, and it's due next week. No doubt he'll come crawling out of the wood-work then — but how likely are we to spot him when he does? That shop in Ashford last night drew a pretty large crowd of gawpers — he was probably right there gloating, laughing his fool head off. Of course, the fire people keep a lookout for anyone turning up at every blaze looking pleased about it, and we try to get a few plainclothes types to prowl around as well, but nobody's reported anything or anyone suspicious yet."

"The shop was pretty badly damaged, wasn't it, sir? And the contents almost completely destroyed?"

"Quite right." Brinton eyed him sourly. "You're thinking it could have been rather too convenient damage and destruction, are you?"

"Well, sir, the insurance angle shouldn't be forgotten."

"If you were Detective Constable Foxon, laddie, I'd damn your impudence for hinting that I'm an old has-been who lets the obvious solution escape him, but as you aren't, I'll just remind you that I'm the superintendent, not you."

Sleaze looked abashed, but only slightly. He permitted a faint grin to cross his face as Brinton scowled his most ferocious scowl, and wondered briefly how Foxon was coping with Inspector Harry, the Fiery Furnace, who on his bad days made Attila the Hun appear saintlike: it was good training.

"Sorry, sir," he said. Brinton glared at him.

"And so you should be. There's life in the old dog yet, and I warn you now, if someone hasn't already, that my bite and my bark are equally fierce. But for the moment I think I'll save my energies for the firebug, when we catch him — or them. And *if*," he added glumly. "If we don't strike lucky soon, I'll start to think we'll never catch him . . ."

Sleaze, who had cheerfully accepted the assignment which left him temporarily at the tender mercies of Superintendent Brinton, ventured to make the suggestion Foxon had warned him should never be made.

"I suppose, sir," he said, all seriousness

now, "that it wouldn't be worth asking what Miss Seeton thinks about things; would it?"

As Foxon had predicted, Brinton turned pale and clutched at his hair. He viewed his seconded subordinate with a jaundiced eye. "Someone put you up to this," he accused the young constable, who looked shocked.

"No, really, sir, I'm serious. We've heard a lot about the Battling Brolly over in Hastings — not just the stuff that gets in the papers — and the lads here have told me how she was the one who really cleaned up the Dick Turpin affair — and, well, I thought that if she did one of her drawings, it might just give you a hint, sir — as we seem to be, well, stumped, sir."

"You mean you're aiming to use Miss Seeton as an excuse for you not being able to come up with the goods? You must be desperate, laddie, and nothing like the good detective Harry Furneux, heaven help him, tried to tell me you were." Brinton shook his head. "The reports from Plummergen assure me that everything's quiet on the Miss Seeton front just at the moment — and that's how we want it to stay, take my word for it. They're all busy agitating about some strange woman who's staying in the pub there and prowling round the place at night and rubbing everyone up the wrong way — not that it wouldn't be easy to do that, in Plummergen — and Miss Seeton is teaching in the village school and in her spare time drawing a series of sketches of the main street. I'd like to leave her doing just that, if you don't mind . . ."

But from the thoughtful expression on the superintendent's face, Sleaze suspected that he might, at a pinch, consider asking Miss Seeton for help, after all.

Miss Seeton had enjoyed her outing to the Shire Horse Stud at Greatstone, and so had the children. She told them that the next art lesson would be another of the little class competitions they seemed to find so much fun, and that they must go home now to tell their families about the day's excursion, and think about what had most impressed or interested them, ready for tomorrow's pictures.

Miss Seeton herself planned to return to Sweetbriars for a cup of tea and a slice of Battenberg cake, then to examine the photographs of The Street which Sir George, at dinner last night, had handed to her with a modest smile.

"Leave it all to you now, m'dear," he told her as she took the snapshots and murmured her admiration. "Capable hands, I'm quite sure."

Miss Seeton blushed and began to demur, but Lady Colveden was ready with reminders of how the Competition Committee had every faith in her, and that little Miss Armitage, for one would be so disappointed if Miss Seeton at this late stage should feel unable to help. Nigel nodded in the direction of his mother and grinned at Miss Seeton.

"I believe it's called moral force," he remarked, reaching politely behind him for the box of bitter mints which were Miss Seeton's contribution to the evening's jollity, and proceeding to hand them round. "You know my mother" — Miss Seeton smiled, and her eyes began to twinkle — "and how dedicated to improving the world she is. She lets nothing, and nobody, stand in her way or thwart her dire purpose."

"Nigel!" Lady Colveden looked horrified. "As if I'd ever try anything so . . . so impertinent."

"Mother darling, isn't that precisely what you and your cohorts *are* trying to do with dear old Plummergen at this very minute? That hideous golden gnome The Nuts bought in Brettenden — don't tell me Dad's photo makes it leer like that entirely by accident. Once Miss Seeton's produced a picture of some really smart, friendly looking chap with a fishing rod and a feather in his hat, even Miss Nuttel's got to admit there's room for improvement. And if somebody were to pinch the thing —"

"Nigel," said his mother in a warning tone, "don't even dream of it. Excuse him, please, Miss Seeton, you know how frivolous men can be when they've been out in the sun all day long. They make it an excuse for talking nonsense."

Nigel helped himself to another mint. "Harvesting's hungry work," he remarked, "and tiring, too, but I strongly deny that I'm suffering from sunstroke. It's just that my aesthetic sense, no matter what you and Dad may think, is as well-developed as the next person's" — he grinned at Miss Seeton, who sat in the neighbouring chair — "and I'm really keen to see how the old place will look once our resident aesthetic expert's had a proper chance to show her paces."

"I can only do my best," said Miss Seeton, "although I would hesitate to regard myself as an expert. Fortunately, the list of suggestions your dear mother and her Committee have compiled is so comprehensive" — her hands fluttered over the neatly written sheet which Lady Colveden had given her — "that I am emboldened to hope that I might be able to draw, well, something along the lines of what is required."

"Of course you'll be able to," Lady Colveden assured her firmly. "We all have every confidence in you."

"And besides, we're bursting with curiosity," added Nigel, "to see how things might look if everybody joins in. Suppose Miss Wicks goes ahead and asks Dan Eggleden to put wrought-iron rails up the steps to her front door, and that marvellous little balcony along the front, too. My kind-hearted mother," he told Miss Seeton, "has had a word with Dan about it already. Because it's so close to the forge, he says he could use Miss Wicks as a sort of showcase, or do I mean guinea pig? Either way, he'd do it for her at a reasonable cost, he says."

Miss Seeton looked pleased, even as it became Lady Colveden's turn to blush. The elderly spinster was a close acquaintance of Miss Seeton's, and, though the two gentlewomen never discussed financial matters, it was clear to the younger that funds were barely adequate in the little white cottage three doors along from the bakery. The flowers in the balcony tubs were always bright; Miss Wicks and friends who were keen gardeners, forever taking too many cuttings and needing a good home for the surplus. The many panes of the sash windows sparkled bravely; Plummergen's keen troop of Boy Scouts had long since managed to convince Miss Wicks that Bob-a-Job Week came around every month.

But this afternoon Miss Seeton did not intend to begin her series of drawings with Miss Wick's cottage, or, indeed, any of the buildings on the western side of The Street. The blazing summer sun, though still high in the sky, would soon begin to dazzle her if she faced that way. She would start, she decided, on the opposite side of the road, with the post office, over whose plain frontage the Committee were suggesting that Mr. Stillman might like to install an awning, maybe in red and yellow Royal Mail stripes.

Sir George's photograph was clipped to one corner of her easel, the Committee's list to the other, and her umbrella was hooked over the wooden peg as Miss Seeton positioned herself just outside Lilikot and set intently to work. She was not conscious of the way The Nuts, from behind their net curtains, were peering out at her.

"Eric, do come quick! That Seeton woman's lurking right by our front gate," Bunny had complained to her friend when she first observed the newcomer. "Blocking the path with all her painting gear — the nerve! Why should people have to walk on the grass to get past?"

"Damaged enough already, with the heat," agreed Erica Nuttel, "not to mention the virus." For Plummergen's rare Brown Wilt was spreading daily, ever wider. "Could all be subterfuge, of course." Eric had come to join Bunny at the plate-glass peephole and was frowning in thought. "Casing the joint — liable to robbery, post offices."

"Oh, Eric, yes! Remember a few years ago, those motorbike people, and the cheese? And how Miss Seeton walked up and simply took the gun and started firing it at us? Everyone tried to make excuses for her, but I've always had my doubts — too suspicious, and too much of a coincidence."

Miss Nuttel agreed with her, and The Nuts settled to a long afternoon's spyholing through the white net curtains of Lilikot.

Miss Seeton did not notice them, and would have taken it as mere neighbourly interest if she had; nor did she hear the giggles of the small group of children on their way from the council houses at the top of the village to catch tiddlers in the Royal Military Canal, who stopped behind her to stare.

Miss was busy drawing — the post office, it was, and she'd got her paints with her, and after she'd done drawing, she might paint it to look real nice, and maybe if they asked her tomorrow, she'd let them use watercolours, too.

Miss Seeton was absorbed in her task of delineating the basic view, leaving until later the addition of the little extra touches the Committee hoped would be improvements. She smiled to herself as she thought of dear Lady Colveden, and how amusing young Nigel could be, and the number of mints he could eat without putting on weight; she brooded on the box of chocolates Miss Maynard had given her, and how few were left, and how much she'd enjoyed eating them and sharing them with various visitors. Miss Wicks, with those so unfortunate false teeth, had whistled her delight in the confectionery through a mouthful of caramel, and for one dreadful minute Miss Seeton had feared that the old lady would clamp her jaws to an embarrassing standstill, requiring the services of a dentist.

Miss Seeton paid no attention to the arrival of the bus back at its home base of Crabbe's Garage, a few doors along from the post office; one or two interested parties crossed the road to watch what she was doing, but nobody liked to disturb her while she was clearly so busy. Plummergen has a healthy respect for Miss Seeton and all her works.

"Why an umbrella?" came the sudden query from behind. "Doesn't look at all like rain." Miss Seeton slowly turned. "Good light, with no clouds," continued the voice, a voice she did not quite recognise. "Going well?"

"Miss Hawke," murmured Miss Seeton, dragging herself out of her creative mood with difficulty. "Er — good afternoon. Yes, I believe I may say it is going reasonably well, thank you. I, er, trust that you are enjoying yourself? This is a delightful part of Kent for a holiday, is it not?"

Mel Forby had, some time ago, decided to throw herself wholeheartedly into her Rural Revival series; she gave up the struggle to learn more about her fellow guest at the George and Dragon, saying she believed the woman to be no more than someone on holiday who took midnight walks for the freshness of the air and the privacy. "Guess you and I know only too well, Miss S.," said Mel, "how valuable a spot of privacy can be in a place like Plummergen . . ."

Oh, dear. Miss Seeton blushed. She had

almost forgotten dear Mel's comments about privacy, so absorbed had she been in her work. How unforgivable, to appear to have been prying! "I do beg your pardon, Miss Hawke," Miss Seeton said as Miss Hawke now fixed her with a suspicious stare. "That is to say . . . I do beg your pardon."

Miss Hawke uttered a barking laugh and patted the bulky shoulder bag which not a soul in the village had seen her open. "Holiday?" she echoed briefly; then at once changed the subject. "Odd perspective," she remarked, peering over Miss Seeton's shoulder at her pencilled outlines. "Wider panorama," and she waved her free arm towards the southern end of The Street. Miss Seeton's glance drifted along and fell upon Sweetbriars, standing full-square on the corner where The Street narrowed, facing the whole village and, she felt, welcoming her even at a distance. "Insufficient focal interest," Miss Hawke dismissed Miss Seeton's study of the post office and strode off in the direction of the George and Dragon.

Miss Seeton felt duly rebuked — deservedly so, perhaps, for she had (without meaning to, certainly, but she had), or so it must have seemed, been attempting to pry into Miss Hawke's business in the village. Which could be regarded as an impertinence, even though it had been merely polite and idle chat after being unexpectedly interrupted at one's work. Miss Seeton felt rather upset and decided that she had done enough sketching for today. Flustered, she folded her easel, collected her bits and pieces, hooked her second-best umbrella over her arm, and headed homewards.

"Did you see, Eric?" Norah Blaine was still keeping watch. "That woman who's staying at the George and Dragon got off the bus and came over to talk to her, and as soon as they'd made contact, Miss Seeton stopped even pretending to draw a picture and followed her back down The Street! Mark my words, she's up to no good in Plummergen . . . either of them," concluded Mrs. Blaine darkly.

And Erica Nuttel nodded her grim agreement.

chapter
11

It still did not rain. For the rest of that week, scorching day succeeded scorching day; hosepipe bans were rumoured, to the fury of Plummergen gardeners. No cure for the sinister and still-spreading Brown Wilt had yet been found, and now a plague of moles seemed to be poised to devastate the flower beds and (even worse) what remained of the lawns of the village. Murmurs against Jacob Chickney, the area's miserly and misanthropic Methuselah of a mole catcher, began to be heard, although nobody dared to come right out and accuse him of professional sloth. Jacob was not popular, never had been, and knew it. He did not care. For years he had been able to quell any complaint with one beetle-browed glower and a few choice curses — so choice that, for full understanding, an Anglo-Saxon dictionary would be required. Old age had not dimmed this dubious ability.

Miss Seeton continued with her series of sketches; Lady Colveden and the Committee made arrangements to display both

Before photographs and After pictures in the village hall: posters to this effect were put on display in various Plummergen stores and tacked to telegraph poles so that there could be no excuse not to attend the Great Exhibition, as Nigel called it.

Farmer Mulcker lost a barn in an arson attack; further outbreaks destroyed, to a greater or lesser extent, shops and one factory in Ashford and Brettenden and Murreystone's church hall. Murreystone chose to blame Plummergen for this loss, and villagers were sent on scouting expeditions to the rival territory to learn what they could. Superintendent Brinton, however. had by now concluded that insurance fraud was likely to be involved, as well as (if at all) the Choppers, and dreaded reading each morning's reports.

"One thing we've got to be thankful for," he told Sleaze Arbuthnott, still on secondment from Hastings, "is that so far we haven't had any kinky ones . . . touch wood," he added. He ran a finger around the inside of his collar. "If only it would rain," he muttered. "It'd calm the blighters down a bit, and we need all the help we can get . . ."

One of Mr. Alexander's mysterious mistress's Borzoi dogs jumped into the Royal

Military Canal in an attempt to cool down, and discovered too late that the water, its flow much reduced by the weather, was brackish and green. Mr. Alexander walked back through Plummergen with Boris, smelly and dripping, at the fullest extent of the lead, and then tied the two dogs on separate hooks outside the post office. He bought a large bottle of dog shampoo and tried hard to join politely in the amused banter of the regular shoppers. Once he had departed homewards to The Meadows, however, amusement gave way to suspicion.

"He's forever walking them dogs down The Street, instead of letting 'em run about the garden, and with its great high walls there'd be no fear of 'em escaping, that's for sure," said Mrs. Skinner. "So it's likely he's got good reason for always going that way — plotting something with that Hawke woman along at the George and Dragon, mark my words."

"And everyone knows *she's* in league with Miss Seeton," Mrs. Henderson remarked. "Taken great care not to be seen together in public, they have, but there's no denying it — and then there's that reporter female as is friendly with Miss Seeton, she's at the George, too — writing her articles about us, so she says, but I have my doubts," and she nodded a portentous nod and looked grave.

Everyone agreed that they, too, had their doubts about what was going on. Something, they felt sure, was brewing. They looked around for The Nuts, who could always be relied on to produce suggestions and speculations as good as any — but Miss Nuttel and Mrs. Blaine still cowered inside Lilikot, waiting until the huge Russian wolfhounds were well out of range before venturing forth.

Lady Colveden was glancing through Miss Seeton's contribution to the Competition. As she finished each picture, Miss Seeton had placed it, with the appropriate photograph paperclipped to one corner, in a folder; on the outside of the folder she fastened the Committee's list, with each idea ticked off in pencil as she had incorporated it into her drawings. It was almost a professional portfolio, and Lady Colveden was impressed. She'd known all along that Miss Seeton could produce what was needed, and to the very highest standard. Every picture was competent and clear . . .

Every picture except the last.

"George, do look." Lady Colveden riffled through the pile of sketches once more. "Yes, this is the only one — how very, very strange."

Sir George joined his wife at the table, upon which she had laid Miss Seeton's work carefully as she withdrew each drawing from the folder. "Little woman's done a grand job," Sir George said. "Knew she would." He ventured to preen his moustache for a moment. "Photographs helped, of course. Give Cedric Benbow a ring — be interested to know."

"Never mind Cedric Benbow for now, George. Just take a look at this last picture — well, I suppose it would be the very first she painted, as it's at the bottom. She told me she just did them and filed them and went on to the next." Lady Colveden shook her head. "It's — I suppose you'd call it sinister — all the smoke, and the flames — almost as if that end of The Street had been set alight."

"Post office is clear enough." Sir George was studying the picture which had so disturbed his wife. "Probably grew tired of filling in the background and sloshed around a lot of grey paint to save time."

"Miss Seeton would never slosh anything, George. She's simply not the type." But Meg Colveden's response had been automatic: she was still busy staring at the picture. "Of course," she comforted herself, "there's the smithy at that end of The

Street, and Daniel Eggleden's been working all hours to make wrought-iron railings and flower stands and lamp brackets and things — you always have smoke and sparks from a blacksmith's forge. She might have been watching him before she started this picture, and then, as you say, grown tired after she'd painted the post office — and doesn't the awning look smart? We were sure it would — Miss Seeton does tend to paint what she sees, doesn't she . . ."

"Unless," her husband reminded her, "she's in one of her queer moods. No telling what she'll come up with then, is there? Often wondered if she's psychic. Afraid she may be starting up again, aren't you?"

"It's happened so often before," explained his wife, in a voice that was not quite steady. Sir George favoured her with a shrewd look.

"No need to sound so apologetic, m'dear. Couldn't agree more — uncanny." He stared hard at the smoke-filled, flame-wreathed distances of the post office picture. "Could just be because of all these arson attacks in the local rag," he suggested, not very convincingly. "Subconscious memory — or the forge, as you thought."

"You don't believe it any more than I do, do you." This was a statement, not a question. "George, what should we do about it?"

"For one thing, not show the picture. Put ideas into people's heads — irresponsible, this hot weather."

"Miss Seeton's bound to notice and wonder why. You know how she takes such a pride in her work. And maybe, if we were to ask her, she could explain why she's shown — oh, no we can't." Meg Colveden looked most upset. "George, she's shown the southern end of The Street on fire — and that's just where Sweetbriars is! She'd be so worried . . . George, where are you going?"

"Kitchen," explained the major-general, his accents as decisive as when he won his DSO. "Wait there." Mystified, his wife waited.

"Don't you think ritual suicide's rather a drastic solution to the problem?" she asked as he came back bearing a large carving knife. "And really, I'm not *that* bothered by this picture —"

"Couldn't find the scissors," replied Sir George with a flourish of the knife towards the dining-room table and the pictures which lay upon it. "Must have been tidying again — everything muddled. Better than nothing, though."

He made to seize the troublesome smoke

scene, but Lady Colveden, with a cry of outrage, stopped him. "Not my best carving knife, please! You might scratch the table, for one thing — let me find my embroidery scissors. You know I'm never going to finish that tapestry fire screen — I can't imagine why I even began the wretched — oh, yes, of course, Nigel gave it to me for a joke. Well, I'll admit that he's won the bet, and we can always ask Mr Stillman to sharpen the edges if the paper spoils them."

Sir George chuckled as he watched his wife rummaging in her work basket. Dearly as he and his son loved her, they knew her limitations: it had been particularly cheeky of the boy, all those Christmases ago, to say he'd be deeply hurt if his mother didn't make even an attempt to complete what he insisted, straight-faced, was something he'd always felt was needed to complete the decor of the morning room. Lady Colveden had gamely struggled on, stabbing her fingers with needle points and frequently demanding that somebody should help her untangle the strands of wool, for some weeks before Nigel, choking with laughter, had confessed. Meg Colveden promptly rose to the challenge and said that she would complete the fire screen, though it might take years, or die in the attempt.

"Which means you'd better leave the carving knife behind when we've finished," she said, "so that I can commit, what is it? *Suttee,* or *hara-kiri,* or something. You can tell Nigel he'll have to cook supper, and it's his own fault."

Together, she and her husband studied the picture again, working out where best to sever that disturbing smoke scene from the main focal point of the post office. "We'll simply have to tell her, if she asks," said Lady Colveden, scoring gently with the points of her scissors along the line they eventually chose, "that it got torn, or something, and as it wasn't the important bit, we decided to neaten up the rest of the picture and burn the damaged piece. Oh, dear." Once more she looked stricken. "Burn — I mean throw away, don't I? It's all such a — an uncomfortable feeling . . ."

Sir George, who knew Miss Seeton of old, nodded. After a pregnant pause he said: "Think I'll give Brinton a ring, at Ashford. Can't be too careful, where fire's concerned. Can we?" And he picked up the discarded portion of Miss Seeton's view of the post office and stared at it grimly.

"How does she do it?" demanded Superintendent Brinton while Detective Con-

146

stable Arbuthnott watched him turn slowly puce. "How did she know there'd be more trouble — big trouble — with these fires?" He clutched at his hair and groaned. "The only thing that's keeping me sane is that she didn't have the corpse in her blasted picture, but otherwise —"

As emotion seemed to have choked him into temporary silence, Sleaze took the opportunity to point out, daringly, that Miss Seeton's sketch, according to their informant Sir George Colveden, had not been of the Brettenden night club which had burned down in the small hours, but of Plummergen. "Perhaps it's just a coincidence, sir," he suggested gently.

"Be damned to that for an idea," exploded Brinton while Sleaze smothered a grin. "Harry Furneux was right — and so was young Foxon, curse him — and I should have known better. I tempted fate, and this is the result. And let me warn you right now, laddie, that since she's got involved in all this, there's no knowing where it will end. She's bound to *stay* in it — and it'll only get worse. If you'd like to transfer back to Hastings, this is your one chance to get out of what my instincts tell me is going to be a very messy case."

"But an interesting one, surely, sir.

Working with, or should I say in spite of, Miss Seeton must be a unique experience — I'd certainly like to hang around and see what happens. If you have no objection, sir," he added.

"I've every objection to working with a lunatic, which is what you've just shown yourself to be," growled Brinton. "But have it your own way, Arbuthnott, and don't say later you weren't given the chance to make your escape. It won't be coming your way again, I assure you." He inhaled deeply, then breathed out, closing his eyes. "So let's have the full report," he commanded. "Carefully, now . . ."

"Formerly known as The Singing Swan," he told Chief Superintendent Delphick half an hour later. "Recognise the name?"

"Indeed I do." In Scotland Yard the Oracle motioned to Detective Sergeant Bob Ranger to stop messing about with his filing and listen in on the telephone extension. "The far side of Brettenden, in the Les Marys district — my first Seeton case, as I recall — vandalism, dope, and Cesar Lebel just to liven things up. But I understood from my sergeant, with his local connections, that it had quietened down a lot in recent years — gone up-market and attracted an older type of clientele, with a new owner. The previous chap drank all the profits, or so I'm told."

"Yes, he pickled his liver very nicely and ended up an emergency case. Went on the wagon once he got out, which is hardly the best advertisement, is it? Makes the punters nervous. So people began to go for a drink somewhere else . . . And when things got a bit slow, he found it hard to sell, with money being a bit tight, as well as the reputation, which was still pretty unsavoury — no wonder the new bloke — lives in Murreystone, name of Thaxted — rechristened the place. It's the Half Seas Over now — or rather, it was, before last night's little effort."

"Tell me," prompted Delphick, "about last night."

"The usual fire alert — building well ablaze before the brigade got there — firemen eventually put it out and then searched the remains for signs of arson, as they've been doing for every incident during recent weeks."

"My oracular sense tells me they did indeed find such signs," said Delphick. Bob Ranger grinned. Superintendent Brinton's bleak tone would have told a far less astute man than his boss that there was something wrong with the fire at the Half Seas Over.

"They found more than that," Brinton said. "They found a corpse with its head bashed in, buried in the rubble — and I got Records to run a dental check, and he's one of yours, Oracle. From the Smoke. Name of Black, Notley Black, and a versatile sort of character he was, too. Bank robberies, jewel heists, con artist — that was in his younger days —"

"I believe I know the name," said Delphick. "And, Chris talking of artists, I don't suppose —"

A heartfelt oath scorched its way along the telephone wires and set Delphick's head ringing. He held the receiver away from his ear and listened to the gabble of indignation that came pouring out in a metallic frenzy. Across the room at the other desk, Bob Ranger raised his eyebrows and emitted a silent whistle. Well, they called the super Old Brimstone, and he could certainly see why, judging by this present performance. Lucky nobody censored the telephone system, or Brimmers would've had the blue-pencil boys banging on his door this very minute. He caught Delphick's eye and grinned.

When the outburst seemed to be quietening down, Delphick said, in his most soothing accents: "I apologise, Chris, but I couldn't resist it. I take it there really is a Seeton connection? As you predicted all along there would be?"

"*She's* the one doing the predicting, Oracle, chattering on about striking matches and candle flames almost before there's been a word said about arson — and then drawing Plummergen going up in smoke, according to your pal Sir George Colveden. They found it rather unnerving, he said, he and his wife. And so do I."

"You say she drew *Plummergen* on fire? Then why are you so worried about this chap in Brettenden? You can't blame Miss Seeton for him."

"Logically — rationally — no, I suppose I can't, but who can be logical where Miss Seeton's concerned? She seems to have known about the arson outbreak before it happened — the village is buzzing with rumours —"

"When did it ever do anything else?"

"— about mysterious strangers with sinister intentions, creeping about the place in the middle of the night, having secret meetings with Miss Seeton —"

"What?"

"— and generally playing merry hell all over the show," concluded Brinton, breathlessly. "I can't stand it, Oracle, I've told you

151

before. I need someone else to cope with her, and you're the obvious choice. She may only be on the edge of it now, but you know what she's like for getting . . ."

He hesitated, hunting for the right word.

"Embroiled?" supplied Delphick, resigned; intrigued. "The word has the correct overtones of unwitting involvement, I think."

"What *I* think is that the sooner you get down here, the better," retorted his harassed colleague. "Bring young Bob Ranger — he can try sorting out his dear old Aunt Em, if you can't manage it. Because one of you's got to," said Brinton firmly. "I never could cope with her, and I'm not starting now — I'm saving my strength for the worst that's to come."

And nobody dreamed of remarking that the worst might not come. Now that Miss Seeton was on the case, they all knew that almost anything could happen.

chapter
12

The heat of the morning sun made Miss Seeton walk along the easterly side of The Street on her way to school, seeking the benefit of even a slight amount of shade. The George and Dragon, with its creepered frontage, looked cool, but was set too far back from the road for its shadow to reach the pavement. Miss Seeton glanced up at the windows and wondered which room was dear Mel's. The reporter, she knew, was no early riser unless pursuing a story; and how could there be a story in Plummergen? Which was the most peaceful of villages where nothing, thank goodness, untoward ever happened beyond the little parochial excitements that would be unlikely to interest a stranger. Amelita Forby, having earned her holiday, must be sleeping still, and Miss Seeton could not expect to see her peeping out at her friend.

The hot summer nights, so exhausting, barely giving one the chance to recover from the even hotter summer days . . . She must take care not to let the children overexcite themselves at playtime: they might prefer to sit quietly under a shady tree and play some round game, rather than run about in the open. Green, especially grass green, was such a very soothing colour . . .

"Oh, dear." Miss Seeton had now reached the wide grass verge just beyond the George and Dragon, only to be halted in her tracks in some dismay, staring. "Oh, dear, how very vexatious — so many molehills . . ." With her umbrella, she poked cautiously at the nearest little mound of finely turned earth, unsure whether or not she hoped to find the culprit inside. The Committee would be very distressed, especially when the grass was already so scorched and brown. Such an excess of molehills would appear like the last straw — which was what the lawns were beginning to look like, Miss Seeton thought. Yet might it not be possible to sweep the earth together and, well, use it for potting plants, or for window boxes? Waste not, want not . . . Bolder now that no little furry face had shown itself, she stirred the earth with her umbrella point. So very many moles — one hesitated to criticise, of course, but there might well be some justification for those who complained that Mr. Chickney did not perform his duties to everyone's satisfaction. Miss Seeton sighed.

154

"Professional pride," she murmured thoughtfully.

"Caper spurge," came an unexpected voice right beside her. "And plenty of it."

Miss Seeton came out of her daydream with a start, then turned to smile. "Why, Stan, good morning. How is dear Martha today?"

"Fine — and blooming, thank you," replied Stan Bloomer, chuckling as he always did when he made this little punning rejoinder. "Caper spurge," he repeated, and on the repetition Miss Seeton understood.

It had been difficult, at first, to understand much, or even part, of what Stan said in his strong Kentish accents. Not that he'd said much, in the first few years of his acquaintance with Miss Seeton: his wife talked enough for the two of them, and Stan, with a countryman's dislike of hurrying himself, had happily left it to Martha to pass on any family news or general gossip that might interest, or amuse, their friend and employer. (Martha Bloomer cleans for Miss Seeton twice a week; Stan, a local farmhand, in his spare time cares for her garden and looks after the hens, selling any surplus for his own profit in place of wages.)

For some years Stan and Miss Seeton had communicated mostly by smiles, but gradually there had come a greater measure of understanding on Miss Seeton's part. By now she prided herself on being able to make out what he was saying at least half of the time — although it helped, she had to admit, if one had some inkling of the subject under discussion. Now she frowned, and repeated the strange words with which Stan had accosted her.

"Caper spurge? Do you mean — not moles, after all?"

"Get away!" Stan chuckled mightily at Miss Seeton's display of humour. "Gets rid of the lit gennum wheresoever they shows their snouts, caper spurge do."

"Little gentlemen? Oh, in black velvet," Miss Seeton said, recalling history lessons and the Jacobite cause. "Yes, of course, it would . . . if you say so," she added in a doubtful tone. "What exactly *is* caper spurge, Stan?"

"Skeers the critters away, iffen it be planted aright. Handsome leaves, it do have, and with flowers all greenery-yallery."

"Wilde," murmured Miss Seeton, "or do I mean Gilbert?"

"Wild?" Stan shook his head. "You can buy from a nursery if you'm so minded to spend out the cash. Better nor poisoned smoke nor traps, spurge."

"Then if you think we should buy some, Stan, perhaps you could make arrangements," decided Miss Seeton. Poisoning or smoking small creatures to death was not what she wished to encourage, nor did she trust the idea of traps, even though she had heard that newer models merely caught the animal, so that it could be moved to another area alive, instead of crushing it. "As many plants as seem suitable," Miss Seeton said, "and as soon as possible, I think." She stirred the earth once more with her umbrella and sighed.

"Day after tomorrow, most like," Stan told her, climbing back on the bicycle from which he had dismounted to accost Miss Seeton in her brown study. With a grunt of effort, he began to pedal his way up The Street towards the farm where he worked, waving a brief farewell to Miss Seeton as he went past. Remembering that she, too, ought to be on her way to work, Miss Seeton moved off in the same direction.

When she reached the post office, she smiled to think how welcome a red-and-gold striped awning would be on such a sunny day, and hoped Mr. Stillman would approve of the After picture she had painted. Indeed, she hoped everyone would enjoy visiting the village hall to discover how their houses and gardens might look, with a little judicious improvement. For her own part, she had decided that the wooden-paled fence around her tiny front garden should be replaced by one of Dan Eggleden's wrought-iron works of art: nothing fancy, for Mr. Eggleden was already working extremely hard and would have little time to spare for anything too ornate. But the traditional arrowhead pattern should do very well and look neat, although painting it would be a lengthy job — she would have to ask Stan his opinion some time . . .

She glanced across at Lilikot. On the wall beside the front door was displayed the name of the cottage, with all the curlicued splendour that a craftsman in wrought iron could achieve. The Nuts were proud of their nameplate; Dan Eggleden could not produce anything ugly or out-of-place if he tried, and while seeming to humour his clients had ended up giving them what he managed to make them believe they had thought of themselves. Miss Seeton gave the sign an approving smile as she passed.

"Eric," squeaked Mrs. Blaine, busy laying the table for a rather late breakfast, "do come quick! Never mind making the tea for now — Miss Seeton is walking up The

Street, and she just looked over in our direction, and, oh, Eric, she *leered!* Do you suppose she's put the evil eye on us?"

"Never can tell, with that woman." Miss Nuttel, who had almost dropped the kettle when Bunny sounded the alarm, came hurrying in to peer over her friend's shoulder through the window. "Feel any different, do you?"

"I felt a shiver running right down my spine," promptly returned Mrs. Blaine, "and my legs have gone weak." She sat down on the nearest chair, breathing hard. "Oh, Eric, maybe I shall faint. You never saw such a look — staring, I think I should call it, and her eyes positively glittered — Eric," grumbled Mrs. Blaine, "aren't you interested?"

For Miss Nuttel, with a sudden exclamation, had wrenched the curtains aside and was gazing through the uncurtained plate glass at the front garden. "Eric," bleated Mrs. Blaine in some alarm, "what are you doing?"

For Miss Nuttel was pressing her nose flat against the glass, emitting little startled yelps and groans. "Eric," quavered Bunny, "what's wrong? Tell me the worst — has that woman bewitched you, after all? Eric!"

For Miss Nuttel, emitting a word Bunny

had not realised she knew (and which, Mrs. Blaine later decided, she must have learned from Jacob Chickney, the mole catcher), now rushed from the room, flung open the front door, ran down the path, and proceeded to stand in one corner of the lawn, shaking her fists above her head and glaring about her, every bit as glitter-eyed as Miss Seeton had appeared. Bunny gasped at her friend's uncharacteristic behaviour and shivered. Anxiously she looked around for any of the dried witch herbs which *Anyone's*, that popular periodical, had assured its loyal readership would protect against all enchantments. If Miss Seeton, in her passage, had indeed cast a spell over Lilikot and its inhabitants, Bunny Blaine was determined to do all she could to thwart her in her evil purpose.

Unfortunately, the bunch of herbs was, as Mrs. Blaine now recalled, in the kitchen at the back of the house, where she had taken it one thundery day to prevent the milk curdling. And she was so stricken by the peculiar sight in the garden that she could not have left the front window even, she told herself, at the risk of becoming enchanted in her turn . . .

She spent an anxious few minutes at her vantage post while Miss Nuttel did what looked like a little war dance on the lawn and scowled up and down into The Street. Suddenly, when Bunny's nerves were almost in tatters, Eric shrugged her shoulders, stamped, and returned to the house without a backward glance.

"Oh, Eric," quavered Mrs. Blaine as Miss Nuttel, breathing hard, her hands fisted in the pockets of her slacks, marched back into the room after slamming the front door in a very pointed manner. "Eric . . . is something wrong?"

"Fool question," snapped Miss Nuttel. "Think I'm making a fuss about nothing, do you?"

"Oh, no, Eric, I'm sure you're not. But — but when I see you so worked up, and I don't know why, I can't help wondering . . . I mean, wouldn't it be sensible if you, well, told me what the trouble was instead of keeping it to yourself? Too like you, hoping to spare me anxiety, but in some ways I think I'd prefer to know the worst."

Miss Nuttel jerked a bony finger in the direction of the garden. "Spotted it gone after that Seeton woman went by — not that I'm blaming her, but . . ."

Her tone did as much as her cryptic words to alert Bunny to the tragedy that had befallen them. "Eric! You mean our garden gnome's been taken? Stolen? How awful!" She looked at her friend in round-eyed dismay. "Surely you can't think — surely even Miss Seeton wouldn't — I mean, what would she want with it? Too eccentric, even for her."

"She leered," Miss Nuttel reminded her. "Said so yourself. Must have had her reasons."

There was a thoughtful pause. "That garden of hers," Mrs. Blaine said at last, "round the back — such a high brick wall, nobody can see inside, and Stan Bloomer would never tell anyone, would he? He'd be terrified of letting people know in case Martha lost her job." Mrs. Blaine sniffed; she had tried to lure Mrs. Bloomer away from her employment at Sweetbriars when Miss Seeton's Cousin Flora, the previous owner, died at the age of ninety-eight. Miss Seeton did not take full possession of her inheritance for some while, and Mrs. Blaine had tried to point out to Martha that there would be little sense in tending an empty property when there was every chance she would not be paid for her trouble. Martha had retorted that if she couldn't trust Miss Emily, then she couldn't trust anyone, not to mention there were them she trusted more than others anyhow. Mrs. Blaine had not forgotten the exchange, though she maintained that of course she did not hold Miss Seeton in any way responsible.

"Victimisation," breathed Mrs. Blaine, "that's what it is — or do I mean exploitation? In either case, it's too clear that unless we went looking for ourselves, we're never going to know the truth —"

Before she could propose some positive course of action, she was interrupted by the telephone. Miss Nuttel went to answer it, then came back with her eyes wild. Mrs. Blaine leaped to her feet and clasped her hands in anguish.

"What is it, Eric? Don't keep me in suspense!"

"That woman," said Miss Nuttel slowly. "Gone right off her head at last — always said she would."

As she paused to consider how what she had always said was now being proved true, Mrs. Blaine quivered, dumbstruck, her gaze never leaving her friend's face.

"Not just our gnome," said Miss Nuttel. "Mrs. Skinner's bird table as well —"

"Not the one Daniel Eggleden sold her only last week!"

Miss Nuttel nodded, grim-visaged. "Matching pair of flower baskets, too," she said. "Mrs. Henderson's . . ."

"Oh, Eric," said Mrs. Blaine, aghast. "And they've only just bought them! Too dreadful, and so costly to replace — and what can she suppose she's going to do with them all? Someone's bound to recognise them."

There was another thoughtful pause. Miss Nuttel broke it. "Been wondering about that, Bunny. Too many people go into her garden — bound to chatter, even friends. Unlikely to be that woman after all."

"But as it's *only* her friends, they might keep quiet — and with that high wall nobody else can see . . ."

Miss Nuttel was shaking her head to quell Mrs. Blaine's objections. Bunny subsided. Eric said: "Not the only high wall in Plummergen, is it? Remember those guard dogs — that man Alexander — The Meadows . . ."

And Bunny's sudden smile was full of congratulation. "Oh, Eric, you're so right, and I was wrong — it must be the answer. Nobody's really been in the garden at The Meadows since Mrs. Venning left, and nobody at all since that man and his — well he called her his mistress, didn't he? — moved in. We don't know anything about her, do we? Too mysterious — and the way

164

they keep those huge wooden gates shut so nobody can catch her out . . . And he's always walking up and down The Street with those dogs. He could be," breathed Bunny, "spying out the land, don't you think?"

And Miss Nuttel nodded gravely.

chapter

13

This morning was rather cooler than previous mornings, and, though the sun still shone, it did not appear to be quite so merciless and persistent in its beaming. Miss Seeton walked along the western side of The Street on her way to school and, as she passed the bakery, reminded herself to buy gingerbread during the lunch break. It looked most appetising through the clear, sun-sparkled glass of the bow window, and it was, moreover, dear Bob Ranger's favourite. Her adopted nephew had telephoned last night to say that he and Chief Superintendent Delphick would be in the Ashford area for the next few days and hoped to see her before too long.

Miss Seeton smiled as she looked forward to seeing her friends again, then sighed as she glanced across the road at the grass verge where yesterday the moles had been so busy. It seemed that they had been busy again — or else, perhaps, that nobody had bothered to sweep the earth away. She had meant to take a garden broom and a sack to deal with the matter herself, but somehow it had slipped her mind . . . And here were molehills on the verge this side of The Street, as well. She would have supposed that the noise and vibration from the smithy nearby would have scared them away, but they did not seem to mind. Which was a pity. Moles, Miss Seeton reminded herself firmly, were as much God's creatures as any bird or butterfly, but one had to admit that they made a most dreadful mess wherever they had their runs. Or should that be earths? Miss Seeton rather thought that referred to foxes — badgers, she remembered, lived in setts, rabbits had their burrows — but moles, she realised, she was unsure about. Perhaps it might make a suitable little quiz for the children, once she had managed to find the answer.

A scuffling, squeaking, furry commotion in the overgrown hawthorn hedge beside which she was now walking brought Miss Seeton to a halt. The tangled greenery which had obscured Mel Forby's northward view along The Street a few days earlier — and which nobody had yet pruned, Competition or no Competition — danced a furious tango as, at its base, something, an animal or bird, wrestled in a frenzy with some other animal that was not giving in without a fight.

The sounds of mortal combat were loud and distressing, and Miss Seeton did not hesitate. She thwacked her umbrella against the hedge, crying, "Stop that! Stop it at once!"

For a moment the hedge ceased to plunge about, and the angry squawks stopped. Miss Seeton parted the tangle of twiggy branches with her umbrella and bent down to see what the cause of the commotion could be.

"Tibs," said Miss Seeton in reproachful tones as the huge tabby cat glared up into the eyes of the interloper who had spoiled her fun. "Oh, Tibs, how cruel to torment that magpie! Just leave the poor thing alone this instant, do you hear?"

Miss Seeton is one of the few persons in Plummergen who are not wary of Tibs, Amelia Potter's notorious cat. Amelia is scarcely of school age, but can control the creature when even P.C. Potter, her father, is reluctant to approach her; the rest of the village is even more cautious and will give Tibs a very wide berth when she is in a prowling mood — which is most of the time. Tibs has been known to kill and drag home rabbits and, on occasion, hares; rats and squirrels are routine prey: a magpie is a mere snack, easily dealt with.

Not on this occasion, however. With her umbrella Miss Seeton prodded Tibs away from the shivering black-and-white bird; the cat, a brooding gleam in her narrowed eyes, spat once, growled deep in her throat, then thought better of an assault on the neat stockinged legs of her assailant, and, one eye on the umbrella, backed angrily out of the hedge. She stood twitching her tail for a moment, then hissed, and stalked off down The Street towards the Royal Military Canal, where she hoped to encounter Sasha and Boris running free. The two Borzois were well-brought-up, carefully disciplined dogs, and Tibs could tease them with impunity while she regained her self-respect.

"And now to rescue you, you poor thing," murmured Miss Seeton to the magpie, which had fluttered wildly when rescue first arrived, then seemed to freeze in a state of shock. One wing drooped along the dusty ground and dust covered its piebald plumage, but to Miss Seeton's relief there did not appear to be any sign of more serious damage.

"But how am I to get you out of there?" she asked sadly, for in the course of its struggle with the cat, the helpless bird had been dragged, or pushed, deep inside the thickety hedge. It would be a difficult job for even an agile person to reach it and, though her yoga had made Miss Seeton adept at standing on her head, she did not think it would greatly assist her in wriggling into a mass of hawthorn prickles.

"Oh, dear," murmured Miss Seeton, trying to hold back the most offending branches with her umbrella, wondering if she might somehow hook them out of the way and pull the poor magpie to safety. She leaned farther into the hedge with a slow, cautious movement.

"Need any help?" came an unexpected voice behind her as Miss Seeton snagged a tweedy thread on a hawthorn spike and dratted the thing with some force. "Careful, now . . ." it said as she tried to extricate herself, and dropped her umbrella so that the branches bounced back and enmeshed her even more firmly in their embrace. "Keep still," commanded the voice, and at the third time of utterance Miss Seeton recognised it.

"Miss Hawke," she gasped, "good morning — and thank you so very much. These branches, such a nuisance — ouch!"

"Sorry, but do keep still. I can see what I'm doing — you can't. Have you out in a jiffy."

It occurred to Miss Seeton that some explanation might naturally be expected by her rescuer. One did not every day encounter the rear view of a gentlewoman trapped halfway inside a hawthorn hedge; and in her embarrassment she had almost forgotten the cause of her unfortunate situation. "The cat," she said as Miss Hawke began to ease her out of the hedge. "A magpie — a broken wing, I think . . ."

"I was watching," said Miss Hawke. "A grand job — well done. Glad to see other people showing an interest."

"Indeed, yes," fluttered Miss Seeton as she began to see clear daylight once more, instead of leaves. "We are so fortunate in this area — drat — so rich in wildlife, particularly birds — ouch — ah, thank you!" And as she once more stood safely on the pavement, she dusted herself down with a sigh of relief. She bent to retrieve her umbrella, bumping heads with Miss Hawke, who'd evidently had the same idea. They both said ouch simultaneously, then straightened, met each other's gaze, and smiled.

"It's your property," said Miss Hawke, gesturing to the umbrella. "But" — with a look at the hedge, and politely trying not to look at Miss Seeton's tattered state — "might be safer if I got it for you."

"It's the poor magpie I'm more worried

about," said Miss Seeton. "Can't we do something for it? If we leave it here, the cat may come back and catch it again."

"You hold the branches," commanded Miss Hawke, groping in the depths of the hedge for the umbrella, "with this" — she handed Miss Seeton's lost property back to her — "while I fetch out the bird. Fair shares." She slipped the heavy bag from her shoulder to the ground, then plunged back into the hedge on her hands and knees while Miss Seeton strove to hook the handle of her brolly over the most obstreperous of the hawthorn stems, out of Miss Hawke's hair.

"Damfool townie notions," came a voice, gravelled by age and tobacco, from behind the little tableau, and there was a sound of spitting. "Should've left it to the cat, grant the blasted creature its uses — interfering with nature, that's what you clever folk from the town're doing."

Miss Hawke wriggled out of the hedge a great deal faster than she had wriggled in, paying no attention to snags on her clothes or scratches on her hands. With the light of battle in her eyes, she turned to face the newcomer: a wizened old person of immeasurable age, clad in the countryman's heavy string-tied boots, faded corduroy trousers, and thick open-necked shirt. The waistcoat he wore, however, of dark grey-brown fur, was not of a type often seen nowadays. Miss Hawke glared at it, and at the man who wore it.

"None of your business," she informed him, resuming the normal brusque manner which in her exchange with Miss Seeton she had almost abandoned. "Not your bird, is it?"

"Vermin's what it is," the ancient informed her, without removing the blackened clay pipe from his mouth. "You'm all alike, you blasted townies," he said, investing the final word with a scorn that surprised both his hearers. "Vermin — but do you heed that it sucks t'other birds' eggs and kills their chicks?" He contrived to spit once more, still keeping the pipe in his mouth. His audience was so amazed by this feat that neither of them could speak. "Garn!" he continued, and the bowl of the pipe jigged between his teeth. "Magpies! Evil birds, they are — bad luck, a bird that flies widdershins — but you lot, one look at its feathers — oh, such a pretty bird," he mimicked grotesquely, "and you're puking out food for the pesky things. Vermin, I say! Ask any keeper and you'll hear the same."

"Keeper, are you?" challenged Miss Hawke.

173

"Mole catcher." Jacob Chickney seized his pipe by the bowl and jabbed its stem in Miss Hawke's direction. "Moles is vermin, too, so they are. Kill the lot on 'em, say I, and none of your business iffen I do."

"Oh, but Mr. Chickney," began Miss Seeton, who had never spoken to the old man before but had heard much about him from Martha, Stan, and other villagers. Jacob rounded on her at once, stabbing his pipe again.

"Just acause you lives here —"

"Mole catcher?" Miss Hawke's eyes glittered. "I feared as much. How barbaric — disgraceful! God's creatures —"

"Vermin!" roared the old man, drowning her out. "Damned fanciful townie notions — trying to take away a man's very job. Paid well for it, I am, and what right have you got to come prancing round with your blasted pernickety ways? It'd serve you right iffen I got rid of you same way's I sort out they other vermin — poison you right gladly, I would, wring your neck and no questions asked, you interfering besom!"

"Mr. Chickney!" protested Miss Seeton, much distressed by his hostile attitude to one who was, after all, a visitor to Plummergen. Miss Hawke had perhaps been a little . . . blunt in her, well, attack, but there was no excuse to meet bluntness with, well, rudeness, although one must be thankful to have been spared any of what dear Martha had warned of the old man's . . . language, thought Miss Seeton, blushing.

"*Mr. Chickney,*" echoed Jacob, mimicking Miss Seeton's genteel pipe. "And what's Mr. Chickney done to warrant being nagged at by the likes of you? I keeps myself to myself and mind my own business — aye, paid for it, too, I am, though's nowhere near sufficing — but it's an honest day's work, and I'll have no blasted townie peeking down her hoity-toity nose at me telling me how to go about it!" Whereupon he spat nastily once more, glared, turned on his heel, and stumped off down The Street, ejaculating *Vermin!* at intervals until he was out of earshot.

"Good gracious," gasped Miss Seeton as her startled breath returned. "Miss Hawke, I'm so very sorry —"

"Not your fault," said Miss Hawke, staring thoughtfully at the old man's disappearing form. "I'll catch up with him later — mole catcher, indeed. Fascinating little mammals, they are — bite the heads off worms and eat them backwards, like toothpaste. Squeeze the earth out — intelligent creatures. But never mind that for now. Operation rescue time!" And she dived once more into the hedge.

In Superintendent Brinton's office Ashford police division was in conference with Scotland Yard. Chief Superintendent Delphick and Detective Sergeant Ranger had examined every arson report in the files; Brinton had studied all the notes the two Yard men had brought from London concerning Notley Black, the nightclub corpse.

"Well, Oracle, I can't honestly say he sounds much of a loss," Brinton said, tapping the file which contained the photocopied notes of the late Notley's criminal career. "He seems to have been a jack-of-all-trades and master of none — I like a crook to specialise, myself. They take a pride in their work and you know where you are with 'em — but him! Con artist, stolen cars with clocked mileage, bank robber, not very successful — did that jeweller's and left his mate to carry the can — spot of blackmail, dirty pics — you must be glad to be rid of him."

"Certainly, he seems to have been inefficient, judging by the record, but remember that it's all we have to go by, and it's remarkably quiet for the last year or two. Since I find it hard to conceive of his having gone straight, maybe we should consider that at last he found something at which he could succeed — arson, for instance."

"People don't usually bump off a successful Torch — they come in too handy," objected Brinton.

"Perhaps he grew greedy and wanted more than his bosses thought was his fair share — you said there was probably an insurance motive with several of these cases, didn't you?"

Brinton nodded. "It's likely enough, given the circumstances. Some of the financially insecure'd be fools to pass up the chance to try sorting themselves out, and if a Torch from Town was all it took, they'd jump at it. And we had a whisper of London number-plates on a car seen prowling round Ashford Forest the night before he was done in — not that there's anything to insure in there, even if trees'll burn as well as paper this dry weather, I imagine — but if the report's right, it could be a link. Sussing the place out for escape routes, or somewhere to hide, I suppose. It was a member of the public rang in, a woman, in a bit of a state — didn't remember the full number, just recognised it as from London by the letters — bothered by lights in there, moving around, then spotted the car driving away."

"Interesting," remarked Delphick, "if not a direct link; but a possible theory, none the less. The London men drive down to Kent, quarrel, and Notley Black's disposed of in the middle of their latest contract . . . but if that's what it's all about, Chris, then who burned down the furniture warehouse in Brettenden last night, if Notley Black was already dead and his friends gone back to London?"

chapter
14

"All right, all right," growled Brinton, "but it's a theory, isn't it? We have to start somewhere."

"Indeed we do." Delphick regarded his friend pensively. "But you're hedging a bit, Chris, and not thinking entirely straight. We have to take into account the — shall we call it the Seeton connection?" Brinton closed his eyes, and his lips formed the soundless syllables of a curse. The Oracle smiled his most oracular smile.

"I'm sorry, Chris, but we can't escape it. You were the one who called my attention to it, in the first place — and you know how we've often speculated that Miss Seeton might be psychic, in some small way. You tell me she's babbled of flames and drawn pictures of smoke — and last night when the furniture warehouse went up, don't tell me it was mere coincidence that Brettenden fire brigade were coping with another barn fire, right at the limit of their area — in Murreystone — which just happens to be a few miles from Plummergen, their historic

179

rivals. Tenuous the link may be," concluded Delphick, "but, though of course the London connection must be checked, my instincts tell me that Miss Seeton and her friends are going to be involved in this arson business before too long."

Brinton nodded, sighing. "You can't fight fate, not if Miss Seeton's anywhere around. Especially when there are a few more coincidences than you've heard about yet — give you three guesses who lives in Murreystone, for one."

Delphick cocked an enquiring eyebrow at Ranger, who had been listening to every word and wondering if he and Anne might try suggesting to Miss Seeton that she should emigrate — or become a hermit. They'd miss her if she went, thought Bob, but at least everybody could get their blood pressure back to something like normal. Old Brimstone, for one, always seemed to turn a strange shade of puce whenever people mentioned Plummergen, or Aunt Em . . .

"Bob," Delphick's voice broke into his sergeant's train of thought, "as our recognised Seeton expert with the local connections, tell me who lives in Murreystone."

"Er," said Bob, racking his brains to remember what Anne had told him. "About three hundred and fifty people, sir, and all of 'em at daggers drawn with the Plummergen crowd."

"Yes, Sergeant Ranger, we know that already. But out of these three hundred and fifty, is there not one . . . ?"

"Ah, oh, yes, sir. Thaxted, sir — bloke who owns the Half Seas Over, formerly the Singing Swan." He tapped one of the cardboard folders on Superintendent Brinton's desk. "Post-incident interview with him in here, sir, but I take it you want the grass roots gossip." He looked towards the superintendent, but Brinton seemed willing to let him talk. "P.C. Potter could probably give you the real gen, sir, but to judge by what Anne's told me, Thaxted's almost a pillar of the Murreystone community — not exactly squire, though he'd like it well enough, but I don't think even Sir George over in Plummergen thinks of himself in those terms. Thaxted's got the money behind him, though, and he's trying hard — and Murreystone's not slow to take advantage."

"Rustic cunning," agreed Delphick with a nod. "They sneer at him behind his back, but hold the parish fete on the lawn of his house every year, and let him draw the prize ticket for the yearly Church Roof Raffle to make him think he's starting to fit in. Am I right?"

Brinton stirred. "That's the way of it, according to Potter and it's pretty good cover, for whatever he wants to get up to — if he does, that is. We haven't been able to catch him out on anything yet. He seems clean — not that we've looked into his affairs too closely, before now. There wasn't much need — but of course, we're going into everything pretty thoroughly after this fire business, and the murder. There've been rumours that the club wasn't doing too well, but he claims it was more of a tax fiddle to run it almost at a loss — don't ask me how that would work, I'm getting the Fraud boys on the job."

"I expect anguished communications at any moment from Inspector Borden and Commander Conway," Delphick assured him, with a faint smile. "They retain vivid memories of their last two encounters with Miss Seeton —"

"Don't!" yelped Brinton. "Stop saying that name! Just forget I ever mentioned her. Please . . ."

"You called us in, Chris. Do you want us to go back to London? Just say the word — but I warn you, once she *does* get properly going, you may not be able to call us away from Town again. Commander Gosslin, not to mention Sir Hubert Everleigh, could take exception to their officers rushing up and down the motorway to Kent every time Miss Seeton waves her umbrella and sends you scurrying for cover . . ."

Brinton rolled his eyes. "It's a fair cop, guv. You're in on this for the duration — which is what you wanted right from the start, and don't even try to pretend otherwise." Delphick chuckled.

"In your own words, Chris, it's a fair cop. I find that I'm looking forward to Miss Seeton's involvement in the case — and her assistance in finally solving it — with the most eager anticipation. I think," he added to Bob Ranger, "that we must take up your dear Aunt Em on her invitation, and pop along to Plummergen before too long, to find out what they're all doing . . ."

"Nigel," said Lady Colveden to her son, who was passing his father's laden plate around the upheld pages of *The Farmer's Gazette*, "it's silly, but I have to ask you — do you know anything about the missing gnome?"

"Gnome on the range?" enquired Nigel, accepting his own plate with a grin of thanks. "Gnome sweet gnome?"

"Nigel!"

"Sorry, Mother, couldn't resist it. You've, er, always gnome what a ghastly sense of humour I have — sorry again," he said as she took up the carving knife and waved it at him. "I didn't even know one was missing — but surely you don't mean that monstrosity belonging to The Nuts? Has someone pinched it?"

"It seems someone has. And since you say you don't know anything about it —"

"I don't." Nigel spoke firmly, but there was a gleam of amusement in his eyes. "Top marks to whoever did it, though — perhaps they'll hold it to ransom, for charity, or save it up until Bonfire Night and use it instead of a guy."

"I didn't really suppose you did," said his mother, "but your Young Farmers do sometimes have their more frivolous moments, and, well, I thought I'd just mention it. Everyone is very upset about it in the village."

There came an astonished rustling as her husband lowered his journal. "Upset about that garden gnome? Must all be mad — seen it myself. Hideous thing."

"Yes, George, I know you've seen it — you took a photograph and made it leer dreadfully, which was rather naughty of you, though I can't say," his wife confessed, "that I blame you, on the whole. But it isn't just the gnome that's disappeared — all

184

sorts of things have gone. Ornamental things, lots of them from Dan Eggleden — lamp brackets and flower stands and, well, *nice* things. Stolen. Which is why people are upset. It's bad enough having an arsonist on the loose, without other people — if it *is* other people, and of course nobody will know until they're caught — prowling about in the middle of the night. They'll start imagining," concluded Lady Colveden, carefully not looking at her spouse, "that they're not safe in their beds. Until whoever it is has been caught, of course."

"Police job to catch 'em," said Sir George, but Nigel, who was closely watching him, could see the light beginning to gleam in the old war-horse's eyes. "Can't have private individuals setting up as vigilantes — irresponsible."

"Not if they're organised by someone who *isn't* irresponsible. Someone, well, with military training — who could make sure everyone behaved themselves . . . Another helping?" And without waiting for his reply, she nodded to Nigel, who handed her his father's plate with an admiring smile and winked at her. She frowned slightly and shook her head.

There was a thoughtful silence.

Lady Colveden remarked; "This outbreak

of arson is very worrying, isn't it? Especially with the weather so dry."

"I've been hearing that Murreystone think it's our fault their village hall went up in smoke the other night," Nigel contributed, with one eye on his father. "And with being so very close, you can't really blame them, can you?"

His mother favoured him with an appreciative smile. "So close it's rather uncomfortable. How long does it take in a car? Pop a can of petrol in the boot, and away you go. We could try asking the vicar to pray for rain, I suppose."

This was too much for her husband. "Pray for rain?" He lowered his newspaper to reveal a bristling moustache. "All very well praying — does no harm — but the Lord helps those that help themselves. Can't call the padre a practical man — needs a combined effort." Lady Colveden held her breath. Silently she dared Nigel to utter one word.

"Young Hosigg's a reliable chap," mused Sir George, referring to his youthful farm foreman. "Nigel could head up a second party — Stan Bloomer, another — Jack Crabbe and his father from the garage — Mr. Jessyp, of course, he'll make a good two-eye-see . . ."

Now that he'd gone so far as to decide who was to be his second-in-command, Lady Colveden could relax. "I think he's a splendid choice, George. How sensible of you. How soon will you be able to start?"

It was late afternoon, and Miss Seeton was entertaining one of her staunchest allies to tea in the back garden.

"Love this place, Miss S." Mel Forby leaned back in one of those rather expensive, but so comfortable, garden chairs which had been an extravagance Miss Seeton felt was at last justified by the recent spell of fine weather. Mel yawned and stretched. "I could really fall for a house like this — the view, the privacy" — she glanced at the mellow redbrick wall, and, thinking of the absent Thrudd Banner, mused on the fun of nude sunbathing — "and the garden . . . glorious. Almost tempts me into retiring, if I could — but there's only one Sweetbriars. Accept no substitutes — this place is ultra special, and you're one lucky lady. But what's your secret? How come the flowers look so healthy, and the lawn here's so green, when everyone else's looks tatty?"

"I believe it is because of that wall you were admiring, or so Stan has told me. They don't care to dig through the foundations, I believe — the moles, that is. And of course, with being so high, and the trees, there is plenty of shade. The wall, I mean. And the canal — we're so close, and Stan says the water probably travels underground — seepage, would that be?" Miss Seeton frowned, but the correct word eluded her. "And dear Stan is very sparing with the contents of the waterbutts, as well."

"You do a grand job between you. Almost as hard work as farming, or blacksmithing, or the other good old country pursuits I've been finding out about recently — and, hey!" Mel sat up straight. "Did I tell you? I've managed to find out what Miss Ursula Hawke's doing here, as well. Amelita Forby, Queen of Fleet Street! She kind of unbuttoned a day or so ago — not much, mind you, but chattier than she's been before. I caught her prowling round the George in a bit of a state — something to do with the mole catcher setting a cat on a magpie, and she needed a cardboard box or something — I was so amazed she'd got any time for me at all, I didn't take in the full story. But what I did take in was why she's in Plummergen, and why her suitcases were so darned heavy. Care to guess?"

Miss Seeton thought back to that encounter with Ursula Hawke when, between them, they had rescued the magpie from the attentions of Tibs, little Amelia Potter's infamous cat. "Might I guess her to be a naturalist of some sort?" suggested Miss Seeton. "She knows a great deal about birds and other small creatures."

Mel pulled a mock-disgusted face. "Here am I, pleased with myself for having eventually solved the mystery, and you'd cracked it all the time! I should've known better than to try and catch *you* out, Miss S."

Miss Seeton hastened to explain the reason for her happy guess, adding that the encounter with the mole catcher (briefly described, at Mel's prompting) and Miss Hawke's reaction on learning his job had been the first clue. "And then, of course, there was the poor magpie, with its broken wing — she was so very knowledgeable about what to do for it — such a relief to have her there, for otherwise I would have been late for school, setting such a bad example to the children — although kindness to animals, of course, is something of which one should never be ashamed, and we could have discussed the subject in one of our natural history lessons. But Miss Hawke was far more than *kind,* she was of great practical *help,* which the magpie would surely have appreciated much more than my small efforts."

"But you stopped Tibs killing it, didn't you? Without which first step," Mel pointed out, "all Miss Hawke's help would have been thoroughly *im*practical, I'd say. And you're right about her being a bird buff — twitchers, aren't they called? Spend all their spare time travelling around on the lookout for rare specimens. She told me this area's great for wintering smew." Mel grinned. "For a minute there I'd got it into my head she was insulting me, but it's some kind of bird, cross my heart."

"A small species of merganser, I believe," Miss Seeton said. Mel looked blank. "A diving bird," translated Miss Seeton. "In many ways similar to a goosander. Which also winter in the area, I understand."

Mel looked impressed. "If you say so, Miss S. — and no wonder you got on so well with Miss Hawke. I guess with a name like that she just had to be interested in birds — but you're right, she's into animals, too. She knows one heck of a lot about badgers — gave me quite a lecture about them. And she's writing a book about it all, she says. *The Complete Natural History of the Kentish Marshes*, that's the working title. She's brought three pairs of field glasses with her, all different magnifications — no wonder that bag of hers looks so heavy — and pretty well every reference book in the language to double-check anything just as soon as she sees it. Talk about dedication to duty. Plus a camera or two with fancy lenses, for close-up action shots of birds mating, or whatever they do at this time of year . . ."

Mel drifted into a brief daydream of Thrudd Banner, then brought herself sternly to her senses. "The poor woman's scared stiff some rival or other's going to pip her to the post, so she —"

At which point, the doorbell rang.

chapter
15

Miss Seeton was in the act of topping up the teacups, and at the sound of the doorbell started slightly. A few drops of tea splattered on the table. She had been concentrating too hard on what dear Mel had to tell her about Miss Hawke — such a very interesting project — and not enough on what she was doing — but how fortunate that, with the chairs, she had bought a matching table in heavy white plastic. No more need to carry furniture in and out of the house whenever it looked like rain: plastic, though ugly and strictly practical, was certainly waterproof.

"Oh, thank you," said Miss Seeton, as Mel rummaged in her bag and produced a wedge of clean paper handkerchiefs. "Would you be so kind as to answer the door while I mop up this little spillage? And, while you are gone, in case it is anyone coming for tea, I will top up the pot with more hot water. So embarrassing to feel one is intruding, and that arrangements have to be made." She smiled at Mel. "And we can always have another cup ourselves, can we not? So nothing will be wasted."

Mel smiled at the very thought of Miss Seeton wasting anything — that generation seemed constitutionally incapable of behaviour so irresponsible — and agreed to answer the door. "Could be your lucky day, Miss S.," she said as she strolled away. "The postman with your winning Pools coupon, maybe, or a free sample of cornflakes."

"Bert only delivers in the mornings," began Miss Seeton, before realising that it was a joke. She smiled again as she dabbed conscientiously at the spilled tea, counting the number of cakes and sandwiches left on the stand.

Mel emerged through the French windows with a dancing look in her eyes. "Not sure if it's your lucky day or not, Miss S. The boys in blue are here in, if you'll excuse the pun, force — the police have come for you!"

She motioned Chief Superintendent Delphick and Detective Sergeant Bob Ranger to join the party and, while everyone was busily greeting everyone else, slipped into the kitchen to fill and boil the kettle for more hot water. She took it upon herself to retrieve the gingerbread from where she knew Miss Seeton kept her cakes and grabbed another packet of biscuits from a tin in the larder. She collected the teapot from outside and made fresh tea, topped up the milk jug, and hunted for the sugar bowl. Neither she nor Miss Seeton took sugar, but the police needed every ounce of energy possible, chasing crooks all the time.

Or at least, mused Mel, all the time they spent in the vicinity of Miss Seeton — which time surely included right now, she'd bet a sizeable sum. She hadn't missed the cardboard folder under The Oracle's arm, even though he tried to hide it, and she didn't suppose it contained sample greeting cards or Delphick's holiday snaps. Amelita Forby of the *Daily Negative* was going to find out what was going on, and which particular crooks the Yard men were chasing — and she was going to get herself a story.

She carried the laden tray out to the garden, and everyone stopped talking to offer their help in laying the table. "Don't worry about me," Mel said sweetly, "you just carry on and pretend I'm not here," and she bustled about, trying to be unobtrusive. When everything was ready, and Miss Seeton was pouring more tea, Mel very pointedly helped herself to another cup and a further slice of cake, and looked ready to sit in the back garden of Sweetbriars until midnight.

Delphick, who had a decided soft spot for the reporter — and who also knew that unless they applied bodily force he and Bob Ranger could hardly evict her, Miss Seeton's invited guest, from Miss Seeton's flagstone patio — grinned at Mel as he selected a sandwich and said: "Relax, Miss Forby. It's too hot to argue, and we're all friends here. You might even be able to help us, though it's really Miss Seeton we came to consult."

Thus called to duty, Miss Seeton sat up straight and put down her cup. "Anything I can do to help, of course, I will be only too glad to. That is . . ." She remembered the school at which she had spent recent days teaching, and to which she was more or less committed until the end of term. "That is — of course I will help, where I can, but . . ."

"Is something wrong, Miss Seeton?" Delphick leaned forward to put his plate on the table and pick up his cup. In passing, he touched Miss Seeton comfortingly on the arm. "It's nothing more painful than a sketch or two, as usual — there's really no need to look so anxious. I'll start to think you're regretting asking us to tea — and young Bob'll feel virtually orphaned if his favourite aunt makes it look as if she doesn't want him."

Oh, dear. How very awkward, that one should give the unfortunate impression that

Mr. Delphick and dear Bob were unwelcome. "It's because of the children, you see," Miss Seeton began to explain, turning pink. Delphick turned an amazed look upon his baffled sergeant.

"Children? Plural? Are you keeping something from me, Bob? Have I missed out on the drama of your drive through the night to make sure Anne reached the hospital in time? Are congratulations in order? And what happened to the fat cigar which I understand is regulation issue to the proud father's friends and acquaintances? I am hurt, Sergeant Ranger, after so many years not to have been thought worthy of confidence. I must restore my feelings with a cup of Miss Seeton's, I beg her pardon, Mel's excellent tea."

Bob was goggle-eyed with mingled protest and astonishment, stuttering as he tried to deny all knowledge of any offspring, while Mel, thinking of Miss Seeton's recent renewal of the pedagogic life, choked quietly over a crumb. Delphick patted her on the back and smiled at Miss Seeton, who was pinker than ever.

"I must apologise for my sense of humour, Miss Seeton. Put it down to the hot weather, and the excitement of meeting old friends again." He completed his first aid by slapping Mel briskly across the shoulders, then said, "If you're worried about the teaching, please don't be. Yes" — he paused as she broke off her rambling attempt at explanation and looked surprised — "we know all about it. Superintendent Brinton has already put us fully, if you'll excuse the pun" — and he grinned at Mel — "in the picture."

Indeed Superintendent Brinton had: repeating the content of his almost daily telephone calls to Scotland Yard with a blow-by-blow account, once reinforcements had arrived safely in Ashford, of everything Miss Seeton had said, done, or drawn (according to reports from various Plummergen sources) since the arson outbreak began. Delphick, intrigued, had made a mental note to visit the Colvedens to examine that picture of Plummergen in flames which had so troubled Sir George; he resolved to have a word with the major-general about the Village Watch scheme which Brinton said the old boy felt might be a good idea; and he persuaded the superintendent to supply him with a set of photographs of what remained of the Half Seas Over. These, insisted Delphick, must be enlarged from the best shots on the files, clearly and with as much detail as possible . . . Which explains why

Chief Superintendent Delphick came visiting his friend and colleague, Miss Emily Dorothea Seeton, with a cardboard folder under his arm: a folder whose contents, after tea had been cleared away, he laid on the table in front of her.

"Oh, yes," murmured Miss Seeton. "I believe Martha said something — such a strange name for a nightclub, although I understand it to be a jocular reference to intoxication. Poor man. To be drunk in a building which catches fire . . . so very unwise — and of course he died, didn't he? Which does seem rather a . . . an excessive judgement on him."

"Don't waste too much sympathy on him, Miss Seeton. He was a small-time London crook who won't be missed — though we'd like to clear up his death, if we can." Rapidly, Delphick explained the minimum he felt she needed to know, then continued: "I'd rather like you to try sketching me your impressions of the photos — the nightclub — perhaps even your idea of the murder with which I'm dealing, at Superintendent Brinton's request. The poor man," he told her gravely, "is rather perplexed by it all, and he'd be grateful, I know, for any help you and your sketches could give him. But take your time. Ask me any questions you

198

like, and I'll do my best to answer them . . ."

He caught Mel Forby's eloquent eye and hesitated. Mel, who was sitting near enough to lean over to look at the spread of photos in front of Miss Seeton, pointedly leaned over to look. Delphick laughed.

"You win, you persistent newshound — the scoop, when it comes, is yours, so long as you promise to play fair now. Wait until, with Miss Seeton's help, we've solved the case, and then you'll get an exclusive."

"It's a deal." Mel cheerfully spoke above Miss Seeton's little cry of protest that she certainly couldn't promise to solve any case, much though she recognised that her duty lay in helping the police to the best of her abilities. "Don't you worry about a thing, Miss S.," instructed Mel, "you'll do fine, the way you always do, and I'll get my banner headlines again. Just wait and see if I'm not right . . ."

Miss Seeton, she noticed in some amusement, well before the end of the little speech of encouragement had begun to drift away from the conversation, suddenly concentrating on the photographs lying before her. Something had caught her attention: she looked back at an earlier photo as if for comparison; held another farther away, frowning slightly; stared, and stared again, and sighed. As she set the last photograph back on the table, her fingers began to flutter, her hands to fidget. "Attagirl, Miss S.," breathed Mel, who recognised the signs.

So did Delphick. With a quiet sigh of relief — there'd come a time, he knew, when Miss Seeton's abilities, and consequently the police luck, would run out, but the time was not yet — he smiled.

"Why not go indoors for your sketching block?" he said as Miss Seeton realised what her fingers were doing and sat reluctantly back on her chair with her hands folded in her lap, trying not to look embarrassed. "Go on," coaxed the chief superintendent. "We're all friends here — we won't mind if you leave us for a few minutes. We'll understand — we can take care of ourselves for a few minutes — and you'll feel better afterwards, once you've drawn it out of your system. Off you go, Miss Seeton . . ."

And, with a murmur of apology for abandoning her guests, Miss Seeton went into the house.

chapter
16

"Well," said Mel, "while we're waiting for Miss S. to do her stuff, we could talk about the weather, I guess. Or shall I start interviewing you now, Oracle — save time for when the story finally breaks?"

Delphick smiled. "You have as much faith in Miss Seeton as I do, don't you, Mel? She hasn't let us down yet — and I know that you've never let her down, either. Your articles in the *Daily Negative* are models of restrained reporting —"

"Praise from a policeman, yet. That I should live to see the day!" broke in Mel, grinning.

"I'm serious. You make a good story out of what happens — but you don't betray Miss Seeton's privacy, and privacy is very important to her. Some people might enjoy seeing themselves plastered all over the papers, but not Miss Seeton. I don't believe you've used her full name even once in your pieces, have you?"

"The Battling Brolly," murmured Bob with a chuckle, and an approving nod for

Mel. Mel was overwhelmed by this twofold vote of confidence: an observer might have supposed her to be almost blushing. "Gee, thanks," she muttered, then could have kicked herself for feeling embarrassed.

"So much for the hard-nosed newshound," said Delphick. "But I mean what I said, Mel. When it comes to stories about Miss Seeton, I trust you more than anyone else to play fair, both with her and with the police. And I've already promised that, as soon as the case is solved, you'll be one of the first to know — and certainly the first reporter. But until then I'd rather not say anything definite . . ."

Mel grinned. "I'll hold you to that, Oracle — as soon as the case is solved. As for now, shall we talk about the weather?" And she proceeded to do so.

They had time to try several other topics of conversation, comfortably, as old friends will, before Bob Ranger's keen ear caught the sounds of Miss Seeton's return. Delphick motioned to his subordinate to continue chatting with Mel, while he himself rose to his feet and turned to face the french windows.

"Oh, dear," said Miss Seeton, "I'm so sorry to have been such a long time, but —"

"But you found that the first sketch you

made didn't look like the sort of thing in which the police would be interested, didn't you?" prompted Delphick. "So you had to draw another, which came harder than the first — and it's that one you've brought for me, isn't it?"

Miss Seeton nodded, slightly pink. "The first one just didn't seem to make sense, not really — it must have been because I knew it was a nightclub, you see. But I don't believe that anyone today — even the very young people, such colourful costumes — though it might have been fancy dress, of course. Not that you, or Martha, mentioned a party. So why I should have received that impression . . . which is why I felt you might prefer, well, something that looked like the photographs —"

She held out her offering to the chief superintendent, who smiled kindly as he took it from her, but did not look at it. "I'd honestly rather see the other, you know. Even if it seems not to make sense — it may not to you, but to us it may. We know the full story, you see," and Mel's eyes glittered as she looked at him. He shook his head gently, and she subsided as he went on: "Please, Miss Seeton. The other sketch, not your copy of the photographs — Superintendent Brinton will have as many copies as

I want run off for me whenever I ask for them. Your talent's not meant to be wasted on doing what a machine can do . . ."

"Strange," mused Mel as Miss Seeton yielded and went to collect her original sketch, "how she always needs bullying — make that coaxing — before she comes up with the goods. I can't believe she's ashamed of her stuff, but her reaction puzzles me. She never seems to realise, does she —"

She broke off as Miss Seeton, pinker still, emerged from the french windows with another sketch in her hand. "Would anyone," she enquired, uncomfortable, "care for another cup of tea?" Evidently she had no wish to watch while they all studied her *sketch that didn't seem to make sense.* Taking pity on her, everyone said that they would indeed care, and, relieved, she went back into the house, leaving her three friends to pore over her drawing.

"Strictly speaking, Miss Forby," Delphick said, politely placing the sketch directly in front of Mel on the table, so that he and Bob had to lean across to look, "this sketch is official property — by virtue of the fact that the artist is a retained police consultant — and you really shouldn't be looking at it, let alone commenting on it.

Which I am sure, of course, that you had no intention of doing, had you?"

Mel flashed a knowing look at him, but said nothing. For a long moment there was silence.

"It reminds me," said Mel at last, "of *Some Like It Hot* — that era, anyway. The costumes — flappers, fringes, those long bead necklaces — looks as if they're going to start up a Charleston any time now, doesn't it?"

Delphick laid Miss Seeton's second sketch, over which she had studiously laboured, beside her first inspired scene of the nightclub dancers. "This one" — he tapped it with a thoughtful finger — "is just what I expected — a copy. It looks like what it is — a burned-out building. Any one of a hundred artistic workhorses could have produced it. But the other . . ."

The nightclub scene was swiftly sketched, figures drawn in quick pencil strokes in the background, a general impression of the frenetic lifestyle which had been so skilfully depicted in the movie to which Mel had referred. Nobody was drinking, however: or, if they were, it was restrained, and in the background. The two foreground figures had neither glasses in their hands nor bottles on the table beside them.

"So probably no bootlegging connection," murmured Mel, a wary eye on Delphick. "And most likely no police raid any minute, nor guys with machine guns in violin cases . . ."

"You must brush up on your British history, Miss Forby. England never suffered Prohibition, except under Cromwell and that of another nature altogether," Delphick told her, but absently. This was no time for badinage: he had to make sense of Miss Seeton's drawing, and preferably before she came back and grew uncomfortable again.

A man and a woman stood facing each other in what was clearly a nightclub. She wore, as Mel had pointed out, the Twenties vamplike costume — straight fringed dress, and long strings of beads — the effect heightened by her bobbed hair. With one hand she had drawn the man close to her and looped a knotted string of black beads around his neck: Miss Seeton had somehow contrived to give this delicate fetter a lustrous, expensive air. The imprisoned man regarded his fair captor with a look of burning intensity: in the near background, another man watched them, equally intense, and ignoring the livelier group behind him.

"Wish someone thought *I* was worth a

black pearl necklace," said Mel, thinking of Thrudd Banner and brooding on her birthday. He'd taken her out for a slap-up meal (three weeks late — he'd been away at the proper time), but it would have been nice to have some more tangible sign of his affections. Ordinary pearls, Mel thought, had too much of a twin-set, tweeded, unexciting air: black pearls, she felt, sounded as if they'd make her feel dangerous, moody, interesting, raffish . . .

"Knotted black pearls," said Delphick. "The prominent feature of this drawing — and she'd already heard about the crime before I told her, she said so. Which is probably the simple explanation for all this, and there's no more to it than her subconscious memory —"

"You said yourself, sir," broke in Bob, protesting, "we can trust Miss Seeton to give us what we want. All we have to do is interpret what she's really showing us, and then — well, then we know what she means." He went red, coughed, and pushed back his chair. "I, er, think I'll go and ask her if she wants a hand in the kitchen," he said; and went.

"Bless the boy," said Mel. "Rushing to the defence of his dear Aunt Em and tying himself in knots like that."

"Loyalty's no bad thing," Delphick reminded her. "And he's perfectly right. We mustn't dismiss this as what it superficially appears to represent — oh, it *is* a nightclub scene, and she's echoing what she's heard — Notley Black, and knotted black pearls — it's obvious. So obvious that there has to be some other meaning behind it — which is what sooner — or later," and he sighed, "we have to work out — if for no other reason," he concluded, rallying, with a grin, "than to give you your promised scoop, Miss Forby."

To which Mel replied, with her own grin, as Bob emerged with a tray in his hands, followed by Miss Seeton: "Good for you, Oracle. I knew I could rely on Scotland Yard . . ."

Plummergen, with its strong sense of identity, was not slow to volunteer for Sir George's Village Watch scheme, in view of the various depredations to which it had recently been subjected. There was a strongly held opinion that most of the blame for these occurrences should be laid at Murreystone's collective door: the rival parish being, after all, only five miles distant. Much could be done under cover of dark to sabotage neighbouring hopes of a prize in the Best Kept Village Competition: and Murreystone was known to be harbouring a more-than-usually-intense grudge after the loss of its hall, for which it felt that Plummergen, in some unspecified way, was probably to blame.

Any husbands, brothers, or sons reluctant to offer their services to the Night Watch Men (as the Colveden volunteers were soon called) were given short shrift by their womenfolk, who eschewed the Lysistrata technique for more certain methods. Lumpy custard, late meals, judicious nagging, and aspersions of cowardice soon subdued this feeble pacifist spirit: it was not enough to claim a need for eight hours' sleep a night, or to suggest that there would be enough help without adding more. Plummergen's blood was up.

Everyone was so fired with enthusiasm that Sir George was able to pick and choose his team. Old men, all women of whatever age (Miss Nuttel and Mrs. Blaine were a vociferous lobby on the Liberation ticket, but retired, worsted), and of course all children were denied any part of the proceedings. The night was divided into two-hour periods, the men into groups of four, each group to patrol its given sector until relieved by its successor. There would be a half-hour handover period for exchange of information and tactics, as necessary; thus, apart from the first and last watches of the night, when traces of daylight should lessen the risk of enemy activity, there would never be fewer than six men on duty in any given area.

The standing orders were for the patrols to keep watch on Plummergen's main street and immediate surrounding areas, never forgetting that it was possible to reach Murreystone, and for Murreystone to reach them, by side roads and across fields from the back. "Eyes all around you," instructed Sir George, "and no smoking, in case the blighters spot you and put it off for another night. Need to catch 'em in the act to stop 'em properly. Give 'em a thorough fright."

There was no doubt in the minds of most people that Murreystone had been responsible for the theft of Miss Nuttel's garden gnome and the wrought-iron flower baskets and lamp brackets, though some blamed Mr. Alexander, or (more likely) the mystery mistress nobody ever saw. But Murreystone were the odds-on favourites; and, if they could only have been proved, the recent plague of moles, and even the Brown Wilt, would also have been laid at the age-old rival's door. Mrs. Flax (who lays out for the village, and is popularly regarded as a Wise Woman) led a small group eager to assign the moles and the fungus to Murreystone's harnessing of Sinister Forces. The Nuts, thwarted in their attempt to join the Village Watch, announced that they would be holding a seance in order to ascertain the truth and the best method of combatting it.

Sir George learned with some relief of this proposal, realising that, though it might not work as intended, it would serve to keep the hysterical element out of his way, which could only be a good thing. Nigel suggested that earplugs should be generally issued to deaden the sounds of table-tapping and cries of "Is anybody there?"; Lady Colveden thought that everyone ought to supply themselves with sandwiches and flasks of coffee, which Sir George vetoed on the grounds that it would turn the whole affair into a bally picnic and they'd just forget what they were supposed to be doing. He repeated his warnings about cigarettes, and some murmurs of disaffection were heard.

A muffled figure, trouser-clad and carrying a mysterious package, was spotted making its stealthy way from the George and Dragon southwards down The Street — the package looking, to suspicious eyes, very like a bomb. Jack Crabbe and his troop

211

of farm workers, armed with sacks, stalked the figure as it made for the narrow road bounded on one side by the brick wall of Sweetbriars, and pounced as it drew near the side gate which Miss Seeton was supposed to keep locked at all times. From within the sack loud and furious shrieks suggested that their booty was a woman.

"How — how dare you!" blazed Miss Ursula Hawke, once she had been unwrapped, and the bomb revealed as her shoulder bag, containing nothing more sinister than binoculars, a torch, two packets of sandwiches, and a notebook. "This is unpardonable — assault — private citizen, going about her lawful business — free country — at liberty to walk where I please — inform the police . . ."

They tried to apologise, but Miss Hawke was too angry to listen. If the owls of Ashford Forest, which she had looked forward all day to observing, now eluded her because of this delay, she would make the strongest protest in the highest quarters. Did they not know that their chief constable, who was a personal friend, was also a keen naturalist in his spare time? He had given her every support in her project and would be annoyed enough to hear that her book had been put in jeopardy; he would be even more annoyed to learn that the work of policing his county had been taken out of official hands by a band of amateur incompetents who molested innocent passers-by and took them, however briefly, prisoner. "Unlawful arrest," muttered Miss Hawke darkly, and glared as she opened the side gate, withdrew the bicycle which Miss Seeton had kindly arranged to lend her, and pedalled off into the darkness.

The patrol did not mention this embarrassing encounter to their relief when the time duly came. Plummergen knows how to keep its own counsel.

Nothing else of moment happened for the remainder of the night.

chapter
17

The bus from Crabbe's Garage drew up outside Plummergen JMI School, and a chattering, excited crowd of junior mixed infants surged from the playground to form a more or less orderly line in front of the door. Miss Seeton, umbrella in hand, marshalled the line into proper order, then tapped on the door. Driver Jack Crabbe pressed the lever, there was a rubbery hiss, and with a thud the door folded open.

"Quietly now, children," commanded Miss Seeton. "Climb the steps one at a time, and sit down in the first empty seat you come to. No pushing, please."

The embarkation commenced. There were minor problems.

"Marcus, you have dropped your packet of sandwiches. Don't tread on — oh, dear. Are they very badly squashed? . . . Henry, you are not to push poor Biddy so roughly. You might knock her over, then she would hurt herself . . . Helen and Katherine, one at a time, please . . . Now, who has left their anorak on the gatepost?"

But eventually everyone was settled, and the excursion to Ashford Forest set off.

Miss Seeton had recently been brushing up on her natural history. Once she had learned from Mel of Miss Hawke's secret enthusiasm, she had ventured to ask the naturalist for advice on what she might best show the children during their trip; Miss Hawke, still starchy and abbreviated with people, was prepared to unbend a little in Miss Seeton's case after the episode of the magpie and barked several helpful suggestions at her before requesting the loan of Miss Seeton's bicycle one moonlit night. There were barn and other owls to be seen, she felt sure, in Ashford Forest — not that Miss Seeton and her horde of children could hope to see them in daylight, and if the school excursion was planned for this week, it would be better for serious observation purposes if Miss Hawke went there first. "Disturb too much wildlife," said Miss Hawke looking irritated at the thought.

But she had been helpful in sharing her knowledge, and Miss Seeton now silently thanked her once more as she sat in the front seat of Jack Crabbe's bus as it drove out of Plummergen and headed for Ashford Forest. The bus had set off more or less on time; nobody had been left behind, nor had any item of food, clothing, or scholastic equipment been forgotten. The children were excited, of course, but on the whole were behaving very well, and a good brisk walk through the trees, never straying too far from the bridle paths, should help them work off their surplus energy.

Jack Crabbe parked the coach neatly in one of the wide gateways to the forest and settled down, once everyone had climbed out and those who were absentminded had climbed back to retrieve their belongings, to compile another of the cryptic crosswords which he regularly sold to the literary periodicals. He nodded a cheerful farewell to Miss Seeton and her band, telling them not to fret, he'd be happy enough till they got back, and no need to hurry themselves. They were to have a good time, and if anyone found a wild bees' nest, they were to mark the tree and let him know, because wild bees gave the best honey and his great-grandfather swore by it for his rheumatism.

Miss Seeton was a conscientious teacher and had read as much as she could about the Kentish woodland before the day of the excursion. "Look carefully at the trees which mark the boundary of the forest, children. They are hornbeams, and you may recognise them by their bark — so very smooth and grey, isn't it? Almost the colour of lead. And such an unusual way the trunk of the tree sometimes grows in grooves — fluted, we might call it. It would perhaps make an interesting picture — some of the twisted shapes, that is." Everyone obediently turned to study the silver-trunked trees with their curious leaves, very dark green above but, when you stood underneath the tree, looking almost yellow. "Now, these particular hornbeams have been pollarded," Miss Seeton said, clearing her throat. "That is, the tops have been cut off about ten feet from the ground —"

"Why did someone cut them off?" young Marcus wanted to know. Miss Seeton, still imparting the results of her careful study, replied: "So that when the wood grows again from the top, it will grow faster than before, and it may be cut and used earlier than if it had been left to grow by itself."

"What do they use it for?" somebody else asked.

Miss Seeton was ready for that one, too. "Hornbeam," she said, "is one of the hardest timbers, and the strongest, too. People used to make mill wheels out of it, and the hubs of cartwheels."

"But does anybody use it *now?*" demanded Marcus suspiciously, as the previous enquirer fell silent. Miss Seeton stifled a sigh. Education, after all, had many guises: the main point was surely to arouse interest in a child and, once having aroused it, to satisfy it. Besides, she just happened to remember the answer.

"Hammers, for pianos — and chopping boards, and mallets, and skittles, and anything that needs, well, strong wood. So this," she said firmly, "is pollarding. Now, who can tell me what it is called when trees are cut off very close to the ground? We shall see some of these other trees later, inside."

There were giggles and nudgings, but nobody knew the answer to Miss Seeton's question. "Coppicing," she told them finally, "and you must watch out for some very old beech trees which were coppiced many years ago. They have one very large base, called a bole, and several smaller trunks growing out of it."

Miss Seeton marshalled her little army into some degree of order and led the way along the woodland ride into the depths of Ashford Forest. She pointed out the beauty of dancing butterflies, sunlit in a glade of low bracken; she showed holes in tree trunks which might belong to either of the two species of spotted woodpecker, lesser or greater, known to inhabit the wood. She agreed that the small scarlet jewels of wild strawberries were good to eat, but warned that a surfeit might cause some internal distress, and that no child should eat more than six each. "We must leave the rest for the birds and wild animals," she said. And such was the respect in which Miss Seeton was held that not the greediest child ate more than the specified half-dozen fruits, though many more than this number were to be found.

The search for wild strawberries had so delighted the children that, without realising it, they had wandered from the main ride in among the high-fronding, graceful bracken with its furled tips and pale green leaves. Strawberries were forgotten in the excitement of other discoveries. Fallen treetrunks and exposed roots were covered with velvety mosses of various colours and kinds, about which Miss Seeton was forced to confess her ignorance. Narrow beaten paths through the undergrowth were attributed to badgers, or to deer. Helen and Katherine found a dead mouse, while Henry snagged himself on some brambles as he tried to pick blackberries.

"I believe," remarked Miss Seeton, "that somewhere in this part of the forest there are some spindle trees. They were once used," she added, before anyone could ask, "to make, well, spindles, and knitting needles, things of that sort — but nowadays I understand it makes excellent charcoal, and of course we use charcoal sometimes in our art lessons. I think it would be interesting to see where it comes from." Miss Seeton had not been a teacher for many years without learning that to ask *don't you think it would be interesting to* . . . often resulted in nothing but blank stares and shuffling feet.

"In case anyone is not sure," continued Miss Seeton, "what a spindle tree looks like, it has smooth green bark when it is young, and its leaves are shiny blue-green above and paler underneath. At most it will be eighteen feet or so tall, probably less. We will look out for a young spindle tree — suppose we make it another competition?"

Some of the children had a far lower threshold of boredom than others, and, despite the fearsome fate rumoured to overtake those who misbehaved in Miss Seeton's presence, a few began to lose interest in the hunt for spindle trees. A small rubber ball, bright red, was produced and tossed from hand to hand behind Miss Seeton's back.

Miss Seeton turned.

Marcus was just about to throw the ball to Genefer and was thoroughly startled. His aim went awry; the ball flew sideways from his hand into a tangle of brambles.

"You've lost my ball," Biddy said. "I want it back."

Miss Seeton fixed them all with a stern eye. "Nobody had any business to be playing with a ball in the middle of a natural history ramble — but since you were, and it has been lost, we must try to find it again. And then, Biddy, I shall confiscate it until the end of term. Does that seem fair to you?"

"Yes, miss. I'm sorry, miss," said Biddy, adding, "but you will get it back for me, won't you? It was a birthday present."

"Then most certainly I will try my best," Miss Seeton assured her. "But those brambles look — oh, dear . . ."

Miss Seeton knew little about blackberries, except that they made delicious bramble jelly when properly cooked and strained through muslin; Martha Bloomer and Stan had taken her on one or two picking trips, but she had to confess that the prickles were, well, prickly. They caught on clothes, and in hair, and even the crook handle of her umbrella was not always a match for their toils. Miss Seeton had a wary respect for blackberry brambles — but surely even her most vivid memory of the thicketty turmoil never conjured up so excessive a tangle?

"What colour was the ball?" enquired Miss Seeton with a frown, peering into the brambles. "I see something blue . . . Stay there, children, while I . . ." With her umbrella she tried to part the bramble sprays, concentrating so hard that she did not hear the chorus of voices telling her that the missing toy was bright red.

"Oh, dear," said Miss Seeton as the umbrella worked its way through. "Surely — surely not . . . Children, stand well back, and let me . . ."

She worked the umbrella out again, then reversed it, and, using the handle to pull and probe, managed to clear part of the spiky tangle of stems sufficiently to show . . .

"Oh, dear," said Miss Seeton. "Oh, no . . ."

chapter
18

Miss Seeton was sitting in Ashford police station, drinking a cup of tea.

"She likes it weak — by police standards — remember, and no sugar," Chief Superintendent Delphick had warned, having learned that Miss Seeton, in a state of delayed shock, was being brought to Superintendent Brinton for her statement. "She's probably going to be in a bit of a stew about the children, too. Has Jack Crabbe rung yet to say they've all reached home safely?"

"Just a minute ago, sir," said Bob Ranger.

"Any trouble? I shouldn't think so — she seems to have coped admirably with them at the time."

"A little girl was a bit upset, but that was something to do with a lost ball, I think, from what Jack said. There wasn't any time for any of them to see — what Miss Seeton saw. She chivvied them all back to the bridle path without letting them anywhere near."

"Too busy worrying about other people," Delphick said, "to spare time for herself. It must have been a shock — a summer day, a school outing, and suddenly a dead body in a bramble thicket. You notice, Bob, that she didn't succumb to any show of weakness until all her responsibilities had been taken care of? The British gentlewoman at her best."

"Miss Seeton *is* the best, sir," said loyal Bob promptly. Delphick grinned.

"As she's practically a member of your family now, your opinion comes as no surprise. Blood, Sergeant Ranger, will tell, or so they say. By inference, you, too, should consider yourself the best — but don't take that as a compliment," Delphick said cheerfully. "You're large enough already. With a swollen head, you'd be impossible."

"Sir . . ."

Delphick ignored his sergeant's red face and embarrassed feet. "Large or small, you're the nearest we've got right now to a tea-boy. Trot along, Bob, and do your stuff. If that radio message was correct, the car bringing Miss Seeton should be here any minute."

Everyone assembled in Superintendent Brinton's office: the superintendent himself, Delphick, Bob Ranger, and Miss Seeton, grateful for the tea and still upset about her discovery in Ashford Forest.

"It must have made it worse for you," said

Delphick, "as soon as you realised that you knew who it was. Or were you not able to see clearly at first?"

"Something blue — her blouse," said Miss Seeton. "I had been looking for a rubber ball, you see. Sometimes, despite one's very best efforts, they grow slightly bored and start to fidget — and what could be more natural to a child than bouncing a ball? It was a birthday present, she said, not that I would have allowed her to keep playing with it, and they can be very fair-minded, I've found, if one approaches them the right way. I suppose . . . it seems foolish, in the circumstances, but a child cannot be expected to understand beyond its own small world — and I did make a promise to try my best, even though I said I should con-fiscate it afterwards. And she agreed. If the police were to find it . . ."

Delphick responded with a gentle smile to the question in her eyes. "Any rubber balls we find in the undergrowth," he assured her gravely, "will be handed over to you for you to deal with as you think best. But when that will be, I'm afraid I couldn't say. We don't have umbrellas to hook back the stems — we have to make do with secateurs."

"You are very kind." Miss Seeton sat up straight and put her teacup back on its saucer. "Too kind, perhaps, for trying to distract me, when it is clearly my duty to tell you everything I know. Which of course I will, though I fear it won't be much, and Miss Forby was the one who told me in the first place, mostly. Although, after the magpie, I suppose I could claim some acquaintance — and my bicycle, as well. She wanted to borrow it, and naturally I agreed, not needing it in the middle of the night, you see. But I wonder why we didn't notice it on the way into the forest? Children are usually so observant, which is why they can be such a pleasure to teach . . ." She frowned, and looked anxious. "I did my very best not to let them notice the body — they can be too observant, sometimes . . ."

"You did a grand job, Miss Seeton," Delphick told her, and Superintendent Brinton nodded. "They're all back in Plummergen now," he said, "and I've told P.C. Potter to give them a Road Safety lesson — should take their minds well and truly off anything they might have spotted in the wood. He likes 'em to act out the parts," he explained. "Makes them roar up and down the playground being motorbikes and lorries — they won't have enough energy left to worry after that."

Miss Seeton brightened. "Thank you so

much, Mr. Brinton. That is a weight off my mind. I was afraid, you see, that somehow I had failed in my trust — not that I could have known, of course, that there was a body in the brambles, but Mr. Jessyp and their parents had handed them over to my care, and to leave them alone . . ."

"They'll be all right, Miss Seeton," Delphick assured her. Children forget; they'd be all right. But would Miss Seeton? She wasn't growing any younger, and she'd known the dead woman — well enough to lend her . . .

"Your bicycle, Miss Seeton. Can you describe it? We'll have some men to look out for it. And perhaps you'd tell us why this Miss Hawke had borrowed it in the first place. For use in" — Delphick cleared his throat — "the middle of the night. It seems unusual." Although, with any connection to Miss Seeton, the unusual could be almost guaranteed.

Miss Seeton told her story, muddling the magpie and Tibs with barn owls and nature rambles and Mel Forby's discovery that Miss Hawke planned to write the definitive book on the Kentish countryside. But her general sense was clear, and the three policemen knew her of old. Delphick usually seemed to understand what she was talking

about; Bob Ranger tried his best, and sometimes did, but had given up worrying over it
several years back; Brinton grumbled in
public, but privately thought she had her
good points.

"So you see," concluded Miss Seeton,
"while I could not have *expected* to find her
there, it was not, in a way, much of a *surprise*. That she was there, I mean, not that
she was dead. Which was indeed a surprise,
although when I noticed that she had not returned it this morning, I had wondered if
she might have tumbled off and hurt herself
— one sometimes loses one's balance, over
bumpy roads — and I hardly thought that
she might be sleeping late, because dear
Mel, that is, Miss Forby, is staying in the
George and Dragon as well and says that
Miss Hawke asks for sandwiches at the
strangest hours, and poor Doris gets rather
upset. She hardly seems to require any sleep
at all — Miss Hawke, I mean . . ."

She tailed off as she recalled that the subject of her explanation would now sleep for
longer than ever before, and looked uncomfortable. She dropped her gaze to her lap
and clasped her hands to still their unhappy
dance. Delphick sat forward.

"Miss Seeton — has something just occurred to you?"

She looked up at him blankly. As her attention wandered away from them, her hands unclasped and began to dance even more unhappily. "I — I don't really think so," she said.

"Come now, are you quite sure? You haven't remembered something — anything — the slightest impression — that might help us discover who did this dreadful thing?"

Her conscience thus appealed to, Miss Seeton looked from one watching face to another. Bob Ranger, who knew the signs as well as Delphick, gave her an encouraging nod. He murmured, "Go on, Aunt Em," and ignored Superintendent Brinton's quizzical stare.

Miss Seeton blushed. "Perhaps," she faltered, "that is, it really is simply an impression — I tried so hard not to look at her, once I realised . . ."

"But you could draw it for us, couldn't you?" Delphick was looking at Brinton as he spoke. "Chris, have you paper and pencils and the rest of the paraphernalia?"

They left her by herself in the superintendent's office while they repaired to another room, ignoring her protests that it felt wrong for her to be, well, evicting the poor man. "He doesn't mind one bit," Delphick told her, glaring at his friend. "Not in the furtherance of justice — do you, Chris?"

"Not at all," said the superintendent, disguising his true feelings. He liked Miss Seeton — after a bumpy start to their relationship, he'd almost come to admire her — but she made him uncomfortable, her and her drawings. All this psychic stuff was, well, uncomfortable — spooky, if you like — not that he'd admit it to just anyone, but The Oracle and that massive young sergeant of his weren't just anyone, they were the Yard's recognised Seeton experts. If they thought she'd better draw something, then he supposed she'd better draw it; but he didn't want to be around watching her while she did.

"We'll have a chat to young Sleaze in the meantime," he suggested, regaining his composure as they closed the office door behind them. "He's due to report in around now — might be a good idea to check on what the Choppers were up to last night, and where. Though I have to admit," he added, "until now I wouldn't have thought murder was their style."

For murder Miss Hawke's death undoubtedly was: unless, of course, she could have hit herself on the head several times, crawled into the middle of the blackberries, and uprooted the most ferocious stems to cover herself from all but the least casual view. Which seemed unlikely.

Detective Constable Arbuthnott was shocked by the news of Miss Hawke's murder, but able to give his new companions a reasonable alibi for the early part of the night, at any rate. Although, he added, once they'd split up and said they were going home, he'd had to take it as fact that they *had* gone home. He could hardly track all of 'em to their separate lairs; he could only testify that their mood hadn't been one of intent to frolic in the forest and bash on the head any old ladies who happened to wander into their path.

"So," summed up Brinton, once Sleaze had departed, "we'd better not rule out the Choppers. One of 'em might have got in a panic when Miss Hawke spotted him doing, oh, something he shouldn't have been doing — but what the hell you can get up to in a forest in the middle of the night that'd be worth killing for, I can't imagine."

"It seems to have the feel of panic," Delphick said, "even though whoever did it kept his head well enough to take the weapon away with him. Something hard, flat, and with a sharp edge — might be a spade, I suppose, yet it's hard to see why anyone would go to the forest prepared to bury a dead body and then just shove it under the brambles — unless they panicked. She was bound to be discovered once the leaves had fallen — he didn't think it through."

"Preserve me from the spur-of-the-moment random killer," Brinton growled. "They're by far the hardest to nobble —"

"Unless," Delphick reminded him, "the nobbler is helped by somebody who detects crime by similar means, which is to say by instinct. As Miss Seeton seems to do. Suppose we go along and see whether she's had time to finish her drawing?"

The door of Brinton's office was just opening as the three policemen walked back down the corridor, and Miss Seeton's grey head popped out. She heard the approaching sounds of six regulation feet, looked in their direction, and smiled.

"I was just wondering how I might find you, Mr. Delphick, Mr. Brinton — in case you wanted to see my sketch."

"If you've finished it, then certainly we do," Delphick told her. "Shall we all go in and sit down again?"

"I can't imagine," said Miss Seeton shyly, once everyone was seated around Brinton's desk, "what made me think of the book, but something must have reminded me — one of my childhood favourites — and the children were talking about paths made by badgers — and it felt, well, *right* when I completed the drawing, although now — on second thoughts, somehow I'm not so sure — it's, well, not *quite* right . . ."

"*The Wind in the Willows*," said Delphick, studying the drawing on Brinton's desk. "There's no doubt of that — but, now that I look closely, I do see what you mean."

There indeed were the three animal friends from Kenneth Grahame's classic: Mole, Ratty, and Badger, carefully drawn in loving detail. Delphick had known the scene at once. After Mole's terrifying experience of being stalked through the snowy Wild Wood by the Weasels and Stoats, the Water Rat had come to his rescue and taken him at last to the safety of Badger's nearby home. The weary pair of friends had been quickly restored by Badger in his underground fastness — or, thought Delphick, was it so fast, after all? Why had Miss Seeton shown the animals not sitting at their ease around the fire, but looking upwards over their shoulders? Almost as if they feared (from the expressions on their faces) that the ceiling was about to fall in on top of them. Mole, in the foreground, was shown in particular detail, while Ratty beside him was more the impression of a furry, anxious face. The teapot in Badger's hand looked piping hot, the cups were waiting to be filled; the animals were toasting their toes beside the hearth, and the table was laden with comforting food. It was a scene that ought to have been idyllic, and at first glance appeared so — yet somehow was not. The shadows flickering in the corners were just too darkly brooding, the smoke from the fire smelled, Delphick felt sure, acrid, and the sparks would burn wickedly where they fell instead of fading out. The whole room looked as if a dreadful fate awaited it.

Delphick frowned. "I didn't think that the Wild Wooders invaded Badger's home," he mused aloud. "I thought that it was Badger and his friends who thrashed them, right at the end, when they recaptured Toad Hall."

"So they did, sir," said Bob Ranger. "Badger tells them about the hidden tunnel that leads up to the Hall, and they wait until the Wild Wooders're having a great feast and then spring out on them and . . ." He stumbled into silence, turning red. Delphick raised an eyebrow.

"Your previously unmentioned progeny — those of which we had no inkling until the other day — would appear to have a tradi-

234

tional taste in bedtime literature, Bob. I congratulate you and Anne on the way you are rearing them."

"My sister's kids, sir," mumbled Bob in explanation, yet more red. "They've grown out of the Jack the Rabbit stuff but they still like me to read them a story sometimes. So, well, I do, sir."

"I congratulate you again." Delphick smiled. "No doubt you regard it as practice for the future, in any case . . . As for the present, we must concentrate on this picture. Miss Seeton — you're not happy with it now you've come to look at it again, are you?"

"No," said Miss Seeton, who had lost her smile as soon as the policemen had settled down to study her handiwork. "No, I'm not — I was at first, but now I've heard your comments, Chief Superintendent, I know there really is something wrong. It isn't simply my imagination . . ."

And her unhappy expression echoed the anxiety in the hearts of the three policemen who watched her. Something was wrong — something else besides murder.

chapter
19

Delphick and Bob drove Miss Seeton back to Plummergen and agreed to stop for a quick cup of tea and a slice of Martha Bloomer's renowned fruit cake. At the end of their short visit Miss Seeton looked slightly happier than she had done when they arrived; but Delphick and Bob, as they trod down the short path to the front gate, allowed themselves to look anxious again.

"I don't think I like the way this case is going," said Delphick. "That picture was very unpleasant."

"Sort of catches you on the hop, doesn't it, sir? There you are with Mole and Ratty safely in Badger's house, then suddenly you realise it isn't safe anymore. As if somebody is about to break in and smash the place to smithereens."

"And the way that fire looked about to boil over and engulf everything . . . No," as Bob made to cross to the car, parked outside the George and Dragon, where they had elected to stay, "we're going to see the Colvedens, and it hardly seems worth driving. I don't know about you, but I could do with the walk to clear my head."

They walked in thoughtful silence for a few minutes, Bob broke it at last by remarking, "That picture she drew of the south end of The Street going up in flames . . ."

"Yes," said Delphick. "Another of her offerings which, by all accounts, is very unpleasant. If it's rattled Sir George, I want to look at it — need to, in fact. That man's neither a fool nor a coward — you aren't awarded the DSO for nothing. If a chap like Colveden says he's worried, then so ought we to be."

At Rytham Hall they found Lady Colveden on her knees by the open front door. "Hello, and don't come any nearer," she greeted her guests cheerfully. "We're having the Before and After Exhibition in the village hall tomorrow — Nigel and George are down there now, setting up all the folding screens and notice boards we managed to scrounge — and you'd never believe the number of drawing pins there are in one of those little packets, until you drop it. You'd better come in through the kitchen until I've collected them all. I'll lock the door in case of accidents — the light's much better for looking with it open, but it would be just like George to come grumbling back from his good deed and tread all over the parquet. Martha," said Lady Colveden with a smile, "is a dragon when it comes to polishing. I'd be scared to face her if anyone scratched the floor."

"It was about the exhibition that we've come," Delphick said as they settled themselves in comfortable chairs, and refused the offer of tea or coffee. "I understand that Miss Seeton drew, or painted, pictures based on photographs taken by your husband?"

"Before and After," Lady Colveden agreed. "George did a very good job, considering how long it's been since photography was his hobby. Cedric Benbow gave him lots of advice, and lent him — but you're not" — and she smiled at him — "really interested in George's hobbies, are you? It's Miss Seeton's pictures you've come to look at."

"Are they still here, or have they already been taken to the hall ready for the exhibition? I should very much like, if it's possible, to see them — one of them in particular."

Lady Colveden's smile grew knowing. "Let me guess which one that might be. Not Mr. Stillman's post office awning, I shouldn't think, and definitely not the ghastly garden gnome somebody stole from

The Nuts — I can't imagine Scotland Yard bothered about that. There are plenty of other pictures, of course, but my guess would be the one Miss Seeton produced showing the south end of The Street in flames . . ."

"Not a fair guess," said Delphick dryly. "Sir George was worried enough about it to telephone Superintendent Brinton at Ashford, and *my* guess is that the pair of you have been wondering about it all week. May I see it?"

"Indeed you may. Did George tell Mr. Brinton we cut it in two? We didn't want to worry poor Miss Seeton — after all it's her house that's right in the middle of the fire — so we're going to tell her it somehow got torn, if she says anything."

"You haven't thrown it away?" asked Delphick urgently.

"Oh, no, we couldn't do that. It would have felt . . ." Lady Colveden hesitated. "My first thought was to throw it away, but I didn't like . . . I wondered about burning it, but that would have felt even worse, somehow. It's such a very, well, uncomfortable picture . . ."

It was. Lady Colveden retrieved the smaller, smoke-dark and flame-filled portion from the bottom of her needlework box. "Well out of harm's way," she explained. "Nobody ever uses it except me — and hardly ever me, for that matter." She took the remainder of the picture from its place in the exhibition folders and set it down on the table so that the pieces joined to make a whole. Beside them she placed Sir George's photograph.

"That's what Miss Seeton was working from," she said. "And there's no sign of a fire anywhere in that, is there? Not even from the blacksmith's forge . . ."

"Which building is the forge?" Delphick asked. She put a slim finger on the white building with the steep-pitched tiled roof and yellow double doors. "No fire," she pointed out, and Delphick nodded.

There came the sound of clattering outside in the hall. "I told you George would try to come in that way and tread drawing pins all over the house," said Lady Colveden. "It's just as well I locked the door. I hope they have the sense to come in through the kitchen — when men go broody about doing their good deed for the day, they're sometimes quite unreasonable afterwards." She twinkled at Bob. "No doubt Anne would say exactly the same about you."

Sir George and Nigel soon appeared in

the sitting room, looking pleased with themselves. "Mother and her cronies can pin the wretched things up in some tasteful arrangement later on this evening," Nigel said. "Dad and I have done more than our bit for the beautification of Plummergen — and so has Miss Seeton, of course, with her pictures." Then he became serious. "The village is buzzing with the news," he said. "Potter and Jack Crabbe did their best, but you know how gossip spreads in this place. I suppose it's true, and Miss Seeton really did find a dead body?"

"What?" cried Lady Colveden, horrified. "Nigel, no, you can't mean that. George — Mr. Delphick — surely there's some mistake? Miss Seeton, finding a body? Oh" — as from their grave expressions she realised the truth — "the poor thing! How did it happen? Where? And why didn't you tell me —" she turned to Delphick — "instead of letting me chatter on about photographs?"

"I admit that I was surprised you didn't appear to have heard," said Delphick. "Especially in Plummergen, news of that sort travels fast."

"I haven't been to the shops today, and nobody's called — we aren't exactly handy for casual dropping in, here, are we? And so many people have been ringing up to moan

241

about the Before-and-Aftering, and the Competition, and the Watch my husband has set up, that this afternoon I simply took the phone off the hook and decided to ignore the lot of them." Lady Colveden shook her head. "Today of all days — I feel dreadful. But poor Miss Seeton must feel so much worse — how is she? What happened, or aren't you allowed to say?"

Delphick told her as much as he thought advisable, and she looked more upset than ever. "You could hardly have been expected to guess," Delphick consoled her. "And Miss Seeton herself, after the initial shock, is coping well."

"Ought to have guessed," said Sir George gruffly. "Told Charley Mountfitchet, when a guest doesn't come back after a night out, ought to ask a few questions." He looked rather grim as he said this. "Have a word with you about that, in a few minutes."

"I'd be interested," Delphick said, "to hear anything you can tell me that might help — but," he added trying to be fair, "I'm not sure we can really hold the landlord at fault. By all accounts, Miss Hawke was much given to staying out all night and wandering around during the day, which makes it rather difficult to check up on her movements, and to know whether or not to start worrying, and when."

"Erratic, certainly," agreed Sir George. "Makes your job harder, I should think. No regular habits to deviate from — no alibi to break."

"It's hardly Miss Hawke who needs the alibi, Dad," Nigel pointed out to his father. "Mind you, I'm not surprised she got herself bumped off —"

"Nigel!" His mother was shocked.

"Nil nisi bonum," added Sir George, looking as if he was slightly doubtful of the wisdom of this.

"What makes you say that, exactly?" enquired Delphick, a calming note in his voice. Sir George and his wife subsided into an anxious silence.

"She was bossy," Nigel said, after a pause. "Interfered all the time — told everybody how to do things, and annoyed pretty well the whole village. Everyone who met her, anyway — and you needn't shake your head at me like that, Mother. Dad's keeping quiet, but he was one of her first victims, if you can call them that, and I know there were others."

With much throat-clearing and prompting, Sir George told his story. "Tried to make out Cedric Benbow doesn't know his stuff," he said indignantly. "Soon put her straight,

243

of course, but the boy's right. An annoying woman — though not enough to hit her over the head, I'd have thought."

"But somebody did," Delphick reminded him. "Somebody, perhaps, with a less equable temperament than yourself. Who else did she try to, shall we say intimidate, in this way?"

"All sorts of people," Nigel said. "There was a bit of a row with Jacob Chickney when she found out who he was, for one. The village mole catcher," he explained to Delphick.

"There was practically a fight, so I heard," volunteered Lady Colveden. "They were discussing it in the post office when I went in for some sugar — apparently Miss Hawke cornered him in the George and harangued him for ages about the ethics of his job, the horrid old man, and he used the most dreadful language back at her."

"Which is no different," Nigel pointed out, "from the way he behaves to everyone else normally. You can't use that as evidence . . ."

He tailed off as Delphick regarded him with interest. "Indeed, Mr. Colveden?" Nigel winced: it had been some years since the chief superintendent had been so formal with him. "Then why did you feel the need to mention the incident in the first place?"

"You asked," said Nigel after an infinitesimal pause, "who else she'd tried to push around. So of course I said. Not that I believe there's anything in it, though. Old Jake is a miserable, money-grubbing, antisocial oaf with the manners of a pig — which is insulting to pigs — but even so, I can't believe he'd murder anyone."

There was a pause. "Who else?" Delphick enquired with a stern glance round at all three Colvedens. "It's no use saying there are lots of people, then only mentioning one."

There was a further pause. "It's too silly," said Lady Colveden, weakening at last. "But in books, and on television, they always seem to suspect the person who finds the body, and . . ."

"And you were afraid we'd suspect Miss Seeton," Delphick concluded for her. "Why should we do that? You must know she's above suspicion. Apart from anything else, how could she have reached Ashford Forest in the middle of the night, when she'd lent Miss Hawke her bicycle — her only means of transport?"

The atmosphere lightened at once. Nigel grinned shakily at Delphick. "You're right: we didn't think it through. In any case, if

Miss Seeton lent Miss Hawke her bike, it means they must have sorted out whatever differences they might have had — and it was only gossip, anyhow. You know how the village loves to get hold of the wrong end of the stick where Miss Seeton's concerned."

"I do indeed. But what could anyone have said to make you believe Miss Seeton also had a . . . an exchange with Miss Hawke? She never mentioned any such thing to us, and she's the most truthful person, as you know. She explained to us in great detail how they'd rescued a magpie from a cat, or something of the sort — nothing about any argument."

Lady Colveden said, "You see, there was some nonsense about Miss Seeton painting a picture and Miss Hawke telling her how to do it — as Nigel said, the poor woman was really very, well, opinionated and interfering. And annoying. But then other people said they'd been rescuing a cat together, or something — I'm not sure about any magpies, but I gather Jacob Chickney was somehow caught up in that little episode. Anyway, it all seems such a muddle. I don't believe any of us knows what to think."

"You can stop thinking that Miss

Seeton's involved in any way, for a start," Delphick said, trying not to smile. "And then, when you've ordered your thoughts, you can tell me, Sir George. what you were going to tell me earlier — about Miss Hawke's midnight wanderings, I believe."

"Ah, yes." The major-general stroked his moustache and looked thoughtful. "Feel a bit to blame — my men letting her go off to be murdered like that. Bad show."

"It's hardly your fault, George, you were nowhere near," protested his wife at once, but Delphick motioned her, with the utmost courtesy, to silence, and she subsided.

"Do please continue," prompted the chief superintendent; and Sir George explained how the Village Watch had come upon Miss Hawke behaving, as they thought, suspiciously, in the vicinity of Sweetbriars ("Little woman lives alone. Can't be too careful, lunatics on the loose,") and had apprehended her, then let her go. "Go to her death," concluded poor Sir George. "First chance for the Watchmen to prove their worth — and they mess it up. Bad show."

Delphick pressed him for more details, adding that he would be visiting Jack Crabbe and the rest of the patrol to confirm what he was sure was the truth. The Colvedens were now glad to offer what assistance they could, but, despite close questioning, and further study of Miss Seeton's picture, nobody came up with any bright ideas. Lady Colveden offered coffee, and while she made it Detective Sergeant Bob joined Nigel in the hunt for mislaid drawing-pins. In one respect at least, the visit to Rytham Hall proved a success.

chapter
20

Jack Crabbe, and those members of his patrol whom Delphick was able to run to earth that evening, told the same story as reported by Sir George. Miss Hawke had left the George and Dragon in the middle of the night, in perfect health, without mentioning either whether she planned to meet anyone else or even where she intended to go on Miss Seeton's borrowed bicycle. She had been angry, they all agreed, and forceful, but otherwise uncommunicative.

"And they all alibi one another for the rest of the two-hour period," Delphick remarked to Bob as they headed back to the George and Dragon for a snack, a drink, and their well-earned rest. "And I find it hard to believe that any of them brooded for over two hours and then went charging off into the forest to kill her. For one thing, how did they know where she'd be? Everyone's agreed that she never told anybody her plans."

"I wouldn't believe it of Jack, or the others, anyway," said Bob, adopted son of

Plummergen, loyally. "I expect it will turn out to be Mr. Brinton's unwanted random killer, after all."

Delphick shook his head with such a sorrowful expression on his face that Doris, about to serve him with his ploughman's platter, thought he had changed his mind and started to take it away again. This took some sorting out before they were able to resume the discussion.

"About the random killer, Bob — you're not thinking this thing right through. Who in the world is going to be wandering around a wood in the middle of the night on the chance of meeting someone he, or possibly she, could kill?"

"A lunatic, sir," supplied Bob promptly. "If it was a full moon last night . . ."

"Moonshine," came a voice from over his shoulder, and it was followed by a tray with three glasses on it. Mel Forby had intercepted Doris on her second trip to the constabulary table, added her own half-pint of lager, and tipped the weary waitress fifty pence to misdirect any of her reporting rivals who might turn up. "Mind if I join you for an exclusive interview?" enquired Mel, not waiting for an answer. She unloaded the tray, pulled up another chair, and sat down with a bright smile.

"Strictly off the record for now," Delphick said, though he smiled back in acknowledgement of her journalistic impudence. Bob was too busy eating pickled onions to do more than nod a greeting. Mel tapped her handbag.

"Notebook tucked away until recalled to duty, as per our arrangement," she said. "But I've just come from visiting Miss S. over the way — heard a weird rumour about how she found Miss Hawke's body in some blackberry bushes in Ashford Forest, and went to see if it was true — and it was. Poor little soul's not sure what to make of it all, and I don't want her babbling to any of the others and giving the wrong impression — she'd say anything out of politeness, you know she would, and the muckrakers would twist it any old way to make a good headline. I'll take care that when the story finally breaks she doesn't get a mention except as the good old Battling Brolly, and I've told her to keep indoors for the next few days and not answer the door unless she knows for sure who's out there."

Delphick thought back to the first time he and Mel had met; when she arrived in Plummergen to find out how a series of child murders might, or might not, be solved by the power of Miss Seeton's pencil.

The power of Mel Forby's pen had been put to good use in that case, for she had, in her own words. plugged the Brolly angle so everyone would forget the name, and had joined that band of Miss Seeton's protectors who did all they could to maintain her genteel innocence of the world's wicked ways. Delphick knew he could trust Mel to look after Miss Seeton's interests, and he told her as much as he safely could of the case so far.

"*The Wind in the Willows*, you say? Could be she thought of Ashford Forest as the Wild Wood — which it certainly was for Miss Hawke." Mel frowned. "I'm a bit rusty — wasn't that where the bad guys lived?"

Delphick grinned in the direction of Bob, who was just finishing his chunk of pork pie. "Our expert on children's literature," he said gravely. This time Bob did not blush.

"Any conscientious uncle," he told Mel, before she could crack any jokes at his expense, "would know as much — it's where the Stoats and the Weasels live, and the Riverbank folk never go there. It's not healthy . . ."

"It certainly wasn't for Miss Hawke," said Mel. "Maybe Miss S. remembered she was a naturalist — our furred and feathered friends kind of thing. Maybe there's nothing in it out of the ordinary," she said, though she did not sound as if she believed this. She looked quizzically at Delphick. "Don't forget my promised scoop, Oracle. If this turns out to be another Seeton Special — which reminds me, tomorrow there's the exhibition in the village hall. I just saw Lady Colveden driving back after arranging Sir George's photos and Miss S.'s sketches. 'All welcome,' the posters say. You plan to come along in case she's drawn anything else that might be of interest? Hey." Mel sat up straight. "Your eyebrow twitched, Oracle. She's done something, hasn't she, and you know about it already? Come on, give."

And trusting Mel as he did, and hoping that perhaps she might suggest some aspect of the case that had not occurred to the police, Delphick, with some assistance from Bob, gave as much as seemed fitting about Miss Seeton's earlier sketch and the disquieting effect it had had on those who saw it.

Mel was thoughtful. "You hope she's on to something in the arson affair? The south end of The Street in flames? That's kind of spooky, Oracle." She frowned. "Depends on whether it's arson or pyromania, I suppose . . ."

"On whether it's someone after the insurance, or someone doing it for kicks?" Delphick eyed her with amusement. "We had already considered those as distinct possibilities, Miss Forby. And are pursuing parallel lines of enquiry as a result. Known sexual deviants, local businessmen who are rumoured to be financially insecure — Superintendent Brinton is checking up on everyone."

"No need to look down your nose at a poor reporter's attempts to help solve the mystery," Mel told him firmly. "You've missed out a couple of motives, for a start. Your arsonist might not be doing it for the insurance — he's maybe trying to get back on someone, or he's putting the frighteners on someone else. There could be any number of logical reasons — but suppose he's not logical? Suppose it really is a pyromaniac? That's one kinky guy, getting his thrills from watching a fire burn and not caring too much what fire it is." She sat forward and lowered her voice. "Now, this is strictly off the record, Oracle, but I guess you ought to know. The other day, when I was watching the blacksmith at work, there was a man there — makes out he's a Russian, name of Alexander, lives with some woman in that house with the high wall opposite Dr. Knight's place — and he was showing more than what I'd call usual interest in Dan Eggleden's forge. And blacksmiths use fire, remember."

"We've heard about the mysterious Russian," Delphick said, "from Superintendent Brinton, courtesy of P.C. Potter: as you suggest, he might well not be a Russian at all. Anyone can buy himself a couple of Borzois to look the part. The question is, what part, and why? Until now we've rather tended to dismiss the chap as being altogether too mysterious to be worth suspecting, if you understand me. Perhaps we should follow your advice and look more closely at him — his lady friend too, of course."

"Glad to be of service," said Mel with a smile. "Don't forget you heard it from me first."

"The scoop, when it comes, will be yours." Delphick had a twinkle in his eye. "If it comes. He may be nothing more or less than he seems, after all."

"The village doesn't think so — although," admitted Mel "they'd say anything about anybody, given half the chance. But I'd dearly love to know what a Russian's up to in a tiny place like Plummergen, in the middle of the country — which reminds me. Country crafts — I've been writing an article or two, and the blacksmith, for one, has been very helpful. But the mole catcher . . . forget it, Forby. However, if Miss Seeton's picture had a mole in the foreground — and they all say he's one of the most unsavoury characters for miles, and he'd even sell his own grandmother for money . . ."

Delphick looked at her thoughtfully; nodded; and smiled. "If you'll excuse me just a moment," he said, looking at his watch, "I'll slip out and telephone Superintendent Brinton — it's not too late in the evening to disturb him, in a good cause. Tomorrow morning, I think, we'll have a word or two with this unsavoury mole catcher of yours — just to see," he said smiling again, "if you and Miss Seeton are correct. Although I never thought" — he turned to walk away — "the police would ever rely so heavily on women's intuition . . ." And he vanished before Mel could think of a withering reply.

Next day, before driving to Ashford ("We'll keep the blighter stewing for a while — by all accounts it'll do him no harm"), the Scotland Yarders were among the first to visit the Before and After Exhibition. Miss Seeton, fortunately, had drawn various views on paper of different sizes, so that the abbreviated southerly aspect did not stand out too noticeably. Miss Wicks was there, delighted with the suggested improvements to her cottage.

"I shall instruct the smith to supply me with precisely such a balustrade as dear Miss Seeton has so skilfully sketched," she whistled through her ill-fitting false teeth. "I shall insist that speed is of the essence. I understand that the initial selection could be in progress this very instant, you see, Chief Superintendent. Anonymously — though no suspicion attaches itself to you or your sergeant, of course," and she nodded, and smiled, and patted Bob Ranger on the arm before trotting away.

"Strewth," muttered Delphick when she was well out of earshot. Then he laughed. "It's catching, isn't it?"

Bob grinned. "I wonder if she's right — about anonymous spies being competition judges in disguise. I suppose that must be how they have to do it — and I wish any stranger who turns up here the best of luck in trying to stay mysterious. In Plummergen I don't think it's possible."

"Miss Hawke managed, it, didn't she? Nobody found out a thing about her — more's the pity. Miss Seeton seems to have chatted with her a little, but Mel Forby told us more than anyone else, and she's professionally curious."

"So," said Bob with another grin, "is Plummergen."

Delphick chuckled, and they turned to go. As they drew near the door, it was pushed open by a man: tall, erect of bearing, subdued in dress. He eyed the two strangers warily for a moment, then inclined his head in a nod of greeting and passed within to vanish behind a folding screen. Bob looked at Delphick.

"The notices say that anyone's welcome," he hissed as the chief superintendent glanced back in some curiosity to see what the newcomer was doing. "Perhaps he's a tourist, passing through and stopping for a breather . . . or he might be a competition judge, seeing what they've got in mind."

Delphick motioned "Wait" to his sergeant, then strolled back into the hall as if to refresh his memory about some finer point of Miss Seeton's artistic achievement. When he came back, he looked grim.

"Displaying great interest," he reported, "in the pictures of that part of The Street showing the smithy. I wish," he said as they emerged from the hall, "that we had time for a chat with that gentleman. I believe he could be the mystery Russian everyone's been telling us about."

"I'd take a bet on it, sir." Bob sounded confident.

Delphick followed his gaze, pulled a face, and said: "No bet. Because, unless Sir George has taken it into his head to post guards at the gates — and I can't say I'd blame him, in the circumstances — those two dogs tied to that post look remarkably like Borzois to me. But whoever he is, he'll have to wait. We should have been in Ashford half an hour ago."

"What did you mean, sir," enquired Bob as they climbed into the waiting police car, "about in the circumstances you wouldn't blame Sir George for posting guards? I know the old boy's proud of his photographs, and there's always Miss Seeton's sketches, but —"

"I shouldn't think for a minute that anyone has plans to pinch them," Delphick said as the car moved off. "But just think of what's been happening here recently. Plummergen suspects, does it not, that the gnomenapping and related crimes occurred at the instigation of the deadly rival? So wouldn't it be in order for them to worry about someone from Murreystone, doubtless heavily disguised, sneaking into the village hall to check up on their plans? If and when it occurs to him, I'm sure Sir George will post his sentries, because when the competitive blood runs hot, anything may happen . . ."

When they arrived at last in Ashford, Superintendent Brinton greeted them with relief. "He's a miserable old sod, right enough," he said. "Potter had to kick him out of bed with threats I'd rather not know about, officially, and he's been cursing and complaining ever since he got here."

"Perhaps he's just tired," Delphick suggested, "although from what we've heard about Jacob Chickney, it's more likely to be general ill-nature. He'd grumble just as much if he'd had time for a three-course breakfast. Have you offered him a cup of tea?"

"I'd rather offer him arsenic," growled Brinton. "I had to send Policewoman Laver for a coffee break after he'd said his piece to her as Potter brought him in — and Maggie Laver is no shrinking violet, believe me. She's heard the lot, or that's what I'd have thought before this character arrived."

"I look forward to extending my vocabulary," Delphick said. "I take it you've been leaving him to cool his heels rather than asking him questions."

"Waiting for reinforcements, I've been," Brinton said. "Besides, I wasn't sure what line of questioning you wanted to follow. I know," and he sighed, "that it's something to do with Miss Seeton's drawing, but . . ."

Most people would have found it difficult to slouch on an upright chair, but Jacob Chickney seemed able to slouch in comfort. He was smoking his noisome pipe as the three policemen entered the interview room, and did not remove it from his mouth as he greeted their arrival with a hawking mutter, deep in his throat, that sounded very like a curse. His beady, narrowed eyes fastened curiously on the one member of the group he had not seen before.

"Good morning, Mr. Chickney," Delphick said, introducing himself and adding that no doubt Detective Sergeant Ranger was known, if only by sight, as someone who now had local connections. Jacob Chickney grunted. A puff of greasy smoke belched from the bowl of his pipe.

"And Superintendent Brinton, of course, you know," said Delphick as Brinton cleared his throat very pointedly and coughed. Bob Ranger, too, looked as if he were suffering. Delphick, who sat farthest away, received the effects of the blast a few seconds later. "Perhaps, Mr. Chickney, you would be kind enough to extinguish your pipe while we talk? Some of us are not accustomed to tobacco — certainly not to tobacco as strong as yours."

Jacob muttered something which sounded like a reference to fanciful townie ways and contrived to send another rank cloud in the direction of his interlocutor. His eyes, black and glittering, narrowed still further in unspoken challenge — a challenge which Delphick proposed to meet only in an oblique fashion.

Without a word he rose, strode to the window, opened it, returned to the table, and sat down again. A lifesaving breeze from outside wafted the pipe fumes away. The central electric light danced gently overhead.

"Trying to make me catch my death, are you?" demanded Jacob Chickney, and hawked, and seemed about to spit — until he met the eyes of Chief Superintendent Delphick, austere and grey and every bit as resolute as he thought his own to be. For the first time in the exchange, Jacob had a feeling he might have met his match. He did not spit.

He continued to hawk and cough, however, and patted his chest with a gnarled, heavy hand. "Police brutality," said Jacob. "Freeze an old man into his grave — have the law on you, I will."

"Surely, after so many years working in the fresh air," Delphick remarked, "a slight breeze from an open window should not trouble you overmuch. If it does, however, the remedy is in your own hands — or rather, in your mouth. Put out your pipe, Mr. Chickney, and the window will be shut."

For a moment nobody moved. All they could do was wait.

Then Jacob Chickney removed the pipe from his mouth and banged it furiously on the heavy glass ashtray on the table. Bob prepared to leap to Delphick's rescue if the old man showed any sign of preparing to assault the chief superintendent, but the ashtray, full of reeking strands which Jacob stirred with a dirty piece of dowelling from his waistcoat pocket, remained on the table. Delphick had won.

chapter
21

Delphick motioned to Sergeant Ranger to stop taking notes for a moment and to close the window. Jacob Chickney's beady eyes followed the large young man as he crossed the room, and he glowered. He stuck his thumbs in the pockets of his grubby waistcoat and slumped back on the chair, breathing heavily.

"An unusual waistcoat, Mr. Chickney," Delphick remarked. "Moleskin, perhaps? I don't believe I've seen one like it before. Interesting in both texture and colour."

Jacob growled something about never mind interesting, it was his job to catch moles, and a man was surely entitled to his perks, badly paid though he otherwise might be.

Delphick nodded and said: "Is it your job to catch anything else besides moles, Mr. Chickney?"

"Vermin," replied Jacob at once. "And especially rats," he said in a tone more surely than ever.

Delphick had been called worse in his time and chose to ignore the implied insult.

"Moles, and rats," he said with a quick glance at his listening colleagues. They, too, could remember Miss Seeton's *Wind in the Willows* sketch. "Badgers as well, by any chance?" he enquired, and as his attention focussed again on Jacob, he saw the old man's face, weathered and lined as it was, twist momentarily in a spasm of some strong emotion. The mole catcher, sensing the detective's interest, made an effort to smooth the emotion — whatever it was — away — and slumped even lower on his chair, with a drooping of his head that did not suggest contrition, rather a conscience that was guilty, but determined not to confess.

Confess — what? Delphick recognised that he had touched a nerve — but which nerve? Maybe the mole catcher was just naturally shifty, after a lifetime spent loathing, and being loathed by, his fellow villagers. Delphick struggled to suppress the feeling that, in the case of Jacob Chickney, Plummergen opinion was probably right: seldom had he met so generally unpleasing an old personage. In Jacob Chickney's case, the town-held myth of the rustic sage, imparting time-honoured lore to younger generations, was all too clearly a myth. But at least, reflected the chief superintendent, he had spared them the worst of his language: probably used it all up on WPC Laver.

He must try to put the old man at his ease. He must try to remember that, grudgingly though he had come, Jacob was still only a voluntary witness, in Ashford police station to help with official enquiries — indefinite suspicion of him was not enough. He had to be caught off-balance, if such a thing were possible with such a clearly cunning old man, in the hope that whatever he let slip would present an opening through which the police could thrust home.

"How do you go about catching moles, Mr. Chickney?" This seemed as good a gambit as any, and Delphick was unprepared for the flush which surged into Jacob's face. The furious ancient scowled.

"Trade secrets," he muttered after a pause. "None of your business how I goes about mine."

"Generally speaking, I'd agree with you. In this case, however" — for Delphick was growing convinced that, without knowing how, he had come close to a winning question — "you might make things look black for you if you refuse to tell me. I might start to wonder just what it is that you don't want the police to know about." He paused. "The poisons, perhaps? You've been careless with them, and somebody has complained —"

"That's a blanking lie!"

"That," Delphick told him, as after this outburst Jacob said nothing more, "is a suggestion, merely. Then if not poison — the traps, should I guess? Nasty little snappers, aren't they, if what I've seen in hardware shops are indeed traps for moles. You place them in the runs, and the moles are crunched to death between the walls when there's no room for them to back out again. You enjoy your work, do you?"

"It's a living. Don't get paid enough, mind. But someone has to do it. No reason it shouldn't be me."

This was the longest reply, and the most audible, Jacob had produced during the entire interview. Once again Chief Superintendent Delphick wondered just what it was the old man was trying to hide.

He said nothing, as if pondering Jacob's answer, and the mole catcher added reluctantly: "They're vermin, ain't they — always getting in the way. Only one thing to do with vermin — get rid of 'em."

"Just as somebody got rid of Miss Ursula Hawke last night in Ashford Forest?" Delphick's change of tone, from almost casual curiosity to intense probing, startled

Jacob. "Was she in somebody's way?"

"Nothing to do with me, that weren't!" The mole catcher no longer slumped on his chair. "You've no call to try putting the blame where there's none! Libel, that's what it is, and I'll have the law on you!" He rose to his feet, blazing-eyed, and seemed ready to march straight out of the room. Bob Ranger stopped taking notes and pointedly flexed his limbs, strongly muscled after years of playing football. Jacob gave him a sideways glance, as if sizing him up, then subsided, muttering.

"I am the law, Mr. Chickney," replied Delphick sternly, as impressive as Bob could ever remember him. "And it is my duty in the law to find out the truth — just as it is yours to tell it. You were in Ashford Forest last night, weren't you?"

Jacob clamped his lips together and glowered. Silence filled the interview room. It appeared that Bob had not properly closed the window, for a faint sound of bird-song began to make itself heard through the gap.

Delphick said: "Miss Hawke was out looking for birds in the forest last night — we know that. She hoped to find owls' nests — and I hope that she did, before she died. But why did she die, Mr. Chickney? Was it because, while she was looking for the owls,

268

she found you? What were you doing that meant she had to be killed, rather than tell anyone she had seen you?"

"And what makes you so dang-blad sure as I was doing anything last night, whether in the woods or no?" demanded Jacob. Delphick silently cheered. A genuine innocent would have come out with a straight denial: only those with something to hide ever answered question for question and tried to sound outraged to disguise their nervousness.

"We have a witness." Never mind that Miss Seeton had been a dozen miles away: any sketch of hers was worth fifty eye witnesses, in Delphick's opinion. "We have a witness — a witness who places you in Ashford Forest at the time Miss Hawke was killed."

"It's a lie!"

Delphick said nothing.

"It's a mistake," Jacob said, with rather less force.

Still Delphick said nothing. The mole catcher began to look less certain of his ground.

"No," he said, almost to himself, "they'd not tattle to the police, not the likes of them . . ."

"Are you sure?" Delphick looked, and

made himself sound, extremely sure. "You should realise that they'd be happy to put the blame on you, a stranger" — this was a long shot — "rather than on one of themselves." The mole catcher glared at him, and for the first time the light of misgiving gleamed in his little black eyes. Delphick waited.

"Made out it was me, 'ave they?" Jacob said at last. "You got no right to believe them instead of me, the blanking liars that they are."

"Then suppose you give me your version of events," said Delphick, "for comparison. Otherwise" — as Jacob seemed set on a bout of self-preserving silence — "the only version we have must be the version we believe." And he hoped the old man would never learn that, until now, the only version of last night's events was a sketch by Miss Seeton of three characters from a well-loved children's book. "How about it, Mr. Chickney?"

"All of us took our dying oath we'd never tell — but I should've known better than trusting any treacherous townie types, for all they paid me to keep silent, and nowhere near enough, neither." Jacob hawked, then spat to express his disgust before recollecting where he was. He scowled at the watching policemen and reached for his pipe. "Furriners," he snarled, "with their fancy London ways — I can't abide furriners, not anyhow, money or no."

Delphick believed he could live with Jacob's dislike of anyone from London. Living with the fumes from his pipe was another matter, but if the comfort of tobacco made it easier for the old man to tell his story, it would have to be borne. "For what, exactly, did these Londoners pay you, Mr. Chickney — apart from your silence, that is?"

Jacob made a great performance out of lighting his pipe, mumbling over the mouthpiece, and sucking the air through in a series of nauseating pops. He ignored the dottle in the ashtray and took from his jacket pocket a small, battered tin with its enamel letters long worn away, prising off the lid with his thumbnail. Despite himself, Delphick winced.

Having filled the bowl with the oily, pungent strings of black tobacco and tamped them down, Jacob fumbled in another pocket for his matches. He made a great performance of striking one on the sole of his boot, gazing into the flame until it burned almost to his fingers. He sucked and popped again at the mouthpiece of his pipe until at last it caught, and the familiar nauseating reek began to fill the air. It was enough to send shivers down the spine.

Delphick would allow him to procrastinate no longer. "The truth, please, Mr. Chickney, and at once. About these Londoners, and the money they paid you, and what you were all doing in Ashford Forest last night."

"London money's as good as any," Jacob said, "and 'ard earned it was, too — left most of the work to me, they did, and by rights should'ave paid me more." He regarded the palms of his hands complacently. "Work-'ardened, I am, long since, not like these weaklings from the city — couldn't dig the way I could, for all their boastful talk."

Dig? Delphick was puzzled. Miss Hawke's grave? But it had been in no grave that Miss Seeton had found her: maybe, if they had buried her properly, she might never have been found. What other reason could anyone have to pay Jacob Chickney for digging?

To Brinton, the countryman, the old man's meaning was clear. "You were digging for badgers," he said in tones of utter disgust. "For baiting." He glowered at Jacob with as furious a look as Jacob now turned on him. "You and your kind," Brinton said, "you make me sick. Badger-baiting!"

Delphick's blood ran chill in his veins, and Bob Ranger adopted countryman, felt slightly ill. Badger-baiting — no wonder Jacob had been slow to speak of it. Disliked though he knew himself to be, his involvement with this so-called sport must make him more unpopular than ever with all right-minded people.

For sport, a group of men with dogs and spades would lay waste a badger's sett in the middle of the night, when there was least fear of discovery from those who might protest. The men would dig down through the earth to where the badger — often hunted through its own tunnels by dogs driven into the sett with kicks and blows from their owners — stood at bay in its final retreat. Its mighty arms and powerful jaws would help it to fight bravely — for a while. But the sheer weight of numbers would exhaust it, and it would be dragged out, thrown into a sack, and driven off to some isolated place where it would be goaded by men who had laid out vast sums of money into fighting for its life against a dog, or more than one. If it was unlucky, the men would not wrench its claws from its front paws: in this way it would be able to fight for even longer, hoping against hope, before being torn to pieces.

Delphick swallowed. When he spoke, his voice was cold. "So you were involved with a group of badger-baiters from London, Chickney. Presumably they paid you to show them the poor creatures' setts."

"Poor creatures? Vermin!" Jacob Chickney was too busy justifying himself to notice that the chief superintendent had modified the courtesy of his address. "Vermin's to be got rid of, and that's my job, and never mind your townie way of talking. Poor creatures, indeed! A good badger can fight a fair few hours, let me tell you."

"Before it dies," Delphick said. "Tormented, exhausted, and outnumbered — and you find the prospect enjoyable? No doubt you have attended a few such entertainments yourself. The countryman at his age-old pursuits! The word *barbaric* comes to mind, among others less repeatable. I only wish the new Act of Parliament had become law, Chickney, because I assure you it would give me the greatest of pleasure to instigate proceedings against you and your cronies — whether or not" — and his voice became even colder — "Miss Hawke's death was anything to do with any of you.

Which I strongly suspect that it was." He leaned forward, his grey eyes dark with menace.

"So tell me about it, Chickney. Tell me what happened!"

Jacob clenched his teeth and set his pipe jigging as he muttered something. Delphick fixed him with a stern eye.

"Speak up, Chickney. What happened last night?"

"That interfering besom from the George," Jacob snarled. "She'd no call to be poking about the woods in the middle of the night when Christian folks belong in their beds . . ." He caught Delphick's quizzical glance and snatched the pipe from his mouth to jab it in the chief superintendent's direction. "Don't you go accusing me of being a heathen, for a heathen I ain't, it being my job to be out of my bed when others did oughter be in theirs — not that they pay me anywhere near enough for the saving of their sleep, but —"

"But you were going to tell me what happened," Delphick reminded him, tired of the mole catcher's perpetual harping on money. "So tell me."

"She must've seen the torches," said Jacob, "for all of a sudden she comes bursting out of the trees yelling *stop* and a-waving of her arms. Carrying on something terrible, so she was, set the dogs barking and made me drop my spade . . . which was too dark to find it again right away."

Delphick filled in the gaps. "Somebody hit her over the head with a spade to keep her quiet?"

"Not me," Jacob said quickly. Not a vestige of loyalty to his erstwhile employers remained: if the blame were to lie between them and himself, there was no hesitation, no attempt to make excuses.

"Not you — if you say so." Delphick didn't know whether or not to believe him, but knew that, while the old man was in the mood to spill the beans, he would have to press on. He wondered just how badly, by his own standards, the mole catcher had been paid, and how much of a grudge could be relied on to produce the full story. "What happened next?"

"She was dead, that's what happened." Jacob looked away quickly and drew on his pipe. It had gone out. Delphick's penetrating gaze unnerved him so much that he did not try to light it again. "She was dead, any fool could see that, all mangled as 'er head was — and these townies, they asked me what to do." There was a note almost of pride in his voice, pride in his ability to think faster in a crisis than the city slickers. "So I told 'em."

"Told them what?" Delphick was losing patience. "This is a woman's life we're talking about here, Chickney, and a case of murder. Not some so-called sporting event."

"Told 'em to put her where nobody with any sense might expect to go poking for many a month, till the beasts would have done their work and nobody could tell who she was. And if some other blanky inter-fering fool hadn't gone poking about in they brambles, she'd have stayed safely hid and not a soul the wiser — and," said Jacob, re-gaining some of his self-confidence, "a good job if she had. The likes of her's no loss to anyone, fussing about vermin all the time, and a woman, what's more. Time was when they knew their place and kept their mouths shut, but no longer, and more's the pity."

The monstrous old man folded his arms, raised his head, and glared as he delivered what he apparently intended as his final word on the subject. He sucked on his pipe, then reached for his matches, and before Delphick could stop him struck an-other match on his boot. He gazed into the flame with narrowed eyes, and a queer smirk twisted his wrinkled mouth. "I like a fill or two of baccy every day," he said, and set the flame to the bowl, still smiling lop-sidedly.

Suddenly Delphick had had enough. "Make the most of what you've got there, Chickney. It might have to last a long time. We intend to charge you — accessory to murder, concealment, cruelty to animals —" he raised his voice above Jacob's roar of protest — "and that, I assure you, is just the beginning."

chapter
22

The chief superintendent rose to his feet, towering above the grimy, wizened figure on the other side of the table.

"You will give us," he continued, in a voice as cold as his eyes were grey, "the names and addresses of everyone who was with you last night —"

"Can't," snapped Jacob. Then he saw Delphick's expression and hastily added: "Don't know 'em, nor anything about 'em. All I know is they come down from London t'other night and found nothing, so they come back again and asked around and found me, and said as they'd pay me for my help, which I give 'em — and for what? Nothing but trouble, that's what." And, forgetting himself, he spat.

"A woman is dead, Chickney." Delphick spoke with deadly calm. "Which, believe me, will mean the greatest possible — trouble — for whoever was responsible. Whoever it was . . . and, since you claim to know nothing about these people, we must refresh your memory. You will remain here

279

in custody — be quiet, Chickney," as Jacob roared again. "You will stay here until you have studied as many books of photographs as it takes to identify the people who killed Miss Hawke. You will look at every one, and you will tell us what we need to know."

"Wrongful arrest," cried Jacob as Delphick drew breath. "I'll have the law on you!"

"Assisting the police with their enquiries," Delphick corrected him. "Your memory is slightly too convenient, you see. Maybe, if you were left to your own devices, it might bring back precisely the information we require and we shouldn't care to have you warning your . . . associates of our interest in them. You will stay in custody until we have brought all your companions from last night's sordid adventure in for questioning — all of them." And the bleak expression in his eyes convinced Jacob that Delphick meant exactly what he said. His own eyes lost something of their dogged insolence, and he began to waver.

Once the mole catcher had been duly charged and taken to the cells — protesting bitterly when his malodorous boots, with their string laces, were removed — Delphick flung open the window as wide as it would go. "I need some fresh air, and plenty of it," he said. "Seldom have I encountered such a deliberately nasty piece of work."

"The professionals at least take a pride in what they do — they don't like messes, especially killing," Brinton said. "Amateurs like him — ugh."

"He's literally an amateur," said Delphick, "being nasty for the sheer love of it — not an ounce of remorse, nothing but complaints about how badly he's paid for whatever job, whether legitimate or not, he undertakes." He grimaced. "I don't envy your desk sergeant, Chris, having to take the creature his regulation cup of tea and seeing those beady little eyes glaring at him through the Judas window."

"Judas is about right, too," Brinton said. "Shopped his London pals quick enough, didn't he? Oh, he'll recognise a mugshot or two before he's much older, mark my words — he's got that look in his eye. He's just hanging on for a while out of sheer bloody-mindedness — keeping the police on the hop is second nature to the likes of him, but when the time comes, he won't hesitate a minute to save his own skin. A decent crook might have made at least a show of not wanting to split on them — but not our friend Chickney. It's no surprise to me that nobody in Plummergen can stand him — I loathe the man myself, and I'd never met him before today."

Delphick was thinking. "I wonder, though, if he might have been perhaps just a little too quick to split. Didn't you get the feeling that underneath all that nastiness there was something he was still trying to keep from us?"

"If it's something worse than murder, and badger-baiting — which is animal murder, no matter which way you look at it — I shudder to think what it can be. Someone with a mind as warped as Chickney's could have any number of peculiar secrets, and I can't say I'm looking forward to finding out what they are."

"Miss Seeton seems to have known," Delphick said. "Some of them, anyway. Her picture of Badger's home and the lurking menace — it wasn't the fire, it was the diggers who were about to overwhelm the place. The mole in the foreground is as good a pointer to Jacob Chickney as we could wish for, now we understand its meaning." And he made a mental note to pass on the thanks of the police to Mel Forby, who had drawn his attention to that meaning.

Brinton had wandered off along his own

train of thought. "At least he's solved one puzzle — that car with the London number-plates spotted by that woman near Ashford Forest, and the strange lights she saw moving about in there on the night Notley Black was killed in the Half Seas Over fire. Coincidences do happen, and I'd say this was a good example — no connection at all with the murder, just those damned badger diggers on their first unsuccessful visit from Town, when the poor brutes were left in peace."

"I suppose so," Delphick said. "But, if that's the case — we're right back at the beginning with the arson business, aren't we? Jacob Chickney will point us in the right direction over the Hawke murder, sooner or later, but what other leads do we have for the fire-raising?"

Bob cleared his throat. Brinton and Delphick turned as one to look at him: for someone so large, he could render himself remarkably unobtrusive when the mood took him. But now he had a suggestion to make.

"The fires, sir — suppose it's not crooks cashing in, but someone, er, kinky. I thought — well, whenever he lit his pipe he stared at the flame on the match, didn't he, and, well, it seems weird. Chickney, I mean

283

— and you did say, didn't you, sir, that you thought he had something else to hide besides the Hawke murder."

"Miss Seeton," said Brinton glumly, "stares at flames in her yoga practice, or so she told me. Which is what started this whole affair in the first place, remember?"

"I think we may safely acquit Miss Seeton of any form of deviance," Delphick said, with a placatory grin in Bob's direction. "There's nobody more conventional — and nobody," he added in reflective tones, "more remarkable. The superintendent was joking, Sergeant. But he's reminded us that there is indeed a Seeton connection to consider: her sketch of the nightclub scene, with the Twenties costumes, the woman wearing the black pearl necklace, the man she held in her toils — if you'll excuse the fancy language — and the other man looking on from close by. If we could interpret the picture properly, we'd be a lot closer to solving this outbreak of arson, I believe."

"*If,*" Brinton said heavily. "That's your job, Oracle, as well you know. It's why I called you into the case in the first place — *she's* why I called you in. I'd rather do what I'm doing, which is all the by-the-book routine work — I've not the Fraud boys checking up on everyone who's lost anything through fire in this area over the last month, even that farmer from Plummergen" — he glanced at Bob, frowning — "what's his name? Mulcker? I can't seriously imagine he's the centre of an insurance conspiracy, or whatever they're up to, but I'm taking no chances. I've asked for every detail to be checked, and checked again, and young Sleaze is being pulled off the Choppers' surveillance, if that's what it can be called, to go through every report with a fine-toothed comb. He may look a mess, but he's a good copper."

"Suppose," Delphick said, "it's neither an insurance fraud nor vandalism — though I agree with you, the Choppers are small-time operators to be involved in something as big as this — but is, in fact, the sergeant's kinky candidate? Not necessarily Jacob Chickney, but, for instance, the Russian gentleman with such a keen interest in Plummergen's smithy. As witnessed by myself, in the exhibition of Before and After pictures — and by Mel Forby, whose opinion I've come to respect over the years. I suppose a journalist's instincts about people must be almost as well-tuned as a detective's — if she says there's something strange about him, I'm prepared to believe there might be."

He turned to Brinton. "Chris, what, if anything, do you know about this mystery man in Sonia Venning's old house?"

"Only what Potter's told me, which is almost nothing. He — they — whoever this woman with him is — moved in a few weeks back, and nobody's seen her since. Which of course has led people to speculate that he's done the poor soul in, even though he's been buying enough food for two all the time — they think it's a cover-up."

"I know what they're like," Delphick said. Bob snorted. Brinton rolled his eyes.

"So do I, so when Potter told me what they were saying I said he'd better go and make sure the wretched female still walked the earth. Potter's a good man. Said he'd already been to The Meadows and had a chat with her — very gracious, he said she was, as far as he could understand her, but she had a foreign accent — and he didn't mean Scottish or Somerset, he meant foreign as in different continent, probably."

"Potter's a good man, certainly, but not what you'd call cosmopolitan. Mel Forby has spoken to the male half of the mystery, and she's of the opinion he's too stage Russian for belief. He walks two Borzois, of all dogs — otherwise known as Russian wolfhounds — up and down The Street every

286

day — Boris and Sasha, apparently. We spotted them tied up outside the village hall while he was inside looking at the exhibition. And did Potter tell you that the man claims to be called Alexander? I'm inclined to agree with Mel. What business have a pair of Russians in Plummergen, of all the unlikely places? I think we should take a closer look at them, Chris. Yes, Sergeant Ranger?" For Bob had stirred once more.

"Well, sir, I was wondering — if this woman's never seen about the place — and The Meadows has that enormous wall and those huge gates — suppose she was being kept inside for her own good? She might be a lunatic, sir, or perhaps not quite as bad as that, but odd, anyway — and this Alexander chap's doing his best to keep an eye on her, only sometimes she gets out and, well, sets fire to things, or whatever form of oddness she's being restrained for. Sir," concluded Bob in an embarrassed way.

Delphick nodded thoughtfully. "A possibility, of course — but would a pyromaniac also indulge in petty theft, such as the infamous garden gnome — how I wish we'd had the chance to see it — and the wrought-iron flower baskets? It's my understanding that deviants don't usually manifest more than one type of aberration at a time."

"If the gossips are right, sir — and I suppose they must be sometimes, according to the laws of probability — then it was the Murreystone lot who took the gnome and all the other bits and pieces. Sir George's Watchmen hope to nobble them one night soon on another raid, even if they don't catch the fireraiser." Bob looked knowing. "From what I've heard of Murreystone, nothing would surprise me, sir."

Delphick grinned. "I bow to your superior local knowledge, Sergeant Ranger. Chris, would you agree?"

Brinton grunted. "So long as nobody gets in a punch-up, good luck to 'em. What's a few garden gnomes compared to a firebug and two murders?"

"One of which," Delphick pointed out, "you seem to be on the way to solving, with Jacob Chickney's assistance — not forgetting that of Miss Seeton. Suppose we leave you now to pursue your chosen lines of enquiry while we return to Plummergen and investigate the Russian aspect of our affairs? No doubt they will maintain their impersonation, if impersonation it is, by offering us tea from a samovar, or vodka in glasses we will be told to hurl over our shoulders, and the atmosphere behind the high wall will be one of permanent gloom whether or not the mystery woman is" — he nodded with a smile towards Bob — "a lunatic. Everything I've ever read of Russian novels warns me what to expect."

"Sooner you than me," Brinton told him. "Even if that means I end up coping with Jacob Chickney. Make sure you're not slipped a Mickey Finn or whatever the Russian equivalent might be. The Russians managed to invent booze that didn't taste of anything, so I wouldn't put it past them to have come up with a poison nobody notices until it's too late."

Delphick shook his head. "There's no need to worry," he said. "Disposing of one body would be difficult enough, as Miss Hawke's attackers found out. But with two — especially when one would be the size and weight of Sergeant Ranger here — I feel that even the most desperate criminal must refrain from murder."

A remark which managed to make even Brinton smile.

chapter
23

Delphick chuckled quietly to himself for much of the journey, but as the car passed the Gibbet Oak and came into the approach to Plummergen he said, in a thoughtful voice, that it might, on reflection, be better to be safe rather than sorry. "Mr. Brinton knows where we're going, but he's fifteen miles away in Ashford. Perhaps we'd do as well to let P.C. Potter in on our plans — just in case."

"The dogs seemed harmless enough, from what we could see of them, sir. And I would have thought" — Bob sounded hurt — "that you and I should be more than a match for a woman and a middle-aged man."

"I, Sergeant, am a middle-aged man." Delphick frowned. "Nevertheless, I would hope to acquit myself well in any fisticuffs which might become necessary — not that I expect them to — and it's always possible that Mr. Alexander feels the same way." He glanced sideways at Bob, who regarded him quizzically. "Nor, Sergeant Ranger, am I scared of those dogs despite your baser suspicions."

"Sir, I never dreamed of —"

"It is simply," Delphick told him firmly, "that, since we're now on Potter's patch, he could feel somewhat peeved if we didn't keep him posted as to what we were doing and where we were doing it. Drive on down until you reach the police house, and we'll have a quick word with him."

Bob drove past his father-in-law's nursing home and the narrow lane opposite, at the end of which The Meadows stood behind its high brick wall. Plummergen's police house was situated on a gentle curve on the right-hand side of The Street, facing south, just after a row of council houses: an excellent vantage-point for most of the comings and goings of the village. But P.C. Potter, so Mabel Potter informed her husband's colleagues, was not at home, even though his car was parked outside.

"He's slipped along to the hall for a quick peek at the pictures — not that there's anything we'd be allowed to do to this place, seeing as it's official property, but we're interested to see what Miss Seeton's done, of course, and all the photos Sir George took, too. Besides, he says if that lot from Murreystone come snooping, he can chivvy them away, and he wants to keep an eye on the parking, what with trippers passing through and seeing those notices with *All Welcome* and thinking they fancy a look round. Block The Street something dreadful, they can, for all it's so wide."

Bob glanced over his shoulder at the unmarked car in which he and Delphick had driven from London. Mabel gave a mischievous giggle.

"Best not to leave that where Potter'll find it, or like as not he'll hand out a ticket, knowing it's not local from the number. But the hall's quite close — well, you being married to Anne Knight, you'd know that, wouldn't you, Sergeant? So why not pull your car into our yard and walk down there — shouldn't take two minutes. And then ..." Mabel Potter was as shrewd as her husband and guessed that the Scotland Yarders had an ulterior motive in visiting Plummergen's police house. "You'll enjoy looking at Miss Seeton's pictures, won't you?"

Mabel had been right: the walk took no more than the two minutes she had promised. "Handy for keeping an eye on any trouble brewing at the local hop," Delphick said, remembering how the Ashford Choppers had run amok so many years ago, and the monumental punch-up that filled The Street and, as a direct result, Dr. Knight's nursing home. His own part in the proceedings had been a metal wrench, applied by the enemy to his temple, and a nasty gash which had left a faint scar. He touched it now as they reached the hall, and hoped that history was not going to repeat itself.

P.C. Potter was giving directions to a group of people who had stopped off en route to Ellen Terry's house, and wanted to make sure they were not lost. Potter reassured them and waved them on their way to a further dose of culture. As he spotted his London colleagues approaching, his face widened into a welcoming smile.

"Thought we'd be seeing you here before too long, sir. Hello, Bob. Business, this visit, is it? Miss Seeton's in there now, if you want to catch her. Pleased with the turnout, she must be — day trippers we've had, strangers all, dropping in on account of the notices and thinking it to be a proper exhibition. One even wanted to buy her picture of the George and Dragon, so they tell me."

Delphick explained that they had already called upon Miss Seeton and would not trouble her now. Their interest was in the new inhabitants of The Meadows. What did Potter know of them? Were they likely to be there now? If the man was not, would the re-clusive lady let them in? Potter told them that he thought now would be a good time to catch them, since Mr. Alexander walked the dogs only twice daily and did the shop-ping after lunch while the lady (so Potter be-lieved) took an afternoon nap.

"Delicate, he says she is. Troubled with her nerves, poor creature, needs peace and quiet and plenty of rest." Potter shrugged. "Hard to tell if it's working, seeing as how she was hid behind a veil when I spoke to her."

Bob shot a speaking look at Delphick, who nodded. "They sound an unusual pair," he said. "But then, Plummergen does seem to thrive on the unusual."

Potter muttered something about the Murreystone lot being a sight more un-usual, if the truth be told, than any amount of Plummergen folk, and certainly not to be trusted an inch. There'd already been at least one of them sneaking in to look at the pictures, and what with the gnome being nicked, and Mrs. Henderson's flower bas-kets, and other matters of that nature, he'd a regular job of it to keep proper watch on the devils, begging Delphick's pardon for his language, and he was downright glad of Sir George's help, though it seemed a strange thing for a policeman to admit.

"But that's at night," he concluded, trying to look on the bright side. "It's quiet enough by day, thank goodness. And light enough for me to take a good look at their faces when they come marching in here, bold as brass — and if I'd only known them notices'd give a welcome to all, I'd have spoken a few words about that in good time. But it's too late for such conversion now, so all I can do is the best I can," and P.C. Potter sighed, shaking his head. So engrossed had he become in his lamentation that he had forgotten the august rank of the person to whom he addressed his plaint. Delphick smothered a grin and made sympathetic noises. Bob Ranger folded his arms and frowned at a large blue car that drew up outside the hall, disgorging yet more people anxious to learn Plummergen's intentions for the Best Kept Village Competition. Not one face was known to him. He suddenly felt very sorry for P.C. Potter.

Inside the hall Miss Seeton was paying close attention to the various comments of friends and acquaintances moving from one picture to another. Those who had made suggestions were delighted when these had been acted upon, depicted in her drawings and sketches. Those whose ideas had not found favour with the Committee were, one hardly liked to use the word, but *sulking* would be what one would say if a child in one's class behaved in such a fashion. So fortunate that in Plummergen the dinner break lasted a full hour. There would be time for her to listen to almost everyone who chose to pass comment on her work, and dear Sir George's photographs, of course. If Cedric Benbow were to appear, it would not be all that great a surprise, for he had shown such interest in the whole project, according to Sir George, and his comments and opinions would indeed be worth having.

But there were opinions enough, and to spare, floating about the hall. Mrs. Stillman had taken time to pop along from the post office and buttonholed Miss Seeton with an eager air.

"You've made our place look real smart between the pair of you, you and Sir George. Just wait till I let Stillman know about this — he'll be on the phone to the post office people as soon's you can say *awning*, and no wonder. You're wasted teaching the kiddies, that's what I say, Miss Seeton. You ought to be selling your clever pictures in some place in London."

As the unknown man standing near them

heard Mrs. Stillman's words, and looked across in admiration of her artistic skills, Miss Seeton blushed with mingled gratification and embarrassment, murmuring a modest reference to her very ordinary achievement, really, although of course one had done one's best, and it had been a pleasure to work for the good of the village that had welcomed her so kindly. It was the very least she could have done . . .

"Why, how strange." Miss Seeton had been drifting about the hall as she intercepted the various remarks everyone was passing. This was the first time she had paid any close attention to the post office picture. "How strange — surely I did not — the proportions, that is. Most unusual." She turned to Mrs. Stillman. "Leonardo da Vinci discovered it, you know, and many great artists used it — Michelangelo's *The Last Supper* is a splendid example. The divine proportion, they call it, or the golden mean — nobody knows why this should be the most pleasing, aesthetically, but so it seems it is. Nor does it matter which way up it is, either."

Mrs. Stillman blinked at the tip of Miss Seeton's umbrella as it moved around the edge of the painting, pointer-fashion. Miss Seeton was so engrossed in her little lecture that she had quite forgotten she was no longer in school. "Five by three," she said earnestly. "That's what it should be — only this isn't, and I find it very strange . . ."

"You mean," Mrs. Stillman decided after a few moments of careful thought, "that it's a funny shape?"

"It's the wrong shape," said Miss Seeton, unconsciously echoing another seeker after truth. "Someone has taken off one side of the painting, and it looks most odd. I wish I could remember what was there before."

Mrs. Stillman shook her head. The post office was, after all, the only thing in the picture of interest to her. "You probably just filled it in rough-like, and the Committee saw no need for it, with all the other places having pictures of their own, and not needing another. Dan Eggleden's ever so pleased with that anvil you've painted in over the doors of the forge. He says he's going to make one with the very same curly bracket, and all thanks to you."

"Yes, of course, that was it." Miss Seeton had been too struck by sudden memory to point out that she had only been working to the suggestions of the Committee, who were therefore the ones Dan should thank. Her normal modesty was forgotten in her pleasure at solving the puzzle. "Dan's forge, you see — so very interesting, and the sparks so very dramatic, although somewhat uncomfortable," and she glanced at the umbrella now back in its accustomed place over her arm. "Rather unnerving, indeed, with the smoke and flames as well. Especially with the shocking affair of the fire-raising in this area, not to mention the dry weather." She sighed, and frowned. "I remember painting the southern end of The Street engulfed in flames — or, rather, I remember that I did paint it like that, not the reason why I did so, although no doubt I was influenced by the proximity of Mr. Eggleden's smithy. And the smoke drawings in class, as well. Most distressing. No doubt Lady Colveden thought it wiser, in the circumstances, not to encourage anyone's thoughts to turn to fire. In such warm weather people may do unfortunate things." She turned away from the picture and almost bumped into the stranger who had been smiling at her earlier, showing natural curiosity about the artist who had brought beautified Plummergen so skilfully to life.

But he was not smiling now.

He was staring after her as she moved away, still frowning a little as she worried about whether it had been wise, in the circumstances, to teach the children how to draw the Accidental Smoke pictures they'd had such fun with. She did not notice the man, apart from murmuring a polite apology to him when her umbrella, swinging as she turned, caught him on the shin with a light blow.

But it did not appear to be this genteel assault on his person that made him regard Miss Seeton so intently.

In Ashford, Superintendent Brinton was on the telephone to Central Records.

"You'll be snowed under," he was told. "Millions of ugly mugs, we've got. Any one of them might fancy a spot of nastiness one night."

"Not as nasty as this. It's your really hard-nosed chummie who'll get involved in badger-baiting. Most of our villains think twice about bashing a copper over the head, let alone an elderly woman. They'd just tie her up to keep her quiet, and skedaddle back to the Smoke so's once she got free she couldn't find 'em to identify them. But this lot" — and he invested the words with so much loathing that Sleaze Arbuthnott, working at a desk in the corner of the room, saw the superintendent's face turn purple — "they're the bottom of the heap, make no mistake. If you've got those pictures of yours graded one to ten, these'd be the elevens."

Records promised to do whatever was possible as soon as possible and rang off. Brinton drew breath, but before he could speak the telephone rang back.

"Forgotten to pull the switchboard plug," he muttered as he picked up the receiver. "What? Who? Oh, Borden, hello. Anything to report?"

Inspector Borden of Fraud seldom allowed his voice to become animated, no matter how startling the news he had to impart. He had found, over the years, that relentless exposure to the baser side of human nature — mostly greed — had rendered him almost impervious to surprise, or to any other emotion. Even now there was hardly a quiver as he said, "We've completed nearly all the checks, and most of your candidates seem to be clean. Glad of the money when the insurance pays out, no doubt, but then anyone would be, wouldn't they? However, there is one rather interesting snippet we've dug out. Your man Thaxted. He isn't."

"Isn't?" Brinton's empurplement intensified alarmingly. "Isn't what? You mean he's dead? It's the first I've heard about it."

"Isn't really called Thaxted," Borden informed him with a very slight tremor of mischief in his tone. The superintendent's apoplectic nature was a byword in police circles, and sometimes those in a freakish mood would see how far they could push him towards explosion. But Borden was freakish, as he was everything else, in moderation. Those who handle affairs of finance cannot afford to be seen as lightweight personalities.

He grew serious. "I'm assuming, of course, that we're talking about the same Thaxted. Norman Thaxted?"

"That's him."

"No, it isn't. Well, it is now, but not formerly. Your Norman Thaxted used to be called Sampford, Posthumus Sampford, would you believe? Only son of 'Snatch' Sampford, whose name may be familiar to you."

"It certainly is," breathed Brinton, recalling what he knew of the legendary jewel thief and cat burglar. "So he's Snatch's son, is he? Well, well. What a modest son he is, too — never a word of this to me."

"I'm not surprised." Borden coughed. "There's more you ought to know before you go questioning him again — it was Pommy Sampford who carried the can, fif-

302

teen years ago, for a big jewel heist that went wrong. Well, his father never got around to teaching the kid all the tricks of the trade, so you'd expect Pommy to miss out once in a while. So, he was unlucky — but his partner got away. And his partner was one Notley Black . . ."

chapter
24

Brinton banged down the telephone to break the connection and immediately picked it up again. "I'll send Potter to bring the brighter in faster than he can blink," he growled, "and if he tries playing any more games with me, I'll scalp him. Pommy Sampford, indeed! Norman Thaxted!"

Mabel Potter answered the telephone and promised to run down at once to the village hall to relieve her husband of his self-imposed duties there and to direct him to Murreystone and the residence of would-be squire, Norman Thaxted. She also said that Delphick and Ranger had collected the car and driven off about half an hour ago, but that she hadn't seen them and had no notion where they were headed. Brinton replied that he had a good idea of their destination and that he'd like her, if she saw them again, to tell them to return to Ashford as soon as possible.

"And tell Potter the same," he reminded her as he rang off with another furious bang. "Pommy Sampford!"

P.C. Potter had spent more time by the road outside Plummergen village hall, directing tourists to other places of interest, than he had spent inside the exhibition: with the result that he failed to spot the stranger who had displayed such interest in Miss Seeton leaving the hall to stroll, studiously casual, down The Street and into the post office. Where, still more casual, he bought a box of matches — and a packet of cigarettes, as a decided afterthought — and made enforcedly light conversation concerning the artist whose pictures had made such an impression on him. Indeed, he had hopes of persuading her to sell him one. Did she live close by? What was her name? And when would he be likely to find her at home?

Mrs. Stillman, who might have recognised the stranger and wondered why he had not approached Miss Seeton while she was yet in the hall, was herself still there, chatting with her friends and making the most of her snatched free time. Mr. Stillman it was who, delighted to be of assistance to Miss Seeton, a favourite customer, told the stranger that she was currently teaching at the school, and his best course of action would be to approach her at home either in the afternoon, or (even better) the evening. "She won't be going anywhere tonight," said Mr. Stillman confidently. Plummergen knows its neighbours' business every bit as well as its own. "You'll catch her then, I'm sure."

And he wondered, briefly, after the man had thanked him and left, why the look in his eyes was more of apprehension than pleasure. But then Emmy Putts, slicing bacon, almost lost a fingertip as she pouted after the disappearing stranger and felt ignored; and in the resulting commotion, Mr. Stillman forgot all about the man who had shown such an interest in Miss Seeton.

The Meadows was much as Delphick and Bob remembered it from that earlier adventure: isolated at the end of a narrow lane about a mile out of the village, behind a high brick wall partly covered with honeysuckle and ivy. Set in the wall were two large wooden gates, and a small door to the left of them without bell or knocker, but with a ring-handled latch which Delphick lifted. The two policemen passed within. On the concrete path, their feet made no sound.

The front door was of plain oak, and also without bell or knocker. "They don't seem to be expecting visitors, do they?" murmured Delphick, raising his hand to rap. As soon as he did so, there came an explosion of barking from inside the house and sudden scratchings from the other side of the door as if the wolfhounds were trying to break through. Bob saw Delphick flinch, but said nothing.

From one of the windows on either side of the door came a flicker of movement as a face — male? female? — peered out and studied the newcomers carefully. The Borzois continued to bark. The policemen waited. A command was issued, and the dogs fell silent. Delphick's shoulders relaxed.

There came a rattling from the other side of the door as bolts were drawn, and the latch lifted. The door, opening, swung outwards. Delphick took a step back, and the face of a man looked cautiously at him.

"Yes?" The man had not opened the door wide; only his head and one shoulder were visible. He was evidently ready to slam the door in the visitors' faces if necessary. "You have," went on the man, "business with me? I cannot think what this could be. Possibly you are mistaken. This is a private house."

"Mr. Alexander?" enquired Delphick politely, pausing for a split second between the two words.

"I am he."

"We are police officers, sir, from Scotland

Yard. Here is my identification . . . and that of my sergeant here. We'd like to talk to you for a few minutes, if we may."

Mr. Alexander studied the warrant cards closely, looking from one face to another. "The good Potter, of course, is known to me," he said. "But is not Scotland Yard the — the big noise?" He produced the slang with some amusement and relaxed his grip on the door. "We had wished," he said with a sigh, "to remain unnoticed here, but if it is a matter for the authorities, you had better come in. Excuse me."

He turned back to issue another command to the dogs, and opened the door wide enough to admit the two detectives to the house. "My mistress," he went on, ushering them into the spacious hall, "I would prefer not to be disturbed, if this is possible — we do not" — he gestured towards the two Borzois, on guard at the foot of the stairs — "encourage visitors, you understand."

And he led the way through to the sitting room.

P.C. Potter drove along the B2080 southwards in the direction of Murreystone, racking his brains and trying to put a face to the name. He had ignored the lure of the longer, though better, route to the north: Superintendent Brinton's message had sounded urgent. He must want this Thaxted bloke in a real hurry — but who was Thaxted? Potter's beat covered more than the immediate Plummergen area, and he prided himself on knowing almost as much about other villages as he knew about his own. But Murreystone, the deadly rival, was a natural exception to this knowledge, the place he tended to avoid except when absolute duty called — as it did now.

He did not waste time hunting for the address: the Big House of any village was where the squire lived, and Potter could remember that Thaxted had played the squire last year when he captained Murreystone's cricket team. He'd shelled out for a complete new set of whites, and they'd put him in to bat at number eleven, just to keep him happy.

Potter passed through Ivychurch with a grin on his face as he remembered how he'd caught Norman Thaxted at silly midon for a duck, and how even the Murreystone team had been applauding behind the wretched man's back. But what, thought Potter, of his face? Suppose he came to the door, took one look at the uniform, and said that Mr. Thaxted was out and he had just come to read the meter?

Still frowning in thought, he turned into the drive of the manor house and drove slowly over the gravel towards the central steps which, aping their betters, sported stone lions couchant at either end. The door at the top of the steps was very firmly closed . . .

And nobody responded to Potter's knocking. If Thaxted was in, he wasn't at home to visitors: Potter trod around the side of the house and peered in at the kitchen window and tried the back door. It was bolted, and every window on the ground floor was closed. Maybe the man really was out: it wasn't so unreasonable, after all. The world and his wife had been enjoying the sun today, dropping into Plummergen's picture show and —

Potter stopped dead. He closed his eyes. He concentrated. "The man at the exhibition," he muttered, conjuring up in his inner vision the face of Norman Thaxted — last seen in Plummergen village hall.

And now wanted for questioning by the police . . .

"In my own country," said the Russian slowly, once Delphick had explained his interest in the inhabitants of The Meadows and promised confidentiality, "I would by rights call myself the Count Alexei Vissarionovitch Goncharov. But I am not in my own country, and yours has received me kindly. Therefore, I prefer to be addressed by your compatriots as 'Mr. Alexander' — it is easier" — and he smiled bleakly — "to speak on the tongue, is it not?"

"It certainly is." The chief superintendent glanced at Sergeant Ranger, struggling over his pot-hooks, and grinned. Poor Bob would never be able to spell it, even if he could read the shorthand back phonetically. Come to think of it, he'd be unlikely to do any better, himself. He cleared his throat, and enquired: "The lady of the house — your wife?"

"My mistress. The Princess Katerina Andreyevna Stakhova — my employer, I believe I should say. My family have given loyal service to hers for many generations, but now we two are the last of our respective lines. The Revolution — very much blood was shed, and very many lives were lost. We were fortunate in that our elders heeded the warning signs and took what some at first saw as the way out of the coward, though later, too late, others wished they had done as we. The princess's mother was a distant cousin of the late Tsar, you understand, and there were fears for the safety of the whole family. The princess was a child in arms when she was taken to Switzerland, where she has lived ever since."

Delphick's attention had been caught particularly by the final sentence. "Switzerland? I suppose you didn't meet a Mrs. Venning out there, by any chance, did you?"

Mr. Alexander smiled. "My cousin Sonia — again, distant, but we share a heritage. Her family fled to England before the Revolution — her grandfather, who married an English wife, and his sister, who entered the convent of a strictly enclosed religious order. There is a dark intensity to the Russian character, as you may know" — Delphick remembered commenting upon gloomy novels, and nodded — "which in my cousin's grand-aunt, and also in my cousin, manifested itself in waywardness of spirit. My cousin's aunt sought to purge herself of the spirit through perpetual devotions — my cousin, I understand, took a less . . . honourable course, she confessed to me. But this, no doubt, you know of."

Delphick nodded, but did not explain all the details of his acquaintance with Sonia Venning. "Please continue," he said, fascinated by Count Alexei's story. Bob Ranger had stopped taking notes and was listening in amazement.

"We White Russians perhaps cling to one another and the past too much for our own good, but we are as we are, and can do little now to alter our ways. The princess, in particular, has relived repeatedly a past she does not remember, that she knows only from what she has been told. When we chanced to meet my Cousin Sonia as she convalesced in Switzerland, and heard the sad story of the loss of her only daughter, the princess became . . . confused about what had happened and feared that the Bolsheviks, having assassinated once, would come to do so again. Behind every tree she saw enemies, and in the face of every stranger. My cousin tried to reassure her, and did some good — but the princess would not be entirely persuaded. She craved the complete privacy it was not possible, without much money, to obtain for her in Switzerland — we émigrés are not as rich as those who speak of us would believe. The long-lost treasure of His Majesty Tsar Nicholas does not lie concealed in a bank vault for the support of his followers, I fear."

He paused. "This is of interest to you? I wish only to give a full explanation for our presence here. Your Foreign Office — a man called Corymbe was truly cooperative — have been kind enough to permit our stay in this village. Where my Cousin Sonia owns this house, you understand — a house of high walls and safety, a house visited by few persons from the outside world, and where my mistress may reassure herself that there is nothing to fear. Already she is greatly improved in her spirits. The dogs protect her, and they are a reminder to her of home if anywhere can be home to one who is a permanent exile from a forbidden land . . ."

"Did you believe him, sir?" enquired Bob, after they had taken their leave of Mr. Alexander and were sitting in the car outside in the lane. "It sounded to me just like one of those historical romances some women read all the time. And we didn't get to see this princess of his, did we? Suppose she's more queer in the head than he's letting on, and it's turned her into a firebug? He wouldn't want to let us meet her then, in case she somehow gave herself away."

Delphick fastened his seat-belt before answering, while Bob's hand hovered over the ignition, keys jingling. "I've had dealings with Corymbe," he said at last. "That business a few years back when Miss Seeton went to Geneva. Although it sounds almost unreal, I believe he'll confirm Alexander's story — he gave us names and addresses,

didn't he, and too many to be phony —
unless someone's planning an incredibly
complex crime, requiring the back-up of a
large organisation and set up over several
years. Which nobody, surely, would come
to Plummergen to carry out."

"Nobody in their right minds, sir," said
Bob, starting the car. Having put forward
his theory, he was reluctant to abandon it.
"But he as good as told us the princess, if
she *is* a princess — well, the woman, whoever she is. He told us she was a bit cracked.
Which could mean anything."

Delphick smiled. "You think it might not
only be the English who are given to under-
statement? A healthy touch of scepticism is
what every detective should cultivate, Bob,
but in this instance I'm prepared to give
Count Alexei — or Mr. Alexander, if he pre-
fers — the benefit of the doubt. As soon as
we're back in Ashford, I'll put a call through
to the FO and have a word or two with
Corymbe . . ."

But it was not as soon as that. Brinton
greeted them in a whirlwind of demands to
know where they had been and what they
had been doing, followed by commands not
to tell him as he had far more important
news for them than theirs for him.

As he had. Delphick was more than interested. "Chickney has found some faces he remembers? And Thaxted's in the frame for the Notley Black killing? Things are looking up."

Brinton glowered. "Oh, no they're not. Not until we can find him — because Thaxted has completely disappeared . . ."

chapter
25

Posthumus Sampford had never had an easy life of it. Childhood friends mocked him for his unusual Christian name: it took years for him to persuade them to address him as Pommy, and after an Australian boy came to the school, he wished he hadn't. He fought grim and bloody battles at playtime to remind everyone that he was *not* of illegitimate birth, and that his mother was a respectable widow, and his father had died before he was born. Died before he could show his son any of his professional tricks: so that Pommy was left to find things out for himself.

Pommy was a slow learner, yet he never failed to achieve his goals in the end, even if it took him longer than it would have taken anyone else. Recognising his weakness, he preferred not to work on his own; accepting his limitations, his friends knew how far he could be relied on. The system worked well — until Notley Black persuaded him into robbing a jeweller's shop that would set them up for life . . .

Pommy didn't go to prison for life, but any sentence is grim when your partner has escaped at the first eruption of the new burglar alarm neither of you knew about, and you are left to take the blame; more especially so, when you learn that, consoling your girlfriend for your loss, he has stepped into your shoes and even married her. When Pommy came out of prison, the iron had entered his soul. If he had chanced upon his treacherous ex-partner in crime, he would have given Notley Black far more than a bloodied nose, but Notley (who had abandoned his pregnant wife after some years spent ill-treating her) took great care to keep well out of Pommy's way. Pommy began to drink, and to gamble: he brooded over his Pools coupons, and studied *The Sporting Life* fervently. He began to win — then it seemed he always won. His luck had changed.

So had his name. Pommy Sampford disappeared, and Norman Thaxted became a noted race-goer whose opinions of horseflesh were increasingly respected. He mixed in circles more reputable than before, although he never lost complete touch with old associates: he decided that he liked being a pillar (albeit shaky) of society and began to call himself a business man. He cut back on the booze, but thought it a shame not to make use of his experience: he bought half a share in a London nightclub, then sold it at a profit to his partner when he heard about The Singing Swan. He bought the club and moved to a large house in the country, determined to put his inglorious past behind him and play the part of one who has always been decent, legal, honest, and truthful. Even in his ownership of the newly named Half Seas Over, he resolved to operate according to the letter of the law: no underage drinking, no sidelines like prostitution . . .

But he hadn't learned as much about running a club as he thought he had. He began to lose money: he began to blink a Nelsonian eye when made-up young women arrived at the door with elderly gentlemen by their sides. The private rooms were hired out to parties who conformed less and less to the respectable ideal he had sought — yet still he lost money, and at a faster rate. There was a limit to the extent he could increase his prices and keep his clientele: he went over that limit, and now he was really worried.

He wanted to keep his manor house and what he thought was his position in the community; he couldn't find anyone to buy the Half Seas Over when he put the quiet word around, and he dared not advertise for fear of bringing creditors down upon him. He resolved to have the place destroyed by fire, one night when it would be closed for redecoration — a workman's carelessly stubbed cigarette, a spillage of paint stripper — and there was no risk to anyone's life. He would arrange a foolproof alibi for the period during which a professional Torch from London did what had to be done, and the insurance settlement would solve all his problems.

The best people to help him, he decided, would be those same old friends who had trusted him to help them, in former times: and help him they did. He was advised to burn down a few unimportant items before the Torch arrived, establishing rumours of a fire raiser at a time when he himself would be utterly above suspicion. He duly obliged by destroying a couple of haystacks and, with resentful memories of his days at school, Brettenden Secondary Modern — at night, when he could be sure there was nobody inside. He did not wish to have anyone's death on his conscience and was worried when a spate of copycat fires broke out, although he suspected that some, at least, were started by business owners with similar problems to his own. He told London that he wanted to go for the big one as soon as possible . . .

And the Torch, when he arrived, turned out to be Notley Black: sent by a school friend with a warped sense of humour to burn down a nightclub for a client whose true identity he was not told. The two former partners, when they recognised each other, quarrelled, and fought, and in the fight Notley, utterly by accident, was killed. Pommy panicked and tried to make Notley's death look like an arson attack that had gone disastrously wrong — but was as bad a planner as he had ever been. Police suspicions were aroused almost at once, and so, very soon afterwards, were suspicions in London. It was put to Pommy, with some force, that by his actions he had rendered his friends short one Torch, thereby losing the consultancy fees to which they felt entitled. Business, he was told, was business, and contracts — with emphasis — were to be honoured.

The unspoken threat of a contract on his life made Pommy agree at once to do as he was told and take over Notley's list of unfinished appointments. Approaches had been made to the late Mr. Black's employers by several persons in the Brettenden area, and

Pommy must oblige them all, without exception, without excuse. Only when his debt was deemed to have been paid would this pressure be withdrawn, and the peaceful life he wished to lead be permitted to continue.

Pommy Sampford, as Norman Thaxted, was by day an upright citizen of Murreystone, by night creeping out to fulfill his arsonical obligations. It was a tiring, nerve-racking time, but he did not dare to let his cover slip. When it became clear that Plummergen planned something remarkable in the Best Kept Village Competition stakes, the would-be squire of Plummergen's rival was one of those deputed to learn what they could of these plans, by visiting the exhibition which was so very clearly marked as welcoming all . . .

Lack of sleep and a twitchy conscience sharpened Pommy's ears, but dulled his judgement. Miss Seeton's wondering words on the subject of divine proportions passed him by, but her (to his mind) persistent harping on fire, while (he felt sure) looking straight at him — and the way she had hit him so pointedly with her umbrella — led him to believe that she had discovered his guilty secret. He would lose everything he had laboured to build up, after his shaky start in life: and he could not bear it.

He resolved to rid himself of the threat, and the world of Miss Seeton . . .

"There's an outside chance it could be a coincidence," said Delphick, "but I very much doubt it, Chris. My money's with yours, on Thaxted."

"You mean Sampford," snarled Brinton. "The time we've wasted because of him! When I get my hands on him — leading us up the garden path like that!"

"In the circumstances, you can hardly blame him. Once we knew of his change of name, we could hardly fail to make the connection with Notley Black — which you did make, after all. No wonder he's disappeared for a while. He's worried, I've no doubt, and thinking up a cover story. I look forward to hearing it once he's been found."

"He shouldn't need to be found! How the hell could he know we were looking for him? Potter was on his way there almost as soon as we knew about Notley Black. Somebody's tipped him the wink, and whoever it is I'll give him the thrashing of his life when I catch him." Brinton breathed in deeply, then out, and the papers on his desk fluttered in a frantic dance. He closed his eyes and groaned. "I might have known," he lamented, clutching at his hair. "*Last seen in the Plummergen area* — it only needed that. You know damn well who lives in Plummergen — she's bound to get involved, don't tell me she won't, and the Lord only knows what the end of it all will be."

"I don't see," came Delphick's mild objection, "why Miss Seeton should become involved in this affair at all. By now he's probably halfway across London, or on his way to Dover and a new life abroad — he's unlikely to stay so close to home, where people will recognise him, now that he knows the game is up."

"Potter's going to keep patrolling," Brinton said, "and he's told Sir George's Village Watch to stay on their toes tonight, just in case." He sighed again, and once more the papers danced on his desk. "We can't be too careful."

"Belt and braces," murmured Delphick, adding, "I suppose it won't do any harm. But Customs and Emigration are on the lookout as well, so wherever he is, he probably won't get far — though, with the start he seems to have had, he must be quite a way from Plummergen by now. I suggest that this time we may forget about Miss Seeton's likely involvement."

"She drew that picture, didn't she? She's

324

already got herself involved, whether we like it or not."

Delphick shook his head to clear it. The resolution of the Russian enigma, and the identification by Jacob Chickney of certain parties who paid him to take him on that badger-baiting foray into Ashford Forest, had made him forget that Miss Seeton had drawn another sketch besides the *Wind in the Willows* scene. "The nightclub, of course," he said, and Bob Ranger exclaimed at his side.

"I've been a fool," Delphick said. "It was all there on paper in front of us, if only we'd been able to recognise it — the rivalry over a woman, the robbery and the jewels — the pearls didn't just indicate Notley Black, they told us about the heist that went wrong — even the nightclub connection. She could hardly have made it plainer."

Brinton grunted. "Oh, it's the same old story: once you know what you're looking at, you can understand what she's on about. But somehow they always seem to happen in the wrong order. I've said it before — you need an interpreter when you're dealing with Miss Seeton. And, mark my words, we haven't seen the last of her in this case just yet . . ."

Thaxted might have lived in Murreystone

for only a few years, but he had come to know the surrounding countryside, for a newcomer, reasonably well. He wanted to be accepted by the locals and to understand what they were talking about when they referred to "the earthworks" or "ruined All Saints" or "the Rhee Wall." Which understanding, once acquired, meant that he felt confident of being able to conceal himself in safety for the remainder of the day, until night fell and he could make his attack upon the Plummergen cottage where he had learned that Miss Seeton lived.

He disliked the idea of killing her, but reasoned that, having killed once, he had nothing to lose. He regretted the necessity, but an elderly spinster would be even less missed than Notley Black, in the prime of life, had been. And this time he would not be rushed into carelessness. He had filled his car with petrol almost to overflowing, and Jack Crabbe, manning the pumps, had sold him what he thought was only a spare can for emergencies. (If this wasn't an emergency, Thaxted didn't know what was.) He'd bought matches from Mr. Stillman, and cigarettes which he chain-smoked in his hideaway as he waited. He was hungry, but had been too anxious to think of food until it was too late: he did not dare go home for supplies, not even for the clothes, dark blue and secretive, he wore when he was doing Notley Black's work for him. He would have to take the risk and hope that nobody would spot him making his way to Sweetbriars and, well, doing what he planned to do: he could not bring himself to say, or even to think, the word for what he planned. He lit another cigarette from the previous stub and looked at his watch for the umpteenth time. When would the sun set? When would the day grow dark — when would it all be over?

chapter
26

Mel Forby had not been her usual ebullient self that day. Her notes for the Rural Revival series were going well, and when she rang the editor of the *Daily Negative*, he had told her to stay there and keep up the good work. She had every intention of doing so, but life was rather, well, flat here in Plummergen just at present. Although Delphick and Bob Ranger were also staying at the George and Dragon, and she saw them almost every day, no front-page story seemed about to break: she was starting to suffer from withdrawal symptoms, she decided. She thrived on Fleet Street pressures, on deadlines, on headlines: Delphick had promised her the scoop when it came, but it was a long time coming.

Lesser women rushed out and bought themselves glamorous hats when in the doldrums: Mel had never been this conventional. She wondered, however, what it would be like to follow yet another old country custom, and resolved that, once she had visited the Before and After exhibition and added a couple of paragraphs to her notes, she would take the bus into Brettenden and see how the other half lived. If nothing else, it would give her another Plummergen Piece for the cartoon strip which had helped to make her name.

"Monica Mary: Milliner" was just the place Mel was looking for: tucked away down a side street, bow-fronted windows, an air of age-old gentility in every flounce of the chintz curtains (tied with bows) and dull gold curlicues of the many, many mirrors along the walls. The carpet was flowered, and thickly piled; the draperies dividing the shop from Miss Brown's workshop were velvet. Mel was entranced, and her fingers twitched with longing to snatch notebook and pencil from her bag to immortalise Miss Monica Mary Brown, and her establishment, in print.

She restrained herself until she had left the shop, with a frivolous headpiece for which she'd paid a startling price hanging over her arm in a hatbox. A hatbox, for heaven's sake. When did anyone last see one of those? And the hat — what had come over her? Monica Mary had been a good saleswoman: she'd seemed to understand precisely the restless mood Mel was in, and talked her out of anything serviceable, anything she might conceivably wear around

Town when winter came. No, this wicked little concoction of ribbons (primary colours, to match Miss Forby's personality) and not much else was strictly a luxury item. She doubted whether she'd managed to sneak it in on her expenses — but there was no doubt about it, it was fun.

Mel ate her lunch, wrote her notes, and eventually took the bus back to Plummergen wondering how many weddings she would be invited to in the near future. In her room at the George and Dragon, she tried on the hat again. No doubt of it: she looked different. It suited her. She felt cheered. She wondered what Thrudd would think. This was certainly a new Mel Forby . . .

She remembered the original Mel Forby, transformed after a few words, and a lightning sketch, from Miss Seeton. Miss Seeton should have the chance to see the new Mel Forby — who was, after all, partly her creation. Thoughts of Thrudd had made her feel rather lonely: she'd invite Miss S. across to dinner, and for a bit of girl talk, and to admire the hat, so very different from that ordinary little number that had got a bullet through it when the post office was raided, all those years ago.

Delphick and Ranger were not dining tonight: they were, unknown to Mel, still with their Ashford colleagues on the hunt for Norman Thaxted, alias Pommy Sampford. Mel and Miss Seeton had the dining room almost to themselves.

"Let me treat you to a bottle of something special, Miss S.," Mel coaxed her guest, who had been quite excited at the thought of her little excursion. Dear Mel had insisted that it was to be her treat, jokingly saying that it would make up for all the slices of Martha's fruit cake she'd enjoyed recently; the *cuisine* at the George and Dragon wasn't noted for being particularly *haute,* but Miss Seeton knew that she would enjoy herself anyway, in such agreeable company.

Doris brought the wine list across and joined in Mel's rather one-sided discussion with Miss Seeton about what they would have to drink. Miss Seeton knew nothing about it at all, and Doris only a little more: Mel just loved the taste of the stuff. They settled for a rather nice Beaujolais, which, said Mel, would go with anything.

"A whole bottle, Mel dear? Surely that's rather, well, extravagant? And," added Miss Seeton, "I'm really not sure that I ought to —"

"I told you, Miss S., this is a celebration. It's not as if you've got to drive home — or even walk very far." An affectionate smile lit Mel's face as she glanced at Miss Seeton's umbrella, which hung over the arm of her turned-oak carver chair. It was a warm summer night, and Miss Seeton had not bothered to bring a coat (or even to wear a hat) for her short journey across the road from Sweetbriars; but the umbrella, as always, had come with her. If a thunder-storm of torrential proportions should erupt overhead, in the time it would take Miss Seeton to open the brolly she could have scuttled homewards through the drops almost without wetting her head; but Miss Seeton without an umbrella would be . . .

"Earth-shattering," murmured Mel, who had treated herself to a solitary sherry or two before Miss Seeton arrived. "I mean" — as a politely enquiring look was turned on her — "flattering. How flattering that you should bring your very best umbrella with you, just for my benefit."

Miss Seeton smiled and blushed. Proudly she stroked the handle of the umbrella which, after their first adventure together, had been given to her by Superintendent (as he was then) Delphick. "It is real gold," said Miss Seeton, smiling again. "I use it on only the most special occasions — and you said, did you not, that you had something to celebrate? So, naturally, I . . ."

She was too polite to make direct enquiry as to the nature of the celebration. Since Thrudd Banner was nowhere to be seen, she assumed that he had not popped the question, as dear Mel, so modern, would be unlikely to phrase it, but Mel's eyes — quite beautiful, now that she had modified her makeup, and emphasised by her cheekbones, so unusual — dear Mel's eyes gleamed with distinct animation, almost mischief.

"You bet I'm celebrating, Miss S. This meal's on the editor of the *Daily Negative*, though he doesn't know it. As a practice run for my hat." And Mel told of her impulsive purchase, promising to take Miss Seeton up to her room after the meal and, if she was very good, allowing her to try it on. They both giggled together at the thought — Miss Seeton had been sipping her Beaujolais throughout the meal almost without noticing it — Mel proposed a toast to her editor, another to her series on the Rural Revival.

It was a splendid evening, if slightly blurred towards the end, when Mel persuaded Miss Seeton to join her in the very smallest *digestif* Doris knew how to pour. Making only a token demur, Miss Seeton joined her: the meal, so surprisingly (one had to say, having heard others speak of the George's cuisine) tasty, had been most enjoyable, if rather filling. And the company, of course, even more so — enjoyable, that was to say. Miss Seeton found her tongue tangling itself over the complimentary phrase and agreed firmly with Doris's suggestion that they might wish for coffee.

"We'll take the cups up to my room, Miss S., then while they got cool enough to drink, you can try on my hat. But mind," Mel warned her, "you're not to tell a soul how much I paid." She placed a finger to her lips and whispered. It sounded unusually loud. "Not a word — promise?"

It was late, Miss Seeton supposed, when she finally trod with great care down the main stairs and out of the door of the George and Dragon. The cool breeze from outside fanned her pinkened cheeks, and she raised both hands to hold her hat firmly down. How silly: she hadn't worn a hat, on such a warm night. Miss Seeton giggled. "A most striking hat, Mel dear, and thank you for letting me see myself in it. Thank you, too, for a delightful evening." The words seemed to come out rather louder than usual, though Mel did not appear to notice.

"A pleasure, Miss S. I'll pass your compliments on to the editor." And she stood on the top step, leaning against one of the white pillars, waving goodbye and watching as her guest trotted, a little unsteadily, across the road and up the short front path to the door of Sweetbriars.

Wow. Mel blinked and took a deep breath. She steadied herself with one hand and rubbed her face with the other. A touch of fresh air, perhaps, before turning in. Charley Mountfitchet would give her a night key, she supposed, in case he'd locked up by the time she got back. She went in search of the landlord and found him in the kitchen, drinking coffee with Doris. They poured Mel a generous cup, and found her a key: she thanked them, took several more deep breaths, and headed for the summer night.

It must be later than she'd thought. Lights were going out in Plummergen bedrooms, and everywhere downstairs was dark. The absence of street lamps made it seem even darker though the moon was rising. Mel decided to walk northwards up one side of The Street as far as the turning for Plummergen Common, cross to the other side, and walk back. Which should set her up nicely for the night. She started off.

She hadn't gone far when she heard a

sudden scuffing behind her and heavy foot-steps. She whirled round.

"Why, it's Miss Forby!"

Her heart thudded down from her mouth and settled, quivering, in the pit of her stomach. "Jack Crabbe," she said, recognising the man from the garage. "What on earth —"

"Sorry if we startled you, Miss Forby, but we're on duty tonight — the Village Watch, you see — just been patrolling down the Old Way, that hedge by the old vicarage could hide any number of people up to mischief — and it's not usual for folks to go for a stroll at this hour, so when we saw you, we did wonder a bit. All right now, are you?"

Her fright had shaken the last traces of the celebration out of her system. "Fine, thanks, Jack. I was just taking a walk before turning in, but now I find I'm not sleepy at all, even though it's so late. How about if I come along with you for a while? I promise not to get in the way, but it might give me a good story for my paper."

Jack Crabbe was no more a match for the new Mel Forby than any of her Fleet Street friends, and after a token discussion with the rest of his patrol, she was allowed to join them as they quartered Plummergen's Street, its one or two side lanes, and neighbouring fields. A barn owl hooted as it swooped on a mouse; Mel thought of Miss Ursula Hawke and shuddered. Jack grabbed her arm and pointed out a dog-fox crossing the recreation ground in the moonlight, barking. In hedgerows and overhanging trees small creatures rustled and squeaked. Mel thrilled to the countryside at night, and wished she'd brought her notebook with her: the moon was bright enough to read and write by.

In turning up a side road the patrol missed the police car's arrival outside the George and Dragon. Delphick and Bob had hunted with the Ashford men until it grew dark, then had obtained a further statement from Jacob Chickney and set various house visits in motion by telephone. Then Super-intendent Brinton grumbled that his death by starvation could hardly be what anyone would wish, and they all went out for fish and chips, washed down by pints of beer. Bob, safely within the limit, drove Delphick back to Plummergen, parked the car with care, unlocked the hotel door with another of Charley Mountfitchet's night keys, and bade his superior good night.

Mel returned half an hour later, com-posing paragraphs in her head, and, yawning, made for the kitchen. Another cup of coffee would keep her alert long enough to write down all her impressions of the night's little excursion before sleep dulled too many of them. From being wide awake, she'd suddenly lost all her zing; but it would be a pity not to put down how the fox had barked and the night-birds had been calling through the dark.

Other birds were calling through the dark: the chickens in their henhouse at the bottom of Miss Seeton's garden. Where nightingales sang sweetly, the chickens squawked: they cackled, and screeched, and flapped their wings at the disturbance. Someone was trying to climb over the wall.

In the main bedroom of Sweetbriars, Miss Seeton slept; maybe she dreamed, maybe her sleep was too deep, but she heard nothing of the commotion outside. It did not last long. Whoever had been trying to climb over the garden wall must have realised that it was too difficult for anyone burdened with a large, full, heavy oblong metal can — and the noise from the chickens was an even stronger deterrent. The chickens, after one final outburst, were left in peace, and fell grudgingly silent. They went back to sleep.

In the main bedroom of Sweetbriars, Miss Seeton slept on — and on. Outside, hardly anything moved.

Mel Forby rinsed out her cup and left it on the draining board, then closed the kitchen door and passed quietly through the hall, up the stairs, and into her room. As one hand stifled a yawn, with the other she switched on the light. She giggled. On top of the hatbox perched her gaily ribboned hat, slipping sideways where Miss Seeton had set it, not entirely steadily, before she left. Mel's eyes brightened. She'd try it on just once more: it would inspire her to write better than ever.

It was as she crossed the room to the mirror that she saw something that halted her in her tracks. An umbrella. Miss Seeton's umbrella: the black silk, gold-handled, number one brolly of which its owner was so proud. It leaned in a most forlorn fashion against Mel's low armchair and looked . . . bereft, Mel decided, was the only word.

She was shocked. Miss Seeton without her umbrella just didn't seem right: her umbrella without Miss Seeton seemed — well, maybe she wasn't quite as sober as she'd thought. But she almost wanted to pat the poor thing and tell it not to worry she'd look after it, and it hadn't really been abandoned for ever.

"So much for celebration," she murmured, feeling guilty. She picked up the umbrella, shook her head, and drifted to her bedroom window. The lights had all been out in Sweetbriars twenty minutes ago, but maybe Miss S. would wake up and remember what she'd done and worry about leaving such a valuable item behind, even in the care of her old friend Mel Forby. Suppose she didn't remember exactly where she'd left it? She might be walking the floor of her room this minute. Mel would go over at once if she saw a light on.

Mel did see light: a red, flickering light. The light of the fire which was beginning to consume the wooden fence around the tiny front garden of Sweetbriars . . .

chapter
27

"Fire!" Mel rushed to her bedroom door, flung it open, and charged into the corridor. Where was the nearest telephone? "Fire!" Which room was Delphick's, which Bob's? Apart from herself, they were the George's only guests. "Fire!" She beat with Miss Seeton's umbrella upon every door as she flew past, her feet barely touching the ground. She hurtled down the stairs, swung round the newel-post at the bottom, and skidded across the hall to the reception desk. She grabbed the telephone and dialled nine-nine-nine.

From the landing above, heavy poundings were heard as feet clattered in her wake, and people appeared, breathless, beside her in Reception. "What fire? Where?" cried Bob as Delphick demanded: "Where's Mountfitchet? How many people are in the hotel tonight?"

"It isn't the George that's on fire," Mel said, starting to shake. "It's Miss Seeton — someone's set her fence alight, and you know the size of that front garden — she'll be burned in her bed before the fire brigade gets here."

"You've rung them? Good girl," Delphick said while Bob turned to run. He wrestled with the front-door bolts which Mel had so carefully shot not an hour ago. Charley Mountfitchet dragged Delphick kitchen-wards. "Buckets!" he cried. "Doris, get out into the garden and bring the hose from the shed. Mr. Ranger —"

But Bob was gone. Mel, regaining her breath, seized an elaborate flowerpot from beside the desk and tore out the cheeseplant by its roots. She flung it to the ground and chased after Bob. Earth was as good as sand for smothering fires, wasn't it?

Bob was galloping up the short path to Miss Seeton's front door, having evidently passed through the flames without noticing them. He battered on the door and began to shout. Mel arrived and threw earth over the flames. They died down a little — or did they? Was it just wishful thinking? — and she nerved herself to ignore them, rushing down the path, past Bob, and round the side of the cottage to the back. She thumped on the kitchen door and added her shrieks of warning to Bob's baritone calls.

There came further shouts from the narrow road outside beyond the bottom of

Miss Seeton's back garden. Sir George and his platoon of Watchmen, patrolling down by the canal, had spotted someone sneaking south from Plummergen with what they were convinced was a guilty look. They had given chase as he vanished into the water-meadows and disappeared. They had failed to find him as he lurked successfully for a while and then doubled back. He climbed into his waiting car, shadowed from immediate sight by an overhanging tree, and, panicking, turned to flee northwards. Sir George's troop, countrymen all, with no need to wait for their second wind, pounded after him.

The car slammed on its brakes at the sight of Charley Mountfitchet's makeshift fire brigade quenching the flames the driver had believed would be unnoticed until too late. There were figures in the road ahead: Norman Thaxted had no wish to add to his list of victims. There were figures in the road behind — and they were closing in on him. Some brandished what looked like pitchforks. Norman gritted his teeth, pressed his hand firmly down on the horn, pressed his foot firmly down on the accelerator, and shot forward.

"Stop that car!" barked Sir George in the parade-ground voice he thought he'd forgotten. The fire fighters, winning their battle with the flames, shouted and waved their arms. The vicar, whose peaceful dreams had been transformed by the commotion into a nightmare about Joan of Arc, burst from the door of the vicarage with an aspidistra in his arms. Unlike Mel, he had not thought to remove the plant from its pot, and peered frantically between the spiky leaves as he hurried to play his part in extinguishing the fire. On hearing the command from Sir George, he hurled the aspidistra, pot and all, in the direction of Norman Thaxted's windscreen. Earth splattered everywhere. Norman skidded but drove on.

"After him!" roared Sir George, and almost everyone gave chase. Norman, too startled to think of switching on the wipers, lurched as fast as he could up The Street, heading north. Outside Sweetbriars, Bob ceased his battering of the door as the flames died away into a damp, hissing stench.

Mel's shrieks were answered. Miss Seeton opened her bedroom window and peered out. "Who is there?" she enquired cautiously. Being startled from sleep in such a fashion had given her a headache. "Good gracious — Mel, is that you?" She peered into the darkness. "And — surely, that can't be dear Bob with you?" as Ranger, feeling rather superfluous, had joined Mel at the side door. He and Mel together tried to tell Miss Seeton that indeed it was them and to explain why they were there. "I'd better come down," Miss Seeton said. She rubbed her brow thoughtfully. Perhaps a pot of tea would be a good idea.

A car, its lights extinguished, was driving into Plummergen from the north. It drove slowly, its engine quiet. There were four people inside. Each one of them erupted into warning shouts when Norman Thaxted, still blinded by the aspidistra earth on his windscreen, came weaving his way towards them. The driver sounded the horn. Norman, nervous as pursuit neared, drove on unheeding. The car without lights tried to swerve. Norman's car lurched across the road. The lightless car's brakes squealed. The smell of hot rubber and sweat filled the air. Norman, his sense of direction utterly lost, crashed into the darkened car without reducing his speed by one iota.

The metallic embrace occurred almost opposite the police house. P.C. Potter peered from his window, grabbed notebook and trousers, and ran into the road buttoning his tunic, shouting instructions for his wife to telephone the ambulance. He reached the accident as the four men, cursing but otherwise apparently unharmed, struggled out of the tumult of tangled steel. They looked upon Authority approaching them at speed and turned to run.

"Stop!" Sir George and his men were at hand. "Stop, in the name of the law!" In the distance a siren was heard. The four men hesitated. They could not escape to the north: better to attempt to fight it out with the unofficial pitchfork crew heading from the south. They squared up to the Village Watch, prepared to sell their freedom dearly.

The fire engine swept down the road from Brettenden to come upon an astonishing sight. Blocking the road was a mass of metal which might at one time have been two separate motor vehicles. Was this why they had been called out? The message had spoken of fire, and after an accident there was always the risk, with spilled petrol and electrical sparks, of fire. But the men who were engaged in hand-to-hand combat all around the wreckage seemed oblivious of the risks they were running. The leading fireman, spotting a police officer apparently unable to control events, got out of the cab to offer assistance.

"Leave them be," instructed P.C. Potter, brushing aside this kindly cooperation. "That's they Murreystone buggers our lot's sorting out — give 'em hell, lads!" He cheered on his own side without stopping to consider his official position. Sir George, urging moderation in a quiet voice, stood ready to call off his troops only if slaughter seemed likely to ensue. The fire crew, scratching their heads, asked if there really had been a fire. Delphick, previously busy with Charley Mountfitchet and his team, now arrived on the scene. He said that there had, but that it was safely out. The fire engine would find it difficult to squeeze past the scrimmage in the street until tempers had cooled: he was a police officer and would take full responsibility. Suppose (if they insisted on checking the ruins of Miss Seeton's fence for smouldering sparks) they turned round, went back up The Street, turned left, left, left again, and then sharp right? They would thus reach Sweetbriars without disturbing anybody else, leaving himself and his colleague — he indicated P.C. Potter — to clear up proceedings here.

And cleared up they were. By the time the ambulance arrived, the Murreystone quartet had been utterly vanquished and added to the criminal collection begun by

347

P.C. Potter, who recognised Norman Thaxted as he crawled at last from the ruins of his car. Bob Ranger, who had left Mel to explain as much as she could to Miss Seeton, held Norman by the collar while Potter scurried indoors for his handcuffs: Delphick called after him to bring every pair he had, as Sir George, viewing the situation with a knowledgeable military eye, advised him that the Murreystone contingent were about to throw in the towel. Delphick, Potter, and Bob — with assistance from the victorious Colveden crew — loaded five conquered foes aboard the ambulance, with instructions to take them first to Ashford hospital (just in case) and then on to the police station, where they were to be charged with causing an affray.

"And that," Delphick said, looking straight at Norman Thaxted, "will be only the start, for some of you . . ."

"But what," enquired Miss Seeton as the assembled group in her sitting-room began the postmortem, "was everyone doing? I don't understand why anybody from Murreystone should wish to set fire to my fence." She poured tea while Mel handed round a plate of gingerbread. "How fortunate that I had already decided to replace the fence — one of Mr. Eggleden's clever arrowhead patterns, I thought. For the Competition, you understand."

"Oh, we understand," said Delphick, grinning. "That's the explanation for everything, you see." He had decided to keep silent about Norman Thaxted's designs on her life: let her continue in blissful ignorance. Something always seemed to look after Miss Seeton, and though he feared that one day her luck would run out, this time, yet again, it had served her well. Why worry her with what she had no need to know?

"It was the Competition," he said. "Murreystone wanted to win — still does, I suppose, but I can't believe they'll stand much of a chance when the judges find out what they'd got in the boot of that car." He paused to help himself to gingerbread as Mel passed.

She feinted at him with the plate. "Stop keeping my scoop to yourself, Oracle, or Bob gets every slice of this and you starve. We want the story — right, Miss S.?"

"Oh, yes," Miss Seeton said. "Certainly we do."

"So, what *was* in the boot of the car?" demanded Mel as she removed the gingerbread from Delphick's reach and sat down, wishing she'd brought her notebook.

"Thermos flasks of boiling water and cardboard boxes with moles in them. The water wasn't for making tea — and the moles weren't dead."

"Amazing," said Mel flatly. "Er . . . care to explain some more?"

Delphick explained. The boiling water, poured over any living thing, plant or animal ("Think of ants' nests," he said), would damage if not kill it. Murreystone was to be blamed for Plummergen's mysterious Brown Wilt: which was neither more nor less than scorch marks, and not a virus at all. "Which means that it's safe to put fresh plants in now — there's no risk they'll catch anything to kill them. As for the moles . . ."

Miss Seeton shook her head. "Stan says there have never been so many molehills about the village. He has planted caper spurge in my garden, and of course it is protected by a wall, although I believe they can tunnel underneath, but I seem to have been very fortunate."

"You have indeed." Delphick smiled at her. "Your wall was so high that the Murreystone crowd couldn't let any of their moles loose in your garden — and the foundations of the road would stop them digging in this direction. They went the other way and ruined as much as they could in the time — doing Murreystone's dirty work for them." He paused to allow Miss Seeton and Mel to express their shock at such a display of ruthless rivalry.

"The most depressing part," he said, "is that Murreystone didn't go to the bother of catching the moles themselves — they bribed a mole catcher to do it for them. The Plummergen mole catcher. Yes" — as they exclaimed — "Jacob Chickney, who'll do almost anything for money. And who did," he added in a grim undertone, thinking of badgers, and owls, and Miss Ursula Hawke. He glanced across at Mel. "I think that's pretty well the full story, but I'll fill you in on any details you'd like once we get back to the hotel." He stretched and yawned. "It's been quite a night."

Everyone else yawned, too. In the silence, the sound of rain could be heard, pattering against the windows. "You'll get wet," said Miss Seeton, "crossing the road. Let me lend you my umbrella . . ."

Mel Forby began to laugh. And laugh.